Fran O'Brien and Arthur McGuinness
established McGuinness Books
to publish her novels to raise funds
for LauraLynn Children's Hospice.

Fran's six novels, *The Married Woman, The
Liberated Woman, Odds on Love, Who is Faye?
The Red Carpet, and Fairfields,*
have raised €190,000.00 in sales and donations for
LauraLynn House.

Fran and Arthur hope that THE PACT will raise
even more funds for the children's hospice.

www.franobrien.net

Also by Fran O'Brien

The Married Woman
The Liberated Woman
Odds on Love
Who is Faye?
The Red Carpet
Fairfields

Buy now online www.franobrien.net

THE PACT

FRAN O'BRIEN

Fran

McGuinness Books

McGuinness Books

THE PACT

This novel is entirely a work of fiction. The names, characters and incidents portrayed in it are the work of the author's imagination. Any resemblance to actual persons, living or dead, events or localities is entirely coincidental.

Published by McGuinness Books,
15 Glenvara Park, Ballycullen Road,
Templeogue, Dublin 16.

Fran O'Brien asserts the moral right to be identified as the author of this work.

A catalogue record for this book is available from the British Library.

ISBN 97809549521-6-7

Typeset by Martone Design & Print,
39 Hills Industrial Centre, Liffey Bridge, Lucan, Co. Dublin.

Printed and bound in Great Britain by
CPI Cox & Wyman, Reading, RGI 8EX.

This novel is dedicated to Jane and Brendan McKenna,
and in memory of their daughters Laura and Lynn.

And for all our family, friends and clients who support our efforts
to raise funds for LauraLynn Children's Hospice,
Leopardstown, Dublin 18.

Jane and Brendan have been through every parent's worst
nightmare – the tragic loss of their only two children.
Laura died, just four years old,
following surgery to repair a heart defect.
Her big sister, Lynn, died less than two years later aged fifteen,
having lost her battle against Leukaemia
– diagnosed on the day of Laura's surgery.

Having dealt personally with such serious illness, Jane and
Brendan's one wish was to establish a children's hospice in
memory of their girls. Now LauraLynn House has become
a reality, and their dream has come true.

LauraLynn House Children's Hospice offers community based
paediatric palliative, respite, and end-of-life care in an eight bed
unit. There is also a residential unit for families, support and
comfort for parents and siblings
for whom life can be extremely difficult.

Putting Life into a Child's Day
Not Days into a Child's Life

www.lauralynnhospice.com

PROLOGUE

Threads connect to the past.
To a dark windblown secret.
Sand drifts, blinds, smothers.
Lodges in crevices.
And erases memory.

Chapter One

He was a middle-aged man. Clean. Well dressed. He said nothing. Just left money on the bedside table. For Elena it was a gross violation. This was something which had never happened before and her screams were all in her head.

The next client was hardly more than a boy. In jeans and tee shirt. With glazed eyes. Not even seeing her as a person. All rushing and anxious. And very likely on drugs.

The third that night was older. More demanding. Physically heavy. He left her feeling bruised and battered.

And so her days and nights passed. She lost track of time.

Elena was given instructions by the man who arranged their work. And warned that she must be pleasant to the clients. Do exactly what they wanted. And above all keep them happy. If she didn't perform well, she would pay. So her sweet smile expressed enjoyment. Her dark eyes were warm. She whispered words in her own language and played their game for her life.

When she got her chance to leave her home in Bulgaria, she had grabbed it with both hands. An acquaintance of her brother had said he could arrange for her to get a job in Ireland. She had been educated and hoped that she would learn English quickly and be in a position to repay her father who had given her his precious life savings so that she could travel to this country.

But it didn't take long for her to realise why she was here. And that the friend of her brother had simply used their family for money. Her immediate reaction had been to leave and try to get home, but they had taken her passport. She wasn't allowed a telephone or given any opportunity to write a letter to her parents, and didn't know whether she would even have the courage to tell them her situation, knowing that they would be horrified.

Over the first few weeks she was accepting of her situation, too scared to do anything which would draw their attention upon her. The person who arranged her day to day living had some understanding of her language but he was a rough man, who didn't hesitate to thump her across the head if he felt like it. She was moved around. The distances varied. Spending a week at a time in different places. Travelling late at night with other women. As time passed, she looked for a chance to escape and was determined to get away.

So Elena watched her surroundings. Learned a little of the language of the Russian women who were in other apartments in the building and were moved with her. So at least she was able to talk to them. And grew stronger, knowing more. She recognised towns and cities now. Particularly Dublin. Always taken to the same complex but held in a different apartment. Outside, she looked for police cars. Noted they were white with *Garda* painted on the side. She looked for where they were parked, and could see that there was a station not too far from the complex.

She took her chance one night when her client was a particularly inebriated man, who slept through some of his allocated time, and talked to her in a rambling fashion for the rest 'of it. Quickly she dressed, and helped him to the lift. They crossed the front foyer and went out through the main door. As he stumbled down the steps, she left him and ran towards the gates.

It was after two o'clock in the morning, and there was no one about, just the occasional car travelling past. She moved quickly, kept to the shadows, and headed for the police station. Hurrying now, she glanced over her shoulder frequently, but to her relief the street was empty. She continued on. Her high heels clattered. The building was up ahead. There were two police cars outside. As she swung through the door and leaned against the counter trying to catch her breath, she prayed they would understand and help her.

Chapter Two

Running along the river path by the edge of the Dodder River, Inspector Grace McKenzie put pressure on her body to complete the five km in under thirty minutes, the target for today. Her work phone rang. She ignored it and smiled at Kim as they ran along. Both of them tried to run as often as they could. Kim only available when her two kids were at school. Grace grabbing an hour if it was possible to squeeze it into her schedule. She was off duty this morning having worked into the small hours the night before and felt the better of the run already, the tiredness she had felt after three hours sleep already drifting away. For the last couple of weeks she hadn't had any time off, such was her workload at the moment.

They reached their finishing point at Milltown Bridge, and stopped to do some stretching exercises. Grace and Kim had met at the gym and a strong friendship had developed between the two women over the years.

'Better respond to this call,' Grace said with a rueful grin.

'The Super wants to see you straight away.' Peter was her right hand man, Sergeant Peter O'Carroll, a dear friend who had been working with her for many years.

'Be there asap,' Grace replied. She turned back to Kim. 'Work. Better go.' She was already running in the direction of her home.

'See you.' Kim waved.

Grace lived alone in a red-bricked Victorian house in Ranelagh. She liked the narrow cul-de-sac near Beechwood Avenue. Her corner house, the last on the street, was sheltered by trees and very private. She didn't know her neighbours except for a brief *hallo* occasionally and that suited her. Grace had been in the Gardaí for almost twenty years and had moved up the ranks to the level of Detective Inspector and loved every minute of her work.

Now she showered and changed quickly. Her wardrobe for work didn't vary much. A few plain suits in dark colours, coordinated shirts, and comfortable shoes with a low wedge heel which enabled her to run or walk quickly with ease. No jewellery, or make-up, just a little lip gloss. Wild red hair which floated in a halo around her face was bunched up, and held behind her head with a grip. Green blue eyes were startling against the creamy colour of her skin.

She hurried along the landing to the top of the stairs but then stopped and looked back. A sudden longing swept through her but she closed the door, turned the key in the lock, and quickly made her way downstairs. Before she left she pulled a cigarette from a pack in her pocket. It was a nervous gesture, a slight shake in her hand as she held the lighter to the tip and drew deeply.

At the station, she went straight to the Superintendent's office. Peter was already there.

'Sorry, I was running,' she said and stood beside Peter.

'Sit,' the Super said.

She did as he asked, but actually hated to sit. Detested that waiting feeling. Always needing to be on the move. Making progress.

'This is a case in which neither of you were involved before, but ran to ground without much evidence. We're dealing with the trafficking of women from abroad for prostitution, and now we've got a break. So I'm putting you on the case and you can choose your team. I want to get results.' He picked up a sheet of paper in his hand and stared at it. 'A young Bulgarian woman came into a station a few hours ago. She is badly traumatised and tells a horrific story of being brought here supposedly for work, and finding herself having to provide sex for an increasing number of men. It was only through a fluke that she managed to get away from the apartment block and make her way to the station. She's in hospital at the moment but I want you to interview her, Grace, as soon as

6

you think it's appropriate. I hope she can give us some information so that we can catch the bastards.' He grimaced as he handed her a file. 'Her whereabouts is being kept confidential, they could be looking for her, and I've arranged for a Garda to be on duty outside the room at all times.'

A nurse led the way into the room, followed by Grace, and a translator. The girl, who's name was Elena, lay in bed, propped up on pillows. She stared at them, eyes full of fear. The nurse patted her hand, and Grace smiled, took out her ID and showed it to her. The girl nodded.

She had left it a few days before finally going to interview her, although the translator had been there in the meantime putting her at ease.

Grace sat down by the bedside. The medical staff had said that she was slowly improving, but the smallest thing could send her into a panic. A door opening quickly. Loud noises. The sound of the soft footsteps of the nurses. Even the fact of the Garda on duty seemed to make little difference to the girl.

Gently Grace questioned her through the translator, but found out little more than the Super had told them. They didn't talk to her for very long as she was obviously upset even describing her ordeal, but Grace arranged through the translator to return the following day and continue the interview.

Grace sat at the bar, and sipped a gin and tonic. A crowd from the station were there celebrating someone's promotion.

'Do you think we'll get much from her?' Peter downed the last of his glass of Coke.

'Don't know, she's so afraid.' She stared into space, back in that hospital with Elena, and was only brought into the present again by the barman walking across her vision. 'I was thinking we should bring a psychologist in on the case. Someone like that would get through to her better than we could.'

'What about Mark Williams?' Peter asked.

'Yea, why not.'

'I'll give him a call.'

'Thanks. Another drink?' she asked, and waved at the barman.

He stood up. 'Not for me thanks, I'm off. The in-laws are coming over.'

'The way we work is tough on wives and kids.' Grace raised her glass and the barman nodded. 'I'll come out with you, I need a smoke.' In the street, she lit a cigarette.

'Are you ever going to give up those fags?' he asked.

'I'd like to,' she smiled at him. 'But don't know if I'll ever succeed.'

'You're such a healthy person in every way, you're fit, work out at the gym, run, you could pull down any man. And are you still doing Karate?'

'No time these days.'

'You are a contradiction,' he smiled.

'Perhaps.'

'Why not try hypnosis to get off the cigarettes? That's supposed to be quite good.'

'I have a distinct aversion to anyone delving into my mind,' she actually shuddered.

'Don't want your secrets to be exposed, that it?' he asked.

'Exactly.'

'I'm off, see you in the morning. Going to hang around here for long?' he asked.

'No, I'll be going home now, just have to call a taxi.'

He grinned, and loped off.

Grace finished the cigarette, returned to the bar and as she sipped her gin and tonic, thought about Elena. Normally she could deal with cases in an objective manner, and never let the individual circumstances bother her too much, more interested in finding the culprit and bringing him or her to justice. Now she couldn't get it out of her head. Suddenly, she stared at her hands. It felt as if something crawled on her skin. On her palms. The backs. In between her fingers. Itching. But there was no rash or anything else to be seen there.

She was puzzled.

Chapter Three

John slammed the heavy front door, and marched across the marble-floored living room. 'The bastard let me down, and I had to find someone else to do the job,' he shouted.

'What happened, my love?' Ruth was immediately concerned.

He ignored her, going upstairs and into the master bedroom.

'Fancy a coffee?' She followed him.

'No,' he grunted, as he threw off his clothes which ended up in a heap on the floor. 'I'll have a kip, and get up about twelve, rustle up brunch for that time.' He got into bed.

'Could you let me have some money? I need to shop,' she asked hesitantly. She hated having to do this. When they had moved in together at first he was extremely generous. But lately he had changed. Querying everything she spent.

'I gave you a hundred yesterday, what happened to that?' He raised himself up on his elbow and stared at her.

'I bought food and ...'

'You were buying stuff for yourself?' His voice held accusation.

'It's just a summer top.'

'You know I like to buy your clothes. I choose them. I pay for them.'

'I saw it in a boutique, and it wasn't expensive,' she explained, a rush of guilt in the soft underbelly of her voice.

'Why do you need to buy anything? You've wardrobes of clothes outside. Designed by some of the top people in the business and costing an *arm and a leg* too. I don't know what goes on in your head, Ruth,' he exploded.

'It was nothing, forget about it.' She regretted saying anything.

'It angers me when you go off and do your own thing, it's like you don't need me any longer.'

'No baby, that's not true. I told you I just made a *spur of the moment* decision and I'm sorry about that, I know I should have waited until we were together but ...' She pursed her lips.

The telephone rang. That old fashioned ring tone repeated a couple of times.

'Where's your phone?' he asked.

'Downstairs.'

'You know it should be answered immediately, if there's a delay, they could lose interest,' he barked.

She rushed downstairs, picked it up, and listened for a few seconds. 'Yes, we arrange everything. Let me take your details.' She pulled a notepad towards her, and asked a few basic questions.

Later, Ruth stood in the shower and let the water rain over her. It was hot. Refreshing. She liked it like that, and after a few minutes, turned the temperature to cold with a sharp intake of breath. The shock of one extreme to another. And back to hot again. And cold. And hot. And cold.

She stepped out and wrapped herself in a towel. In the dressing room she slid open the door of the wardrobe and stared at the array of clothes hanging there. He was right. She had an amazing collection of day dresses. Suits. Casual. Evening. All designer labels. She flicked through them, and chose an outfit by *Joseph* in a soft cream.

Before dressing, she picked up a lilac top which lay on the armchair, held it against herself and looked at her reflection in the mirror. It was so pretty. She had really liked it, but knew it wasn't possible to wear it now.

'We'll have dinner at Sonaris, eight,' John announced.

'OK.'

'And don't wear whatever rag you bought yesterday, we'll be meeting some important people this evening.'

'Yea.'

He kissed her. 'Cheer up, I love you.'

'Do you?' She reached towards him.

'Course I do, don't I tell you every day?' John said, laughing as he ruffled her short blonde hair. 'Now tell me what you think of the Armani?' He turned around.

'It looks great.'

'How is the cut? The shape of the shoulders?'

'Perfect. You know you can wear anything.' She had been attracted to him in the first place by his looks. He was dark haired, tanned and brown eyed, without an ounce of spare flesh. In Seville, they had met in a bar where she worked. At first, she had thought he was Spanish, and when she discovered he was English and lived in Dublin, she was thrilled. Being so long out of Ireland, it was like being home again even to talk about the place. They had hit it off immediately. There was something about him she couldn't resist and after a short time she followed him back to Dublin and moved into his penthouse apartment. He owned a lot of property around the country, he said, and although he was in negative equity because of the recession, his rental income was considerable. He asked her to work with him and she was glad to do it. He loved her. And Ruth wanted to be loved. That above all else, and would have done anything for him, just to be loved.

It was idyllic at first. They lived in a large luxurious penthouse in a development at Sandyford, and enjoyed a glittering social life. John had taken her everywhere. While she had travelled extensively in the past herself, these trips with John to Paris, New York, Dubai, Thailand, among many other places, were magical. The hotels they stayed in were at least 5 Star, and higher if it was available. He bought her jewellery, clothes, shoes, all designer labels. Her head was in a spin, never so happy.

But there were conditions. She only became aware gradually.

'What about your parents, you've never said?' he had asked curiously.

'My parents are dead, and I've lost touch with relations.'

'Any siblings?'

'A sister ...but I haven't seen her in many years.'

'That's perfect.' He kissed her. 'I'm not into Sunday lunch with the family.'

11

'You don't have to worry,' she reassured. Ruth had fallen out with her sister. Left Ireland and never made contact again. And was certain that she wouldn't be welcomed back with open arms after all this time.

'You're a woman without connections, exactly what I want.'

But when Ruth discovered exactly how John made his money, she was shocked.

'I don't think I can do this,' she protested.

'It's only the computer, and phone, you don't have to meet any clients. You'll be my personal assistant.'

She was uncertain.

'And there will be some deliveries to various places. It's to keep the business running smoothly.'

'What sort of deliveries?' She was puzzled.

'Just items. Look, stop worrying. I just need you to help me. We'll run the show together,' he cajoled, and kissed her.

'Who worked with you before we met?' She tried not to show suspicion. 'Was it a girlfriend?'

'No. You are the first in a long time. And that's the truth of it. Believe me, my love, you are the only one for me. But I want total commitment. Never speak to anyone about what we do.' He kissed her. 'If you promise me that, I will take good care of you.'

She acquiesced. The strength of her love for him swept all of her scruples away.

Ruth was kept busy on the laptop and phone over the next couple of hours, and then left the apartment. There were daily appointments in various parts of the city and suburbs. Every day, somewhere different. Someone different.

Her first meeting today would take place in a library. The instructions were exacting. Browse for five minutes. Then take a couple of books and sit at a table reading. This was the part of it she disliked the most.

He looked nondescript. His hair was thin on top. Wearing a dark jacket and jeans. He sat opposite. But didn't acknowledge her. The covers of the books they were reading almost touched. She kept her eyes down. Aware that he was flicking the pages.

And then, suddenly, he was gone. But he had left something behind. It was a plain plastic bag which stood on the floor at the end of the table.

Chapter Four

Grace carefully chose the members of the team she wanted to work on the trafficking case. Some had been involved on a previous case a couple of years ago, but most of them had not, and she was anxious to have a fresh look at all the facts.

'Elena is feeling much better now. But it's horrific to think she was treated in such a violent way by those men.' Every time she remembered those huge dark eyes her own stomach clenched, and she could actually feel the girl's fear. Knew exactly what she had gone through. Understood the sense of being held against her will. Screaming for help. Grace stared down at her hands. That irritation had returned. She tried to rub it away. But couldn't.

'Excuse me, I must ...' she turned and left the office. In the ladies room, she held her hands under the flow of water. But that feeling wouldn't go away. She stared at herself in the mirror. Her complexion was pale. Eyes wide. Fearful. She dashed water across her face and dabbed it dry with a paper towel. But then felt weak, and had to lean against the sink to gather her strength.

Feeling a little better after a few minutes she went back to the office and resumed the meeting.

'Elena wants to go home as soon as possible. But has agreed to look at some mug shots. Although she's terrified of going back to the apartment complex, I'm hoping Mark will be able to persuade her to tell us where it is situated. This isn't something Elena will put out of her head any time soon. She might never recover. It will always be there, underneath, eating away ...' she stopped abruptly.

'Apparently the complex is not very far from the Garda Station she went to,' Peter added.

Grace pointed to the map which was pinned to the wall. 'This information should give us a real lead and help us to locate the people who are organising this ring. They're making huge money out of these poor women. They are used and abused by them. Lives are destroyed. And if families knew what was happening to their daughters, very likely they would never accept them back. That's what our girl is afraid of. She's in *no-man's land*.' Grace took a deep breath. 'In the meantime, I want you to go through the files of any previous cases. Look at all possibilities. Examine every detail minutely. And try to think outside ...' she searched for a word ...'the norm, if you can.'

Grace arranged to meet Mark Williams at the hospital later. A psychologist who often worked on cases with them, he was invaluable in his approach, and at times could get more information from witnesses and suspects than the whole team together.

'Elena is very nervous, and I've tried to be gentle with her. But it's awkward through the translator. The words don't come out right,' she said softly.

He nodded. A tall well built man, broad shouldered, ex-rugby player. His eyes met hers, hazel, warm.

They went into the room with the translator.

Elena still looked scared when she saw them, but Grace tried to assuage her fears through the translator. She introduced Mark, but Elena reacted badly. She gripped Grace's hand tightly and tears filled her eyes.

He tipped her arm. 'I'll go, see you outside.'

Grace spoke with her then, and the girl was comforted. After a time, she managed to persuade Elena to take her to the apartment complex in which the men had held her as soon as she felt up to it.

'I'm sorry, but I suppose she was reminded of what happened ...' Grace said to Mark.

'It's perfectly understandable.'

'If Elena can take us to the complex, then it means that we have a good chance of identifying the people who run this trafficking ring. I'd give anything ...' she hesitated.

'This case is very important to you,' he said. 'I can see that.'

'Can you?' she asked sharply, surprised.

'Yes. It's obvious.'

'She's such a gentle girl, I hate the thought of what she had to endure,' she murmured.

The translator followed her out, and said goodbye.

'When you're going to find the apartment I'll come along. She may not react so badly next time she sees a man, Peter will be there as well no doubt?'

'I've explained who you are so she mightn't be so scared.'

'I hope we get those responsible, but it is going to be difficult. These rings are wide ranging, and there are many people involved. They constantly shift and change. If they think you've got something on them they cover their tracks immediately,' Mark said.

'I will get whoever is at the top. Bastard,' she muttered, vehement. 'If it's the last thing I do.'

Grace left the office about eight, and headed home. On the way, she stopped off at a local supermarket to pick up something to eat, grabbing a basket on her way in. Grace did everything hurriedly. Like a person who was running out of time. Her purchasing habit was simply to rush to the delicatessen or chilled food section and chose whatever took the least time to prepare. For Grace it had to be quick. Tonight it was a cooked roast chicken, and some oven chips. Not the best diet in the world, and something which needed to be changed radically, what she was putting into her body left a lot to be desired.

Immediately she stepped through the front door at home she turned off the alarm, put down her shopping bag and hurried upstairs to open the locked door on the landing. This evening all she needed was to close her eyes in that dark velvet space and know that immediately the tension would ease.

Grace sat in front of the television, and sipped red wine. Her dinner was on a tray, the Irish Times spread out on the couch beside her. She held a cigarette between tense narrow fingers, nails tipped white, able to smoke in comfort at home. Everywhere else had some restriction. And while she agreed with the law, reluctant to endanger other people with her own habit, hated having to find somewhere to have a cigarette. A chain smoker, she lit another cigarette from the tip of the first when it had burned down.

She had bought her usual half a dozen newspapers, interested in reading the various journalists on the same subject. Sometimes, the ethos of the newspapers made for quite interesting articles. And she was always keen to see the reporting of crime, particularly in the tabloids. Although knowing quite well the truth was often far from the facts reported, there was always the possibility of a tiny nugget of information which would help her.

She went through the dailies, and the Evening Herald. Speed-reading. The headline grabbed her attention first, and her finger drew her eyes down the lines of type in the article. Breathing fast, she absorbed the words. If something caught her interest, it was outlined in a red marker. There was a lot of newsprint but Grace had done this since she had joined the Gardai. Always anxious to be on top of the job, she had to prove herself, particularly to her family who had never agreed with her choice of career. Every line was read, and she was certain that the vital information could be stored in her file of papers and accessed if ever needed. But that was a long time ago and now it wasn't necessary to read the news in hard copy any longer. The internet could supply anything needed at a click. And there was so much stored upstairs, she couldn't possibly find a particular article at this stage.

But Grace had not been able to shake the habit of buying and reading the newspapers every day and now that obsession overshadowed her life. Like a silent creature it followed her around and terrorised. Later she went upstairs. It was like another world. Into which she brought the day's news. The happenings of the people of Ireland and the world too. Encompassed in these sheets of paper. Life and death. Happiness and sorrow. It was all there.

She went into her bedroom. It was very small now. Where once she had a double bed it had decreased to the width of a single bed by the walls of newspapers which stretched up to the ceiling, and took up all that side of the room, completely blocking the window so that there was no natural light. That left just a foot of space to move on one side of the bed where there were other newspapers stacked. A fitted wardrobe with sliding doors at the end allowed just enough room to take her clothes out. Every other inch of space was filled with piles of folded newspapers.

Grace knew that the basic reason why she read all the newspapers and stored them was to build up information, but in her heart of hearts was aware that this wasn't at the root of it. She had grown up in Waterford, the youngest of four children of Mary and Liam McKenzie, who ran a pharmacy in the city. None of her siblings were interested in following in their parents' footsteps by taking over the business, and all had emigrated and were living their lives in other countries.

Grace wasn't interested either. Always a longing in her to do something else which would mean she could develop her own strengths. Be able to deal with any situation which presented itself. She couldn't explain to anyone why this was, but when it came to her Leaving Cert year and making decisions about which degree course to follow in college, she had to tell her parents that pharmacy wasn't for her, and she wanted to take up a career in the Garda Síochána.

'But why would you want to do that?' Her father had been astonished. 'It's a tough dangerous career. Are you out of your head?'

'I just like the idea of helping people.'

'It would be far better to help them from a health point of view. Sure the chemist is a huge part of the community. You know how many people come in here and bare their souls to both of us every day of the week. Tell us their secrets. Ask for advice.'

Her mother nodded her head in agreement. 'You've always got A's in school, so there will be no problem in achieving the points needed. You've got the brains. You have to use them. Make the most of your talents.'

She had tried to withstand the pressure during that last year at school. It was difficult. Her self esteem was very low. She found it difficult to argue her case. They tried hard to persuade her against

18

the decision but Grace won them around in the end. She was their youngest and they loved her. They couldn't say no.

So she went on. Determined to do well. She would put the past behind her and prove to the family that her choice of career had been worthwhile. More importantly, Grace had to prove to herself that she could handle any situation. To physically put down any man. Intellectually put down any man. And have the power to do so.

Now she went out on to the landing and stared around her. The newspapers were piled here too. And in the other bedrooms as well. She pushed open a door with difficulty, and stood in a narrow space which ran the length of the room between walls of grey. In her arms she carried a large bundle of papers tied with twine. At the end, the column of newspapers didn't quite reach the ceiling and she climbed up on a stool and carefully forced them into the space.

There wasn't much room left. Enough for about a week's collection of papers? What was she going to do then?

Chapter Five

It was almost twelve midnight. Warm. Humid. Unusual weather conditions for Ireland. John reached the complex and pressed the remote. The gates opened and he swung down into the underground car park. The smooth purr of the Mercedes engine made hardly a sound. He looked at his mobile phone to check the time. There was a new consignment coming in and he needed to inspect. Headlights cut a channel through the darkness. A car swung into the area, driving fast. It curved around into a parking space, and jammed on, the brakes applied too sharp.

'Fuck you,' John muttered, and compressed his lips. His smooth good-looking face suddenly ugly.

Car doors sprang open. People climbed out. Laughter echoed. Two men and two women walked towards the lift. The car lights flashed as the alarm was activated.

John leaned back in the seat.

Minutes passed. Headlights illuminated the shadows for a second time. Another car drove into a space close to the lift. The lights switched off. One man and three women climbed out. He went to the boot and lifted out suitcases. The women took one each. They walked towards the lift entrance.

John waited for a few minutes and then walked quickly towards the lift. He pressed the button. It had stopped on the first floor. He pressed again. Impatient. A moment later the door slid back and the lift took him up into the building.

He entered the apartment. The driver of the car came into the hallway.

'How did it go?' he asked.

'Fine.'

He moved to a large mirror and stood in front of it, able to see directly into the living room. The other man stood beside him.

The three young women sat silently in the large room. His eyes moved across their features. He was pleased. They were exactly what he wanted. Dark haired. Eyes large. Fearful. Unsure of their surroundings. 'Let them stay here for a couple of nights. Then we'll move them into the other apartments and put them working. Have you got their passports?'

'Yes.'

He put his hand out. The man handed the documents to him and he slipped them into his pocket.

'Move the other group out now,' he said, and left.

John sat in his car and watched as four other women appeared out of the lift. They carried their belongings in suitcases and black plastic bags and were quickly hunted into the waiting car which then sped off.

He thought about the Bulgarian girl who had run away. Bitch. He had people looking for her. But she seemed to have dropped out of sight. He was angry. She was costing him money. It was expensive bringing these women into Ireland. His complex web fanned out all over Europe. Supplying not only the market here but also those in other countries. He wondered had she run away with one of the clients and that made him even angrier. She was his property and when he caught her, he would make her pay and she would never be able to attempt such a thing again.

Still, one person couldn't destabilize his organisation. He reminded himself. Never. It was tight. Run like a well oiled machine. And he kept it that way.

He drove to the house in Dalkey. This was where he lived really. His own home where he could look out at the star studded night sky and think. The house overlooked the sea. It was surrounded by high walls and trees, utterly private and secluded. He kept his collection of vintage cars here. And also his art and antiques. His main fortune was in Swiss banks. Cash. And diamonds. Although his large property portfolio had collapsed, he was still an extremely wealthy man. He thought of Ruth. Lately he behaved in a cruel way towards her, quite cruel. But he had to keep her where he could watch her. She was important to him. He could trust her and that was everything. She loved him and would never betray him. He told her he loved her when he had first met her in Seville. There was something about her that he had cherished. A fragility. But lately he had grown bored with her, and couldn't even be bothered to let her know when he wouldn't be home. He wasn't too concerned with how she felt, and just used her for his own ends.

Chapter Six

'Happy Birthday, Grace.' Kim hugged her. 'It's great to see you, I was beginning to wonder had you been delayed.'

'There's always something which crops up, you know what it's like. I'm sorry.' Grace handed her a pink gift bag containing chocolates and a bottle of wine.

'Thank you, but this is your birthday, you shouldn't have brought anything,' Kim said, smiling.

'You know, I didn't even remember it, if you hadn't reminded me then today would be just like any other.'

Kim was so glad that her friend had managed to get here for dinner. On so many occasions, she had had to cancel at the last moment because of work, and it had been some time since the friends had been together for an evening. Grace had an unpredictable schedule, and Kim's husband Andrew was an airline pilot and travelled constantly. Between the two of them, it was very difficult to arrange a date to suit. Now, this evening was extra special because it was Grace's birthday.

'To Grace,' Kim raised her glass. 'Another year.'

'Don't remind me. Thirty-eight.' She grimaced.

'It's only a number,' Kim said.

'You're as young as you feel,' Andrew added.

'That's a cliché.'

'You look wonderful,' Kim reassured.

'No more than twenty-one,' Andrew said, smiling.

'Well, thank you, Andy baby, how is it you always know the right thing to say to a woman?' Grace blew him a kiss.

'I've had plenty of practice,' he grinned at Kim.

'She is a lucky woman, isn't she?' Grace said.

Kim blushed.

'Having you and the kids ...' There was envy in Grace's voice.

'You'll be next, why not?'

'Think it's a bit late for all that.'

'You have to think of yourself,' Kim warned. 'Your work uses up all your energy. Don't let it take over completely.'

'Don't remind me,' Grace said. 'Anyway, who'd put up with me?' she laughed.

'I can think of a number of men who would give their eye teeth,' Andrew grinned.

'Send them around.' She raised her glass.

'Blind date?' Kim asked with a teasing grin.

'God forbid.'

'The internet?'

'Meeting all sorts of weird bods, no thanks.'

'One of the women whose kids are at Jason's school hooked up with a fellow on some site. I've met him, and he seems really nice.'

Grace's phone rang. 'Excuse me, guys, must take this.' She left the table.

'I'll just get the coffee.' Kim went into the kitchen, and was followed by Grace who had finished her call.

'Do you have to leave?' Kim asked.

'No.'

'Good.' She set a tray.

'You have such a collection of cookery books, a whole row of them. Do you use them all?' Grace stared at them.

'No, just that one there mostly.' She pointed.

Grace pulled another one from the shelf. 'This is an old one,' She read the title. *Full and Plenty, Complete Guide to Good Cooking by Maura Laverty.*

'That belonged to my mother,' Kim smiled.

Grace flicked through the pages. 'Look, here's a recipe written by your Mum.' She took the sheet of notepaper and unfolded it. 'Pineapple upside down cake, imagine, that must be gorgeous. And there's lots more cut out from newspapers, you should try some of these recipes.'

'I should.' Kim poured cream into a jug.

A small photograph fell out of the back of the book. Grace picked it up. 'It's you. What age were you then?'

Kim looked at it. 'No, that's not me, it's ...' she hesitated suddenly. 'Course it's me, what am I saying?'

Chapter Seven

The plastic bag looked innocuous. Left behind. Like someone's shopping - a few items for dinner. Ruth picked it up, and walked slowly out of the library to the car.

She drove to her next appointment. It was in Temple Bar. She parked the car some distance away and walked through the narrow streets until she came to a small pizza place. A man worked in front of a large oven. She waited until he had finished and turned around. He nodded but didn't really look at her. His eyes were on the bag as she silently handed it to him and left the place. Never wasting time. Reluctant to reveal her identity. Hating the thought that he might think she was one of the women who offered a service? Her body passed from one pair of hands to another like a used rag.

Next, it was a cafe on Dorset Street. A grocery in Rathmines. A newsagents in Walkinstown. And the procedure was repeated more than once. Her last call was at a shopping centre. She walked slowly along the mall towards the entrance.

It was a busy place. A little girl played with a ball. She was about three years old, had dark curly hair and was dressed in a pretty red dress. Two boys fought over a toy. The mother separated them. A group of teenagers sat together on a seat, laughing.

Ruth had a sudden longing for something, but couldn't quite grasp what it was. A sense of loneliness swept through her. She began to cry. Tears streamed down her cheeks, and were dried with a tissue which disintegrated before long.

She was aware of people glancing at her. Dressed in her designer clothes, she didn't think they were admiring her. More likely in these days, it was envy. So many people trying to survive. They couldn't afford designer, couldn't afford to buy clothes at all,

26

except for their children when they needed the basics. What was she doing here? Carrying bags which contained enough to transform any of those lives round her many times over.

Sometimes she wondered if she was followed. Had John put a tail on her? Fear skirted at her heels. How large was his organisation? Were there other women hurrying to and from shops, cafes, libraries, cinemas or even churches, carrying bags in the same way? Clutching the handles tight. So afraid.

'You're late,' John said as soon as Ruth arrived back at the apartment.

She was surprised to see him. He had gone out earlier to a meeting and she hadn't expected him to be back so soon. 'I came straight home.'

'It shouldn't have taken that length of time,' he snapped, grabbing the bag from her.

'The traffic was heavy.'

He stared at her. 'What happened to your make-up? The mascara is all over your face.'

'I got caught in the rain,' She took off her lime green coat and hung it in the cloakroom. Glancing in the mirror she wiped the black streaks with a tissue.

He watched her from the doorway. 'Looks like you were crying.'

'No,' she forced a laugh. 'Am I OK now? All clean?'

'Yea baby, I don't want anyone to make you cry. If they do, they'll have to deal with me. You just mention the name and they're history,' he smiled, and moved towards her. Kissed her. 'There's just enough time to shower and …'

Ruth didn't know what to do. After taking her head off for being a little late he wanted to make love? Still, she rationalised, it could be worse. He was unpredictable in the extreme.

He put his arms around her, and nuzzled her neck. 'Come upstairs.'

She hesitated, and then eased into him. Couldn't say no. Never could.

The evening at Sonaris Restaurant was enjoyable up to a point. The restaurant was part of a chain owned by John and somewhere they were often to be seen. It was very popular, designed in such a way as to give the ultimate in privacy with alcoves around the perimeter and a general open area in the centre. The decor had a Victorian feel, the ambience warm and inviting. This evening the place was crowded. The recession wasn't affecting Sonaris. The two couples with whom they had dinner were strangers to her, but Ruth found them pleasant enough. As the night wore on, there was too much drinking and lots of laughter. She wasn't in the mood for it so just slowly sipped a glass of white wine.

'Come on, darling, let the waiter top you up,' John encouraged, laughing as he leaned across and kissed her.

'No thanks, I've had enough.' She held her hand over the glass. The waiter nodded and moved on to one of the other women.

'Abstemious tonight?' John asked. 'And you haven't finished your meal? What's wrong?'

She shook her head. Embarrassed in front of the others.

'Come on, eat up,' he encouraged.

'I'm not hungry,' she smiled at him. Feeling like a six year old, and now quite unable to finish the pasta on the plate in front of her.

He ignored her and topped up her glass himself. 'At least have another drink. You don't have to drive home, pet, someone else will do that. Enjoy yourself.'

'Got your own personal chauffeur?' One of the men quipped. 'No need to worry about drink and drive, or being stopped and asked to blow in the bag.'

They all laughed.

The attention moved from her on to cars, travel, the economy. She didn't really listen, just smiled and nodded, and longed to be somewhere else. The restaurant buzzed with chat. She gazed around from where they sat in an alcove at the back when a couple rose from a table and walked towards the door. They were striking. He was tall, and good-looking. The woman wore black and was around her own height with shoulder-length blonde hair. She smiled at the manager and they chatted for a moment at the desk.

Ruth stared at her. Shocked. Unable to believe her eyes.

Chapter Eight

Kim looked at the photo. She hadn't seen it in years. Her mother had obviously tucked it into the back of her cookery book among the recipes. The image disturbed her. When was that, she wondered, and did the calculation. They were twelve years old.

'Kim?' Andrew called from the hall.

She pushed the photo into the drawer. 'Yea?'

'The parents are coming over later, can we include them to dinner?'

'Yea, sure,' she said. Normally, Kim was delighted when Andrew's parents called. And she often invited them to lunch or dinner, and they were always pleased to babysit. But this evening she had been looking forward to spending time with Andrew, just the two of them. He would be leaving first thing in the morning.

Their lives had settled into a pattern over the past couple of years. Andrew was based in London and was away most of the time on long-haul flights all over the world. And as the length of time between his flights varied, quite often he stayed in London for the few days instead of coming home. Even yesterday, she had tried to make him understand how she felt about that and suggested that they all move to London, but he had turned that down instantly.

'We want a good life for our kids, and Dublin is the best place for us to live. The education is better, and we'd only be pulling them away from their friends and schools if we left. And where would we find a home like this?'

'But we'd all be together. As it is the kids will grow up without knowing you,' she protested.

'They won't. The kids are quite used to my coming and going. We have a great relationship.'

'And what about us?' she insisted. For once they were discussing things. Usually, it was very hard to pin Andrew down to talk about any worries she had, particularly the subject of his work.

'What about us?' he grinned.

'You never take me seriously, don't realise how much I miss you.'

'Don't you think I miss you?' He kissed her.

She put her arms around him.

'It's the job, love, can't do anything about it.'

'But ...'

'Don't go on about it.' Suddenly, his voice was sharp. 'I'm fed up listening to your moaning. Every time I'm home it's the same.' His mouth twisted, and a look of dissatisfaction flashed across his face. He pushed her away from him.

She felt rejected, and hated to see this side of him. The hard side.

'Thank you for a lovely dinner, Kim.' Her mother-in-law, Dolores put away the dishes in the washer, and closed the door.

'You're welcome.' She scrubbed the pots.

'I'll pour the coffee.' The older woman picked up the percolator. 'Now you sit down and enjoy the cake I baked for you.'

'It looks delicious.'

'Cherry and almond cake,' she smiled and began to cut slices. 'Andrew's favourite.'

They sat together in the living room.

'This is wonderful, Mam.' Andrew finished his cake. 'I'll have another slice if it's there.'

'Sure,' Dolores stood up. She was in her sixties now and still youthful.

'I'd love more as well,' Andrew's father, Noel, added.

'You sit, let me get it,' Kim offered.

'No, I will,' her mother-in-law laughed. She went through to the kitchen, and came back a moment later with more cake and the coffee percolator.

'I'll go up and look in on Jason, I told him I'd tell him a story, that's if he's still awake,' Noel said. Andrew's father was a lovely man, and Kim was very fond of him. She had come to depend on Dolores and Noel, who were always there if she needed help in any way.

'Finish your cake first,' Dolores said.

'I'll have it later.' Noel walked out of the room.

'He's probably asleep by now,' Andrew commented.

'I'll just look in on him, I promised.'

Andrew shrugged, his eyes on the. television screen.

'I'll go up too.' Kim followed Noel.

Although Jason was sleeping, his grandfather sat on the edge of the bed. 'I just like to watch him,' he said softly. 'He is so like Andrew as a little boy.'

Kim tucked the duvet around Jason's shoulders.

'Should have come up sooner. I'm sorry I didn't get to tell him the story,' Noel said.

'Next time.'

'You'll tell him I came up, will you?'

'Sure.'

'These kids have changed our lives, you know,' he smiled at Kim. The kind blue eyes were warm in the craggy face. You have no idea what they mean to us.'

'I think I have.' Kim patted his hand, aware of the raised veins on the skin.

'And having you as a daughter, that's just as special.'

'I'll text you before we take off.' Andrew kissed her goodbye. A brief touch on her lips.

'Will you be back at the weekend?' she asked.

'Don't know, probably not enough time,' he said, looking past her to Jason who came downstairs holding on to the banister.

Kim was disappointed but said nothing. He had gone to bed last night still angry with her, and she lay beside him very upset and quite unable to sleep.

'Mum?' Five year old Jason jumped the last two steps. 'I can't find my shoes.'

'I'll get them for you, love.'

'See you guys.' Andrew hugged Jason, kissed Lorelai, and hurried through the front door.

She stood looking after him. Her husband. On his way to the airport to fly a plane to London, New York and onwards. Disappearing out of her life for another couple of weeks.

'Mum?' Three year old Lorelai stood in the doorway, holding a selection of pads and coloured markers in her arms. 'I want to do a tree,' she announced.

'To draw one?' Kim looked around from the big wooden kitchen table where she mixed flour and butter for pastry.

'Yes.' Lorelai slid up on a chair at the other side of the table.

'My hands are all flour, but you take a sheet of paper and a pen and draw it. Like that one in the garden, look.' She waved towards the large birch.

'That has all leaves,' Lorelai stated, her voice cross.

'They're pretty.'

'I don't want them.'

'Draw the one you want.' Kim added water and kneaded the pastry into a round ball.

Jason came into the kitchen, and ran a toy car along the table. He turned at the end and ran back up the other side, stopping when he reached Lorelai. 'What's that?'

'It's a tree.' She drew a long purple line.

'Doesn't look like a tree.'

Lorelai didn't answer, her lips puckered in concentration. 'That's branches.' She added them.

'Where are the leaves?' He picked up a marker.

'No leaves.' She pushed him away.

'Has to have leaves.' He tried to draw them on.

'Mum?' she cried.

'Jason, leave Lorelai alone.' Kim rolled out the pastry on a board.

'Leaves, leaves ...' he yelled.

'Want to put people,' the child insisted.

'No people on trees,' he said with derision. He ran the car over the drawing, caught the wheels of the little red car on the curling edge of the paper and tore it.

There was an immediate shriek of protest from Lorelai.

Kim intervened, and peace reigned again. Her mind drifted back into the past again. Lately that seemed to be happening more and more frequently. She looked across at the children. Both drew their own pictures at the table now. She went towards them and held them close.

Jason protested, and wriggled to escape her grasp.

Lorelai was happy to hug. Her little girl. Always so loving.

Suddenly, a sense of foreboding swept through her. If she ever lost her two precious children it would simply be impossible to live without them. Above all, she wanted to be there for them as they grew up. See them go to college. Meet their one true love. Have their own families. Her grandchildren. Loving them all the way.

It was almost two weeks before Andrew returned. Tall and handsome in his airline uniform. Kim was so happy to see him. It had seemed ages since he had left.

'You look great, had a good trip?' Kim kissed him.

'Yea, now what have we got for Lorelai?' He opened his bag, and gave the fair haired child a fluffy teddy bear. She hugged it.

'Say thanks to Daddy,' Kim reminded.

She clung to him.

'And now Jason, where is he?'

Kim went into the television room and found him staring at one of his favourite programmes. 'Dad's home, and he's got something for you.'

He jumped up immediately, and rushed into the kitchen. 'What did you bring, Dad?'

'Here you are,' Andrew handed him his present.

'What is it?' He tore the paper off excitedly. 'A transformer.' He jumped up and down.

'And I'll give you a present later, Kim.' His hand slid down her back and he pinched her bottom.

'Thank you,' she said, and giggled.

That evening Kim couldn't wait to put the kids to bed so that she would be alone with Andrew. Always that longing for him when he was away, missing him so much. The weather was pleasant, and she barbequed steaks on the patio.

'Smells good.' Andrew stood behind her, and took the fork from her. 'Let me.' He turned the meat. Just about able to manage that. Generally he wasn't much good around the house, having neither the ability or the inclination.

He opened a bottle of red wine.

'Cheers.' She raised her glass.

'To you, my love. So good to be home.'

'When are you away again?'

'Sunday.'

'Where are you flying to this time?' she asked. Really not wanting to hear it. The long haul trips he made these days were just too hard. She spent her time wondering where he was. Who he was with. Jealous of the time he spent with others away from her.

'Dublin, London, Dubai.'

'Pity it's not shorter ...' The words were out before she knew it, having promised herself that she wouldn't bring up the subject again. But to her surprise, he smiled.

'If that was the case maybe you'd see too much of me. Then coming home wouldn't be so exciting. Who wants a life of nine to five. Boring. Leave in the morning, fly a short hop, and be back in time for supper. It's not for me,' he reached behind him and handed her a bag.

She opened a ribbon, and pushed aside the layers of black tissue paper inside. 'It's beautiful,' she whispered, and held up the short black lace negligee.

'I want to see it on you, come on up, now.' He took her hand. 'We'll leave the dishes until the morning.' His lips pressed on hers, and he took her upstairs into the bedroom, and closed the door.

They undressed each other. His scent was enticing. It did something to her. Always did. He picked up the nightdress, and held it over her, slowly bringing it down over her head until it fitted snugly.

He smiled. 'You're beautiful.'

She leaned into him.

Then they went to bed.

The following morning, she left him sleeping and took the children swimming but on her return he wasn't there. Deciding to change, she went up to the bedroom. Anxious to look as attractive as possible now that he was home, she chose white jeans, pink tee-shirt and matching sandals.

Then she made the bed and hung up his uniform in the wardrobe. Threw the shirt and underwear he had worn yesterday into the wash basket. His flight bag was on the chair, and she checked the contents. There were a couple of shirts and underwear in it but they were clean and she removed them to prevent any further creasing. He usually had his clothes laundered by the hotel wherever he was and didn't bring a pile of washing home. Her phone rang. She began to reach into her pocket but then realised that the ring tone was different and seemed to be coming from the bag. She stared into it but couldn't see a phone. It was empty. But the tone continued. She checked the pockets but could find nothing. Listening carefully she decided that it had to be coming from the bottom of the bag. She ran her fingers around the edge of the leather and managed to lift it up and there, vibrating slightly, was the phone.

It rang off and after a moment, there was a couple of beeps. Someone had texted. Kim stared at it aware that she had never seen it before. And that ring tone wasn't familiar. Her mind was a crazy melee of questions as to why Andrew kept a phone in a secret part of his bag? She reached for it, hypnotised, her fingers outstretched, and was about to pick it up when she heard the front door bang.

'I'm home,' he called from downstairs.

Kim heard the kids shout, and the sound of them all going out into the garden. She left the phone there and went down. Andrew played football with the children and she joined in. There was much laughter. Later, they took a break and sat out.

'I found a phone in your flight bag. Did you get a new one?' she asked.

He looked at her. 'Just bought one to use when I'm in the States.'

'Oh.' She didn't know what else to say.

'I need a spare anyway, can't be without.' He stood up, and rejoined the kids.

Chapter Nine

Grace lay in bed. It was Sunday morning. Warm. Sticky. The heat wave which had descended on Ireland over the last few days was difficult to bear. The stacked walls of newspapers crowded in on her and she experienced a sudden sense of desperation. What was she going to do? There was no space left up here. And she had an overwhelming desire to begin using the rooms downstairs. Metres of space just waiting there. Empty.

For years she had thrown herself into her job. Worked long hours and came home eventually to a cold unresponsive house. While she had met men over the years, none had ever lasted the course. There was never anyone with whom she could share holidays. Christmas. Easter. Birthdays. No one to love. No man in her life. Or children either.

She got up. Showered, dressed, and went downstairs where she had created something very different. With pristine white walls. Pale wooden floors. Colour scheme in shades of beige and cream. Minimalist. Here she could escape. For a time. But was drawn inevitably upstairs again. Held in those stuffy rooms, a prisoner of her own making. But knew if she began to store the newspapers down here, then she would be swallowed up entirely, imagining the piles of newspapers building up in the hall, filling it up with words. And then the sitting room, living room, study, bathroom, every space crammed. Without a doubt, if she gave in to her craving she would lose herself. Grace shivered.

The streets were busy. Grace sat in the back of the car with Elena. Peter drove, Mark sat beside him. She smiled at the girl, patted her hand and hoped she was reassured. Immediately, she clasped Grace's hand and held on tight.

They went towards the Garda station where she had gone on that night, and then followed her directions away from it. While she still had very little English, she understood left and right and managed to indicate to them which way to go. Peter drove slowly. The girl's grip grew even tighter.

'We're nearby,' Grace said to Peter.

He slowed down.

'There, that must be it.' A large gated apartment block came into view on their left. It was five stories high like many of the *Celtic Tiger* developments, but already had began to look rather run-down. She took a note of the name.

'Is that the place, Elena?' she asked.

The girl nodded.

'Drive past and turn,' instructed Grace. 'Don't worry, you'll be all right with us,' she said to Elena, smiling.

The girl burst into tears.

Grace handed her a tissue.

'We won't hang around here, it's too much for her,' she said to Peter and Mark.

They drove back to the station.

'She's been on to her parents, and is anxious to go home. We've arranged a passport for her but it hasn't been issued yet. I feel guilty saying it, but I wish she'd stay around for a bit longer,' Grace said.

'Has she recognised anyone in the mug shots?' Mark asked.

'Not yet, but I'm going to show her some more later.'

Elena stared with extreme concentration at the photographs on the page. Her lips tightened, and there was a frown between her eyebrows. She looked with regret at Grace and shook her head.

'Don't worry,' Grace turned another page. There was an air of anticipation in the room as she watched the girl. Praying she would recognise someone who was further up the line of command. That's all they needed. Just one. They had to get a suspect for this crime. And the continuing crimes which were happening at this very moment. She shuddered. Imagining what had happened to Elena.

Through the interpreter, the girl had used the word *rape* more than once to describe her experience. Although, her expression and the sound of her voice hadn't needed any interpretation. It was quite plain what she meant.

During the interviews with Elena, Grace herself was unexpectedly swept back into a dark place. Caught among shadows, fear licked the edges of her consciousness. She had to force herself to come back into the present. To concentrate on the case. And push away this dread which hovered in her mind. That was when the sensation in her hands returned. And to her alarm, lately it was happening more frequently.

Grace applied for a search warrant and within hours the Gardaí were parked in the underground car park. They had not insisted that Elena accompany them there. She was too frightened.

A woman climbed out of her car, carrying a number of shopping bags. Grace crossed the area to meet her as she approached the lift.

'Hallo,' she took ID from her pocket and held it out to the woman, who looked to be in her thirties.

'We're making enquiries in the area, and wonder would you mind answering a few questions?' Grace always felt a gentle approach was best. But in spite of that, the woman's eyes opened wide, and she looked nervous.

'What's it about?' she asked.

'As I said, just general.'

She nodded, and put her bags on the ground.

'Have you ever noticed anything out of the ordinary around here? Perhaps cars which you didn't recognise?'

'I keep to myself.' She didn't meet Grace's eyes now.

'Have you seen this woman here?' She held up Elena's photo.

'No.'

Grace gave her a card. 'If you do notice anything, anything at all, please let me know. You have my number there,' she smiled.

'Occasionally, there's activity late at night,' the woman explained, hesitantly.

'What do you mean by activity?'

'People coming and going. I'm not a good sleeper and sometimes I walk at night.'

'Down here?' Grace was surprised.

'Just around the area.'

'Would you recognise any of these people?'

She shook her head. 'They were just women getting out of the lift and running to a car.'

'And what happened then?'

'The car drove off.'

'On how many occasions have you seen this?'

'Maybe about three or four.'

'Over what period?'

'A few weeks.'

'Let us know if you see anything else, immediately.'

Grace arranged for Gardaí in plain clothes to carry out surveillance at the complex. She would have liked to raid those apartments and free the women she knew were probably held there, but it was vital that they pick up some of the people involved in running the prostitution ring, so they held back. She felt guilty about that, but had to think of the greater good.

They changed unmarked cars regularly during the day and night. Grace spent some time there too, a video camera at the ready. She was on duty when on the following Monday night a car sped into the car park and quickly reversed into a spot opposite the lift entrance. A man got out, followed by three women who took their bags from the boot. He led the way towards the lift, a sense of urgency in the way the group hurried across the area and disappeared into the building.

Grace grabbed the video camera, pleased as she managed to film them. Although from her angle she couldn't see their faces too clearly, but continued filming. And ten minutes later was rewarded when the man reappeared with three different women. They dragged suitcases on wheels, and two of them carried black plastic bags also, tottering along in haste on high stilettos. Immediately, she requested assistance from a car which was parked nearby.

She waited as the women and the man climbed into the car, and as soon as they moved she turned on the engine. Ahead of her, the car raced up the incline and almost collided with the Garda car which pulled in front of them. Immediately, the occupants jumped out and ran in different directions. She ran after a woman. Catching her as she went around the corner of the building. The Garda apprehended the man. The others had disappeared.

Grace and the team went back to the complex, and interviewed everyone who lived in the place. Although, they finally had to force their way into three apartments and found one woman in each. They were foreign, hadn't got a word of English, and didn't even seem to know where they were.

'These women have been trafficked. Thinking that they were coming here for a job of some sort, they've been dumped into this vile industry. And they have no passports. What does that say?' Grace was angry.

Through the help of translators, they finally managed to obtain some personal information from the women but they were reticent, and not inclined to tell them anything about the way they had travelled here. Who had arranged it for them, or how much money they had paid.

'They're scared stiff,' Peter said.

'We'll have to arrange something for them.'

'See if the Passport Office can help,' said Grace.

'At least Elena has gone home,' Peter said.

'She may not have gone home. Sometimes this is all organised by the local mafia and if she turned up again her family could suffer.' Grace was worried about her. She had grown fond of the girl, and was suddenly aware of how big this whole thing was. The other two women who had run away had still not been found. They had the driver, but so far had found out nothing under interrogation. He had kept his mouth shut tight and wasn't going to talk.

In spite of hours of investigative work, they still had little to go on. Grace was frustrated. She really felt for these women and was determined to get a positive result. There were endless hours spent trawling through the DVD's of people coming through Arrivals at

Dublin Airport. She even went through them herself, and was to be found late in the office on more than one night. It was around four in the morning when she spotted a woman at Passport Control who looked familiar. She increased the size of the image, excited. Then she inserted another from the Arrivals area. Noting the time difference. She should be coming through around now, Grace thought, and held her breath. Then saw her pulling one of those suitcases on wheels and walking directly towards a man holding up a card. Grace couldn't see his face properly. He had his back to the camera.

She switched to another DVD, which showed the outside area now, and watched as the woman came through the doors. There were two other women behind her, and all three followed the man. He was visible now, heavy set, and walked towards a silver car. She couldn't see the registration but knew that one of the team would manage that.

The car was old, 1996, and there was an up to date disc on it for 2013. Now they had a name and address in the south city. The area was mostly flatland. Identified by the number of bins at the front of houses. Rather dismal grey net curtains dragged this way and that in the windows. An occasional pair of trainers on window sills, no doubt requiring fresh air, or drying, and sometimes accompanied by floppy socks, hanging down like they were waiting to be filled by Santa Claus.

They found the house in a cul de sac. There was no car parked outside. Peter took a couple of men around the back and Grace rang the front door bell. She could hear footsteps as someone came down the hall. The door opened.

'Grace McKenzie, Detective Inspector ...' she said and held out her ID to the woman who peered at her around the half open door.

She was pale with straggly grey hair and what looked like the previous day's make-up shadowed her eyes, and lips. She wore a washed out pink jumper and navy trousers, under a green checked apron.

'Are you Mrs. Quirke?'

'Yes.'

'Can I have a word with you?' Grace asked.

She nodded, opened the door a little further and led the way down the hall into the sitting room. The house was probably over a hundred years old, and had little work done on it in the intervening years. It was crowded with furniture which was thick with dust, ornaments, books, magazines, and newspapers were piled on surfaces and on the floor. Grace was taken aback, and had a sudden vision of the top of her own home, and shivered as she thought of what it had become.

She talked to the woman and discovered that the car belonged to her husband who had died a few months ago, but that she had allowed her lodger to use it. All they had was a first name – Silvio, but nothing else.

Chapter Ten

Ruth found herself thinking constantly about the woman she had seen from her secluded corner in the restaurant. A vision in her head which took her back many years to her childhood. Sometimes she knew the woman as if it was only yesterday they had been together, although at other times, she drifted away, nebulous, indistinct, without any form. Her sister Kim.

Ruth wondered if perhaps she had imagined her. Or perhaps the woman could have been someone else. It was too much of a coincidence to see her in a place they frequented so often. How was it she had never noticed her before?

She tried to concentrate on her work and stared at the computer screen. At the lists of names. Passport numbers. Personal details. The phone rang. She dealt with the enquiry. Gave the appropriate information. Did the job she was required to do.

John poured a glass of whiskey. 'Want a drink?'

'No thanks.'

'Meant to tell you, we're moving.'

'What?' she blurted, taken aback.

'To another apartment,' he said.

Tears moistened her eyes. 'But why? This is our home,' she cried out loud. 'I love our penthouse.'

'Because the *Special Branch* are getting too close. One of our drivers has been picked up, and a number of women as well,' he said, his voice curt.

She was silenced.

He gulped his whiskey. Moving around the spacious living room. Back and forth. Again and again.

'I don't understand why?' she said.

'You're dense. When the Gardaí get too close, then the whole organisation comes under scrutiny. It could be the end of us.' He stood at the large picture window and stared out over the city to the sea. 'If it's any consolation, I don't want to move either, but I've no choice,' he murmured. The anger in his voice diminished somewhat.

'We've been happy here,' she said softly.

He nodded.

She moved towards him. Felt it was safe to approach now. While he had never hit her, when he was in a mood she never knew how to take him.

'I love you.' She kissed him.

He looked down at her. His eyes quizzical.

'I'll get on with dinner,' she said after a moment.

'You're a very good cook, you know. Unusual in women these days.'

She was surprised. He had never complimented her in that way before. 'Thanks.' She did enjoy cooking. Anxious from the beginning to keep him happy. What was it they said? *The way to a man's heart is through his stomach.* At least she had succeeded there.

'And even better in bed,' he added with a grin.

So she had come up to his expectations in that area as well. She smiled. Much more pleased to hear that. Being a good cook wasn't exactly a compliment.

But there was something about him lately. Ruth was aware that he kept her at some distance and that upset her. She didn't seem to be able to get close to him. To sit together like any couple and watch a film on television of an evening. To share those precious intimate moments when she might trail her fingers through his short dark hair and kiss him unexpectedly, and know that he was her man.

Now Ruth was left wondering what John was thinking. Did he still want her like she wanted him? Always that need in her to be reassured. The romance of their early relationship had faded without doubt. Something had changed. And it wasn't that problem he had with the *Special Branch*. It was something much deeper.

At three in the morning John woke Ruth up out of a deep sleep.

'We're going,' he said. Pulling on his clothes. 'Get dressed, and be quick.'

'It's the middle of the night?' she complained. 'Pitch dark.'

'Get your stuff packed.' He carried suits over his arm and went out to the lift.

Hurriedly, Ruth emptied drawers of lingerie into a bag. Took down a suitcase, and pulled clothes from hangers. Her hands shook. She was confused. And didn't understand why this was happening. In the bathroom she gathered toiletries, and make-up. Rushed around the apartment, picking up little bits and pieces which meant so much to her.

He returned. 'Don't take everything, there won't be room. And certainly not all those shoes.'

She stared at the collection. There had to be at least fifty or sixty pairs.

'Can we put them somewhere? In storage?' She couldn't decide which ones to choose.

'No.'

She felt disappointed, loving her shoes so much.

'Take a few and be done with it. I've got all the stuff I'm taking. The rest will be dumped. And don't bother taking those bits of rubbish.' He pointed to her little keepsakes. 'Victor will arrange for this place to be cleared without a trace of us ever being here.'

She knew there was no point in arguing with him.

'Get the jewellery,' he said.

She took the boxes from the safe and he put them into a plastic bag.

'And your keys.' He stood waiting, his hand out, as she searched for them.

John drove quickly. And Ruth followed in her car. To another part of the city. The apartment block was very different to the luxurious one they had left. Older. More run down. There was a smell in the lift. Like the residue of boiled cabbage, and urine. Not an attractive aroma.

It was a tiny one bedroom apartment. A galley kitchen as part of the living room. A bathroom off the narrow entrance hall. She stared around.

'It's very small.'

'You'll get used to it.'

'There's hardly room for the two of us, not with all our stuff,' she pointed out, and burst into tears, quite exhausted at this point.

'I'll keep mine somewhere else.'

'What do you mean?'

'What I said.'

'But you'll be living here, won't you?'

'On and off.'

'What about us?' she blurted as panic swept through her.

'There'll always be an *us*. Don't worry.' His remark was perfunctory and didn't reassure her. 'Have to go back, double check.' He kissed her on the cheek. 'Be back later.'

'When?'

'Not sure.'

He left.

Ruth rested on a chair for a couple of hours, but as the morning light brightened the apartment, she noticed that the place was really grimy. She opened the windows. Washed the net curtains and hung them on the shower rail in the bathroom to dry, found some cleaning agent and tackled the kitchen and bathroom. But the appliances were old and worn, and it was difficult to imagine how she would cook in such a cramped space. Luckily she had brought some new bed linen, but the duvet needed to be thrown out, as did everything else in the place. But without much money, Ruth couldn't buy anything new. Had to use the crockery and cutlery that was there. She hated that. Hated the thought that other people had used them before. Fingers had touched. Mouths had licked. She shuddered.

That evening she enjoyed dinner at Sonaris for a change. It was such a relief to get out of that filthy box, and she would have stayed here all night in preference to going back. As usual, they were joined by his friends. Sitting in their alcove she watched the other diners. But didn't see anyone who looked like Kim on this occasion.

John drank too much. One of the waiters dropped them back to the apartment. She didn't even know the name of the street. Just knew how to direct the man. Glad at least that she had noticed the number on the apartment door – twenty-seven. She helped John up in the lift and into the apartment. He flopped on the bed. She tried to take his jacket off, but with little success, and just about managed to remove his shoes, covered him with the duvet, and lay down beside him.

She closed her eyes, but couldn't sleep. The past intruded. Memories of her childhood. Bright days in the sun. Darker times when she and her sister fought like cats. And darker than ever their last disagreement over the family home. She couldn't get away from it now.

Chapter Eleven

'Where's Daddy?' Jason asked.

'America,' Kim replied.

'When is he coming home?'

'In a few days.' Answering his question, she suddenly realised that she didn't know. He hadn't said when he left the last time. Lately Andrew had been more evasive. She couldn't get a straight answer out of him. Even the kids had been fobbed off when they asked innocent little questions about flowers, the moon, the sea, and why is that, and who is this, and a thousand other things they wanted to know. But children don't ask why are you so vague, Daddy? Although there were times she almost expected them to say that. Both children could come out with the most surprising of remarks at any time.

On the surface they were very happy. But out of that came the thought of the phone she had found. He had given her a pat explanation which meant nothing.

When he returned that weekend she had an idea. 'Why don't we all go over to meet you in London for a couple of days?' Kim suggested.

'No.' It was a blunt response from Andrew.

'We could go standby. It wouldn't cost that much in a hotel. And we might visit places together. Enjoy ourselves with the kids. That's all I want.'

'I'm never sure how long I'll be in London. I can't have you all waiting there for me. It's ridiculous.' He was dismissive.

'Maybe we'll surprise you?' she said with a grin.

'Don't do that.' There was a particular emphasis on the *don't*. He frowned.

'Why not?' she persisted.

'Because it's not practical,' he grunted, turned from her to pick up the newspaper, and leaf through the pages.

'Andrew, I've already mentioned to the children that we might be going to see you in London, they're going to be very disappointed.'

'What?' He glared at her. 'How could you do something so stupid? Are you losing it?'

'Of course I'm not losing it,' she snapped.

'Well, just put it out of your head. I don't want you and the kids to come over to London any weekend. It's not going to happen.' He threw down the newspaper and marched out of the room.

She was left stunned. Why had her suggestion resulted in such a violent reaction by Andrew? Why didn't he want to see her and the kids in London? It would only be a short trip.

Grace phoned.

'Just a quick call. How are you all?'

'We're fine,' Kim said.

'Sorry I haven't had time to drop in but it's been really mad busy at work.'

'That's nothing new,' Kim laughed.

'I'll call around as soon as I can, I want to see the kids. I should take them off somewhere for a treat, but ...I love your kids, I miss them.' Her voice was suddenly husky.

'They love you too. Call in, even for five minutes, I want to see you. I really do.' Kim wondered if she would talk to Grace about her misgivings about Andrew? It would be so good just to bounce her crazy ideas off her friend, even if she made no response and dismissed her worries out of hand.

Kim was in the study, filing away a pile of utility bills. Andrew looked after all the payments in their home, which were paid by direct debit, but she did the admin.

It was tucked in with a bunch of other bills. Electricity. Gas. What attracted her to look twice was the colour of the print. A different tone. She pulled it out. Her heart seemed to stop, she couldn't breathe properly. Her pulse raced.

It was for a property in London.

She wondered what this bill was doing there.

She searched for the date.

It was just a month ago.

And was addressed to Andrew Morris.

She was puzzled. What did he have to do with this house? Why was he paying the electricity bill?

Now she had to confront it.

And it was like a wild animal.

And roared at her.

Teeth bared.

Foaming at the mouth.

Chapter Twelve

The next time they went to have dinner at Sonaris, Ruth took her chance to talk to the man on the reception desk while John was having a meeting with the manager in the office.

'There were friends of mine in here a couple of weeks ago. People I haven't seen in a long time. They walked out before I had a chance to say hallo, and I wondered if you could give me their phone number?'

'What date was that?' He opened the booking register.

'Thursday, the tenth, their booking was probably about eight o'clock,' she guessed.

'It was quite busy that evening. Everyone comes at the same time.' He turned the book around to her. 'See if you recognise the name.'

She stared at the list.

Ran her finger down.

Searched for a name.

One she recognised.

But nothing sprang out.

She shook her head and pushed the book around to the manager. 'She was fair, with hair to her shoulders, and he was very tall.

'Let me see.' He stared at the names. 'That could be Andrew and Kim, he's certainly very tall.'

'Yes, that's them.' She was excited. 'Would you mind giving me their phone number?'

'No problem.' He pulled a sheet of paper from underneath the counter, and jotted it down.

'Thanks.' She pushed it into her pocket.

'What are you two chatting about?' John was suddenly beside her.

'I was just asking about ...the menu, I thought they might make a few changes to surprise you,' she said hesitantly, caught out.

'That's very thoughtful of you, baby.' He took her hand and they walked back to their table.

Back at the apartment, she took her chance. They had made love and he was relaxed. 'How long will we stay here?' she ventured.

'Don't know.' He lit a cigar, pulled on it, and then exhaled. The cigar smoke wafted into the air.

She coughed. 'This place isn't exactly up to the standard you usually like.'

'Isn't it good enough for you? Were you a high flyer before you met me? That little one room flat you had in Seville wasn't exactly plush.'

'No, I'll admit that, but I was pulling myself up after a particularly difficult time.'

'Which of the vices had you in its clutches?' he said, grinning. 'You never told me.'

'That's all in the past.' Ruth had tried to put the years since she left home behind her. It had been a struggle admittedly. She never understood why she had been so different to her sister, Kim. She hadn't wanted the safety of a job. The security of a husband and family. Her inheritance gave her the means to search for excitement. All over the world. She could have written books on the countries she visited. But in Spain she had met a man who took her to heights she had never reached before. But then he had dumped her and taken everything she had. 'I hate this part of Dublin,' she said. Anxious to change the subject.

'To inner city Dublin.' He raised his glass of wine in toast. 'Isn't it the heart of what it means to be Irish ...*Oirish*,' he tried to imitate what he thought was an Irish brogue. It was an unsuccessful attempt to cover up his own London twang.

'This place is dirty. Whatever I was, I never liked living in filth.'

'You're not in a position to be choosy, I pay the bills,' he snapped.

'Maybe I might ...' She almost said *leave* but then pulled back. She didn't want to do that. She loved him. With her heart. Her mind. Her soul. Mostly that. With her soul. The deepest part of her. 'Do some redecorating. Get someone in to paint the place. Buy new curtains, and furniture. That would help,' she suggested.

'Na, it's not worth it. We won't be here long enough.'

'That's great. Have you any idea where we'll be going?' She was excited.

'Whatever comes up.'

His phone rang. He took the call.

She watched his expression.

'What?' he barked. Obviously angry.

He listened. 'Fuck. Meet me at the usual place.' He stood up.

'Have you to go out?' she asked, disappointed now.

'Yea.' He left.

Later, she took the piece of paper from her handbag, and unfolded it. She had tried to make the phone call more than once, but always, as she came to the last digit, her courage had failed. What would she say after all these years? There was no way to apologise. And, anyway, would it even be accepted by her sister?

This time Ruth took courage and dialled the full number. The tone rang out for a few seconds. Then a soft voice answered. She recognised it immediately, but couldn't speak at first. She took a deep breath. 'Kim?' Her voice trembled. Tears filled her eyes.

'Who is this?'

'It's me.'

There was silence at the other end of the line. Ruth waited nervously. Tapping the surface of the coffee table with her fingers.

'Ruth?'

'Yes.'

'I can't believe this. Why are you calling now?' Kim asked.

'I saw you recently and I ...'

'Where?' It was a harsh demand.

'Sonaris Restaurant.'

There was an intake of breath.

'How are you?' Ruth asked after a few seconds. Praying that Kim wouldn't put down the phone, and cut her off before she had a chance to explain.

'I'm fine.'

'You were with your husband, or maybe he's your partner.' She felt a little more confident and was able to talk more freely now.

'My husband.'

'You don't seem to have changed at all. It was wonderful to see you after all this time.'

'Thanks.'

The conversation dried up. Ruth couldn't think of anything else to say. 'Maybe I could ring again?' she asked. 'Sometime?'

'Yes.'

She pressed the off button. And only then let the tears flow.

'Grab your things. You shouldn't have so much to bring this time.' John said.

'Where are we going?' Ruth asked.

'You'll find out.'

'Is it better than here?'

'You could say so. But everything's relative. What you like, I don't, and vice versa. Now we have half an hour, that's it. I want to be out of here quickly.' He took his suits from the wardrobe. 'Will you empty the drawers?'

'But we're only here such a short time, why do we have to go, I hate moving,' she complained. Even if it was a dump she found it difficult to motivate herself.

'Get going,' he snapped.

Just as before they departed the small place in a rush. She cleared the kitchen of food and binned it. Hating to leave food there to spoil.

'I haven't got all my stuff,' she said.

'I'll buy you another, whatever it is.' It was a throwaway remark.

She didn't believe him.

The next complex was only a couple of miles away across the river. A newer development. It was much the same layout, and only very slightly larger. The decor was modern but, as before, the cleanliness of the place left a lot to be desired.

She went in, and put down the bags.

'Give me a hand with the rest,' he said.

She did as he asked.

'Right, let's celebrate. There's wine in that box there.' He twisted off the cap on a bottle of red wine. Then he looked in the presses. 'No glasses. It will have to be mugs.'

'Wash them first,' she said.

'They look clean.' He looked into them.

'Here, let me see them. They're tea stained. Gross. Let's just drink out of the bottle, you could catch something from those.'

He took the first slug, and handed it to her.

She laughed, and did the same. Then she sat on the couch which was covered with a grimy throw to hide a large brown stain on one of the cushions. 'Hey love, I think we're turning into a pair of gypsies.'

'Sorry, it's just the way things are. I was able to stay put in the place in Sandyford for quite a while, but things have tightened up. I have to watch my back now.'

'Is it the Gardaí?' She was startled.

'There are always problems in my line of work. And ...they are putting pressure on us. Some of our people have been picked up.'

'Could we be in trouble?' she asked, and leaned across to kiss him.

He shook his head. 'Na ...but there are a lot of people involved in our organisation and I can't trust them all. Someone will surely snitch, that's the problem.'

'You can trust me.'

'I know, love, I know.'

Ruth made her first pick-up in a cinema today. In the early afternoon the place was virtually empty. It was dark inside. That velvet darkness that was impenetrable when you first come in. She stood inside the door for a moment or two until her eyes adjusted to the lack of light and slowly walked forward. This was important. She had to sit in a particular row, and with her left hand counted down the backs of the seats until she came to the sixth from the back. She sat into the second seat, holding a large box of popcorn on her lap.

The film had already begun. It was one of those thrillers. Criminals. Police. Violence. She had heard about it, but had no interest in seeing it. Now as it unfolded, she became caught up in the plot, and when someone sat beside her, was suddenly annoyed at the interruption, before realising who it was.

He reached for some of the popcorn. Ruth pushed the box towards him and he handed her a bulky envelope. She slid it into a large bag she had with her. He sat there eating the popcorn. She tried to concentrate on the film but couldn't escape his chomping. He finished the popcorn completely, put the box on the floor, and left. She was out of there a few moments later. The plan always had to be followed to the letter.

John took very little notice of her. Seemingly caught up in his business. The instructions for her pick-ups each day came from someone who called her at nine each morning. On the dot.

She asked for money and to her surprise John gave her a roll of notes, and she was able to shop for things for the apartment. Threw out the old curtains. Bought a new throw, delph, cutlery, pots and pans. She rearranged everything. Enjoying it. Maybe they would be here for a while. Maybe she could call it home.

More morose than ever, John didn't even seem to notice the improvements in the apartment. He wasn't home very often. Still, she tried to be there for him. Unobtrusive. Quiet. A gentle lover. She cooked their evening meal around seven as usual, but more often than not he didn't appear. Often she awoke suddenly in the middle of the night, her hand outstretched across the bed, to find it was empty. Cold. She lay back as tears filled her eyes and she curled up. Lonely. Abandoned.

Chapter Thirteen

Grace instructed the team to continue surveillance on the house in Rathmines until the man Silvio returned. Then to follow him whenever he moved out again. She went for a run, anxious to shake off the stress of the day. The night was cool but she enjoyed the exercise, and returned home feeling much more refreshed.

When the call came through from the team, she was already in bed and woken out of a deep sleep by the sound of the phone.

'We're on his tail,' the sergeant reported.

'Stay out of sight, we don't want him to realize we're there.'

Grace threw on some clothes, made herself a cup of coffee and lit a cigarette. Excited and hopeful that they would make progress on this case. She went to the car, took a map of the country from the glove compartment, came back inside and spread it out on the table. Marking the progress of the team which kept in touch during the night as they followed the car which travelled through the midlands, its circuit finally ending back in Dublin again at the house in Rathmines.

'We should bring him in,' Grace said to Peter. 'He's involved in this ring. But we have to get him to talk. If he refuses, and his English is poor, we will have a problem, and even if we have an interpreter something could be lost in translation.'

'We have everything on video, so there is evidence, and that's all we need.'

'Right, let's pick him up.

Grace looked at the man through the two-way window.

He was sullen.

They went in together, introduced themselves and sat down. She prayed they would get something out of him.

'This interview is being recorded,' she told him.

He made no response.

'We followed you last night and this morning taking groups of women from apartment to apartment in various towns around the country. Why did you do this?' she asked. They had found out that he was Polish and now waited for the interpreter to ask him in his own language.

He didn't reply.

'Do you know these women?'

She had to wait again and found that irritating.

He shook his head in denial and stared at the table.

'We have you on video tape picking up women at Dublin airport. Where were you taking them?'

There was no response from him.

Grace sighed.

'My client knows nothing about this,' the solicitor interjected.

Peter took over. Asked the same questions in a different way. Tried to trick him. Force him to say something. But this man was clever.

'He doesn't organise this ring. It's much bigger than him. He's only a pawn. There's someone far more powerful at the top,' Grace said at their meeting later.

'Hopefully whoever it is will be rattled by the fact that one of his men has been arrested.'

'We'll keep him as long as we can.'

'Driving women around isn't against the law,' Peter pointed out.

'Unfortunately,' Grace said. 'But we have surveillance on each of those complexes now,' she said, trying to be positive.

'But we have no proof of what's going on inside.'

'If someone could follow them, we might find out the exact units.'

'But what if they change their movements because we picked up one of their men? Maybe they've already moved away from those particular apartments,' Grace said.

'Maybe one guy will make no difference to them.'

'But they won't know what he told us. So scared, he could just blurt it all out while we hold him.'

'Maybe he might still do that. We could wear him down. We've got another few hours.'

But although time passed and they continued with the interrogation, he kept his mouth shut. Grace became frustrated, and although she was sharp, neither Peter or herself could get anything out of the man. They had to let him go.

She left the station then, and on her way out bumped into the psychologist, Mark Williams. They talked briefly about Elena, the Bulgarian girl, who had now gone home, and the man who had been followed during the night.

'We've got nothing,' she said.

'Pity.' He seemed sympathetic.

She nodded.

'Would you like to have a coffee?' he asked, with a smile. 'You seem tired.'

'Haven't had much sleep.'

'I was just going around to that place on the corner.'

'Yea, sure.' She pulled a pack of cigarettes from her shoulder bag, and offered it to him.

'No thanks, don't smoke.'

'Lucky you,' she grinned as they walked together. She took a few pulls and then put the cigarette out before they went in.

He ordered coffee and they sat together, chatting generally.

'How's the case going?' he asked after a time.

'We haven't got very far. It's exasperating.' She took a sip of the latte. 'I just want to find out who's at the top of this ring. Who organises it. And then I intend to put him away for a long time,' she said.

'It seems to mean a lot to you.' He picked up the mug of coffee.

'More than most other cases,' she admitted.

'Why is that?'

'It just does. That girl Elena ...I felt for her. Can't bear the thought of what she went through, and all the other women too. It's just vile.' She felt that weird roughness on her hands again. It was uncomfortable.

'I agree. It is vile. And I can think of a few other words to go along with that,' he grimaced.

She looked down and stirred the coffee slowly, aware that her eyes had moistened. She felt awkward and embarrassed.

'Perhaps you shouldn't let yourself get too involved,' he said softly.

'I don't ...normally,' she whispered, recovering.

'You'll be able to handle the case better if you're more objective.'

'You giving me advice?' she asked, with a grin.

'Sorry, I didn't mean to.' He shook his head, and smiled.

'I shouldn't have said that, it's what you do.' Her fingers played a rhythm on the table in an effort to shake off whatever was adhering to her skin. Anxious to have another cigarette, she stood up and searched in her bag for money. 'I'd better go.'

'I'll get it.' He went up to the counter.

'Thanks. I owe you.' Grace went outside, immediately lit up, and took a deep drag. After a moment or two she began to feel better and ran her hands along the smooth wool surface of her jacket. The feeling of discomfort eased.

'Some time, would you like to have dinner with me?' he asked.

Grace stared at him. Taken aback. Shocked into silence, which was unusual for her. 'Thank you, but I ...' She wanted to add her usual quip - *don't mix business with pleasure* - but held back. There had been plenty of invitations over the years from men she met through work and she always kept to her rule. But somehow this was different.

'It's just dinner, Grace,' he said, with a wide grin. 'And we can discuss the case ...if you like, among other things.'

'All right,' she couldn't help laughing. There was something about him that she liked. But couldn't explain exactly what it was.

'I'll call you.'

Chapter Fourteen

Ruth had settled in to the new apartment. But John was extremely irritable, taking her head off for the slightest thing. One evening, he received a call just as they were sitting down to eat.

'What?' he barked, and then listened for a few seconds. Growing anger quite clear in his expression.

'Something wrong, love?' Ruth asked, concerned.

'Bloody fool. That's all we need. Get over here now.' He pressed the off button. 'I'll need privacy,' he ordered.

'But we haven't finished our dinner.'

'Take it into the bedroom with you.'

'I don't want to eat in there.'

'Get in there, with or without your dinner. I don't want to eat anyway so you needn't worry about me.' He pushed away his plate. 'Get out, I have to think. Go on.'

Ruth disappeared inside, sat on the bed but didn't close the door fully. She felt claustrophobic in this place. In comparison to the spacious size of the rooms in Sandyford, these two small rooms hemmed her in so much sometimes she found it difficult to breathe. But now she watched what was going on in the other room through the slightly open door.

After a while there was a ring on the doorbell. John opened the door.

The man was small, and dressed in black leather. He held a crash helmet in his hand and put it down on the table. There was no talk between them. He pulled a sheet of paper from his inside pocket and pushed it across the table towards John. 'The word is those women who have been picked up by the *Branch* will be sent back home, so we've lost them. The driver didn't open his mouth and has been released. But we'll have to stop using those apartments in the midlands. They have them under surveillance.'

'Rent some replacements. In different towns,' John instructed. 'And get rid of that man they have interrogated, do you read me?' They went out together.

John didn't come home until the following morning, his mood low. Ruth didn't know what to say, wondering whether he was going to continue the confrontation. She decided to behave normally and kissed him.

He sat down at the computer.

She was preparing dinner. Chopping vegetables at the kitchen counter. Her mind a ferment of worry about him. What had gone wrong? Was his life in danger? Her own life?

Now she worried about making the pick-ups and deliveries. It was the one thing she did for him. It made her feel useful. Valued. She shuddered inside, trying not to think of the nature of the business in which he was involved, and in which she was also involved. Up to now she had persuaded herself that it was all to do with something else. Even the pick-ups were to do with drugs. Illegal cigarettes. Protection rackets. Somehow that had made it more acceptable to her own moral standards.

But was John casting her off slowly but surely? His need for her lessening. They had not made love for a few days. She missed that communication through intimacy. Her love rejuvenated every time he pressed his lips on hers, their mouths moving sensually, that aroma of his skin in her nostrils, drawing her in.

She looked across the room at him. His dark hair was spiky from running his fingers through it. His jacket had been flung on the couch, tie over the back of the chair, and the white shirt he wore was creased. The innate neatness in her personality was irritated by the untidiness. She longed to hang his clothes up. Put out a new shirt. Fresh out of the packet. Once worn and then discarded.

For lunch, she cooked pasta with salmon in a white wine sauce. He liked that.

Not particularly hungry, she had a poached egg and toast herself.

During the meal there was no conversation. He was texting. Always texting.

'I think we may have to move again,' John said, without taking his eyes from the screen.

'But we're only getting used to this place. Why do we have to go somewhere else?' she demanded, angry with him.

'It's just the way things are. I've had to make drastic changes.'

'Are we ever going to live somewhere permanent?' she cried, really upset now.

He shrugged.

The pick-up was at a coffee shop in Temple Bar. Ruth had bought a magazine, and looked at the photographs while sipping a cup of tea. He was late today. She glanced at her phone to check the time. She was nervous. There were two entrance doors and he came from behind. Tipped her suddenly on the shoulder. His touch sent her heart racing with fright. He sat in the chair opposite.

The waitress came over.

He ordered a coffee.

They talked about the weather. She hated having to make such inane conversation, preferring the furtive push of a bag under the table. Now she had to look into his eyes and know that he was aware that she was involved in this. It was sick, and suddenly, Ruth didn't know how long she could keep it up.

As soon as he had gone, she called Kim.

Ruth made an effort with her appearance. Went to the hairdressers. Wore one of the few designer outfits she possessed. It was a taupe suit with a short skirt, matching sandals and bag. John had said he would probably be late tonight. She hadn't bothered to question him. Had just about given that up.

She was there just after eight and sat in a corner of the bar. It was a quiet place. She ordered a gin and tonic, needing something to give her confidence. Suddenly she saw Kim come through. Her heart leapt into her throat and tears filled her eyes. She stood up, almost knocking over the glass in her haste. They put their arms around each other and held tight.

'Sorry,' she wiped her eyes. Embarrassed.

'It's lovely to see you,' Kim whispered.

'How long has it been?' Ruth asked.

'About fifteen years I think,'

'Too long.'

Kim waved at the bar man.

'I'll get it,' Ruth said.

'No, let me, will you have another drink, what is it?' Kim insisted.

'Gin and tonic, thanks.'

'I'll have a glass of wine.'

The drinks arrived and they talked at length. Catching up on the years which had passed.

'I couldn't believe my eyes when I saw you that night in Sonaris. You really haven't changed at all,' Ruth said.

'Neither have you, except for the short hair, when you left we both had hair half way down our backs, remember?' Kim laughed.

'That was a long time ago. I hardly remember. Have you kept in touch with all the people we knew then?' Ruth asked.

'I'm ashamed to say I haven't,' Kim admitted. 'I moved to London and met Andrew there, although we moved back here after a couple of years. I always hoped to hear from you.'

'I'm sorry. I was travelling all over the world. I had cut myself off. And when the money from the sale of the house ran out I was ashamed to come back,' she said, emotionally.

'I understand,' Kim nodded.

'I gave money to people, charities, the poor ...' she tried to explain. Knowing that she had spent it mostly on herself, and other people. 'Until there wasn't any left.'

'I hope it wasn't too tough for you?' Kim put her hand over hers.

'No, I lived with various people who helped me. You could say it was a hippie life in places like Nepal so it was all yoga and meditation.'

'Don't think I'd mind doing that, do you still keep it up?' Kim asked.

'No. Doesn't fit into the lifestyle,' she grinned.

'Are you happy now?'

'Yes,' Ruth nodded. It was hard to give the impression that she was head over heels in love. A few months ago it would have been much easier.

'I'm looking forward to meeting your partner,' Kim said.

'You're obviously very happy with Andrew. He's a gorgeous guy. Those pilot types have something special about them. It must be the uniform.' Ruth changed the subject.

'You'll have to meet Jason and Lorelai,' Kim reached into her bag, took out a photo and handed it to Ruth.

'They're really gorgeous ...' she whispered. 'Lorelai is beautiful, and Jason is a mischievous little fellow by the look of him.'

'You can be sure of that,' Kim laughed. 'Now when are you and John coming over to see us?'

'I'm not sure, things are a bit unsettled at the moment ...we may be moving apartment.'

'Hope it's going to be somewhere nice.' Kim took her hand.

'So do I,' Ruth said, with a grin.

Chapter Fifteen

The pile of papers grew larger as the week went on. No matter what Grace was doing, or what time she went to work or came home she bought them. So busy at the moment with the case, she hadn't time to read them all, only glancing at the headlines if she had a chance. The broadsheet journalists talked about recession. Reported about politicians shouting at each other in the Dail. More hair-shirt budgets were threatened. GDP. GNP. The Euro zone. Economic recovery. Investment in jobs and growth. In the pages of the tabloids, there were boobs, bottoms, actors, actresses, footballers and their wives, lurid descriptions, and caricatures of government ministers.

But for Grace, time was running out. Space was running out. In her head, she carried an image. A plan of her home. It occupied a particular part of the brain. She wasn't sure whether it was frontal lobe, or that delicate spot behind her ear, or right in the middle. But wherever, she was forced to make a decision. Would she move this or that, and so create a few inches of space. The upstairs bathroom, the landing, and each bedroom were full. The attic was the same. And when she added the last few days' newspapers, the remaining space would be filled completely.

Mark Williams called her, and asked if she would have dinner with him on Saturday night. She was surprised to hear from him and hadn't really believed he meant what he said. At the end of the call he asked if there was any particular food she disliked? And that was very considerate in her opinion. The conversation was short, but he sounded pleased when she agreed to meet him.

Grace wondered why he asked her. And why she accepted. Was it a date? Her social life was always around her work. Usually a few drinks with other Gardaí which she could leave behind at will. Without strings. But there was something else in her life which didn't allow competition. That entity which demanded her soul. Now she put that aside. For once.

'You're looking wonderful.' Mark stood on the doorstep, and handed her a bouquet of flowers.

Roses. Iris. Chrysanthemums. And others she couldn't identify. 'Thank you.' Grace felt good in her black suit, with a short skirt, gold sequined top, and black six inch high heels. She accepted the flowers, and ushered him inside. 'I'll just put these in water before we go.' She found a large vase in the press and took the flowers out of the cellophane covering. 'They're beautiful.'

'Glad you like them.'

She smiled and put them on the table.

'Right?' he grinned.

'Do you fancy a drink before we go?' she asked.

'Thanks but I've asked the taxi to wait.' He led the way outside and she locked up.

They sat into the car. Closer to him on the back seat than she had ever been to him before. Their shoulders touched. It felt strangely intimate.

'I don't think we should discuss work this evening,' he said, with a smile.

'Probably not,' she agreed.

'I can think of much more interesting things to talk about,' he said. His voice had a deep timbre. Velvety.

Grace felt self-conscious. So this was a date then, and did she want that? It would have been better not to start something from which she couldn't extricate herself down the line. But it was only one night and that could be it. 'Where are we going?' she asked.

'Surprise,' he said, with a grin.

Grace smiled. Now she was excited. It was a long time since someone decided to surprise her, and brought flowers as well.

He took her to the Rasam Indian Restaurant in Glasthule, somewhere she had never been before. They were quickly welcomed in and ushered to a table by the owner, Nisheeth, whom Mark obviously knew.

'This is a lovely restaurant, such a warm ambience.' Grace glanced around her. 'And I love the tables in the alcoves. Really nice if there was a group of people.'

'Wait until you taste the food,' Mark said as the waiter handed her the menu.

She read down the list of dishes. 'They're so different, it's such a change.'

The owner arrived at their table. She was introduced, and they chatted for a few minutes. Then he took a bottle of Champagne out of the ice bucket.

Grace looked at Mark in surprise.

'Thought we'd celebrate.'

The cork was popped, and their glasses filled with the sparkling liquid.

'Slainte,' Mark clinked his glass against hers. 'To ...an enjoyable evening,' he smiled.

The meal was delicious. A mix of starters to taste, followed by their main courses. The choice of wines complemented the food. It was perfect. They talked at length. Grace found herself revealing more about her life to him than she had ever done to anyone else. What was it about this man, she thought more than once.

'I don't go out that often,' Grace had to admit. Amazed at how relaxed she was with him. Probably the affect of the Champagne and wine, she thought.

'You're a workaholic,' he said.

She nodded, and smiled.

'Maybe we'll change all that.'

'Work demands and I have to follow.'

'Sometimes, it's too easy to let that happen.'

'It's my life.' She stared across the room at the other diners. Groups of people. Families. Friends. Couples. There were no people sitting alone. Would she have come here on her own to have a meal? The answer was obvious.

They took a taxi home, and he came to the door with her.

'Would you like to let the taxi go and come in for a nightcap?' she asked. 'We can call another later.'

'No thanks, it's late.'

'It was a lovely evening, I really enjoyed it. Thank you,' she said.

'My pleasure, maybe we'll do it again?'

'Love to.'

'Thanks, I'll call you.' He reached down and kissed her. His lips were warm. Moist.

He went down the path and waved before he climbed into the taxi.

She waited there until it had disappeared and then went inside. To say she was astounded was an understatement. She had not expected this. Not at all.

Chapter Sixteen

Kim was in a daze. Emotional. About Andrew. The electricity bill. The address in London. And about Ruth too. But she got on with things. Worked out at the gym. Jogged. Looked after the house and the garden. Cooked. Baked. Took care of Jason and Lorelai and kept busy. She missed Grace. They hadn't been able to meet in a while because she was too busy at work. Although Kim would have given anything to have a chat about what was going on with Andrew and ask her advice.

He was due home the following morning. Kim didn't know whether to ask him about the bill or not. Since finding it, her mind had been in chaos. Last night she hadn't slept. In the middle of the night she had turned on the television and flicked through the channels. Staring at the screen, not even aware of what was on. She went into the children's rooms, and stood looking at them, deeply asleep, her little innocents. Then made a cup of hot chocolate and went back to bed.

Kim had looked through the rest of the files but found nothing else. She photocopied that one bill, and returned the original to the file. Now it lay hidden in one of the pockets of her large handbag and was carried around with her. Those words printed on it shouted out loud. It was an address where someone else lived. Another person's home. She wondered what went on in that house. How many people lived there? Was it a family? Or just a couple? All the time her mind went around in circles imagining how she might ask Andrew about it. But it was like writing a difficult letter. Trying to compose sentences which would adhere to each other and make sense. Create something which would prevent the emotion which churned within burst through and give her away.

She watched him now. Carefully. Searching for something different. Wondering would he slip up in his chat about work? Where he had been? Who he had met? She talked constantly. Asked questions. Hoping for something. Anything. She was aware of sounding hyper, but couldn't help herself.

He seemed tired. She pushed him on that. 'What are you up to? Burning the candle at both ends in New York?'

'It's jetlag, my love. Sometimes it catches up.'

He always used that excuse, she thought. 'What about parties with the cabin crew? All away from home. Free of encumbrances?'

'I've outgrown cabin crew,' he dismissed the idea, with a wave of his hand. 'I have to be able to control them all on board, can't do that if I'm playing around with one of them. I'd never manage to get the plane on the ground,' he laughed.

'No, suppose you wouldn't.'

'I've never gone down that route, have I baby?' he reached to kiss her.

'Don't know,' she shrugged.

'What's this?' He stared quizzically at her. 'You're jealous?'

'No, I'm not. It's just I don't see you often enough.' She put her arms around him. Persuading him. Persuading herself. That she wasn't jealous of anything, and there was no reason to feel that way.

His couple of days at home flew by fast. Back on a Wednesday morning. Away on a Thursday afternoon. One night only. That time so precious she lay awake, her arms around him, listening to his deep even breathing. If only she could hold on to him, and never let him go from her again.

But in the darkness of the early hours, an idea occurred to her. It was crazy. Mad. And she was swept away by her own audacity.

Chapter Seventeen

For Grace, it was back to the drawing board. To look at all the evidence they had gathered. She called a meeting of everyone on the team.

'How will we work up to the top? To find the people who control this.'

'Crawl up bit by bit,' Peter said.

'Let's try every one of those websites selling sex,' Grace suggested. 'I'll offer my services and see what happens. Do you think I could sound foreign?'

'You could try,' someone said with a laugh.

'You'd have to be very careful,' Peter warned. 'Could be dangerous.'

'I will.'

'If you go anywhere under cover, you must wear a wire. And have back-up.'

'Yes, of course,' she was enthusiastic now. 'Whatever.'

The team trawled through the sites. Many were individuals promoting themselves. Others offered high class escorts. But Grace was looking for the site which offered a countrywide service.

Some of the men on the team called the mobile phone numbers. Explained that they would be travelling around the country and that they might require service in various towns and cities.

Responses were vague. Yes, we think we could arrange that. Others were more positive. These they noted.

Appointments were made but not kept. They checked out apartments or houses. Anxious to see if any of them used those addresses they had noted already. Put surveillance on them. There was a long list. But they went through each one meticulously.

Grace herself made calls. Tried a foreign accent. An upmarket one. Even something resembling her own.

One particular woman interested her. She was well spoken, and articulate. Grace was impressed. If she wished to work with them, they would pay her commission on the money received from the clients. And the woman remarked that the money was good and it was possible to do very well. There was a price list for the different services. Someone would meet her to discuss that. They would allocate an address, and send the clients. But she must be prepared to move. Perhaps just a week in one place and so on. Did she mind moving around the country? Transport would be provided.

That's what took their attention.

Grace met Mark in the office a couple of days later. They passed each other on the corridor. She smiled. But was rushing to a meeting, and just said a quick *hallo*. He said something but she didn't catch it, too anxious to get away. It was awkward, and she was aware of cutting him off rather abruptly, but just didn't know how to deal with the feelings which had dominated her since that night they had dinner.

She liked him a lot. And it disturbed her. By now, the idea of having a relationship with any man had been something which just didn't figure in her life. Still, she had wondered more than once since Saturday whether it was possible to spend some time with Mark without opening herself up to him entirely. They were both mature. He had been in a long term relationship for many years but had been living alone for the last three. Maybe they could date without taking it any further?

He called her on the phone that evening.

'Hey, thought you didn't know me today,' he said.

'Sorry, I was in a hurry,' she murmured, feeling guilty.

'So I haven't been given the cold shoulder?'

'No.' She could sense the humour in his voice, and felt herself melting. Giving in. And laughed softly.

'What a relief,' he said.

'You weren't that worried surely?'

'You've no idea.'

'Come on,' she joshed.

'Fancy meeting for a drink?'

'I'm very busy at the moment, hard to get the time.' She was truthful.

'Just one drink?'

'Well ...'

'I'll call for you, say in half an hour?'

'Tonight?' She was taken aback.

'Why not?'

He came over. She opened the door, and invited him inside. They stood looking at each other. Then without any preamble, he reached out and suddenly his lips were on hers, passionate, searching. Their breaths mingled. His aroma was all around her. He pulled her close to him. His hands gentle. She could feel him. Wanted him. Held his face in her hands. Their mouths sucked. He unbuttoned her blouse. Bent his head and kissed her breasts. Her pulse raced. She gave herself to him, and after that it all happened very quickly. They took each others' clothes off and threw them on the floor. Naked they moved into the living room, and on the rug they lay together and let it happen.

For Grace it was something else. She had not made love with anyone for years. Had forgotten what it was like. She screamed out loud, her body tense, pushing hard against his, as waves of pleasure swept through her. Their breathing raced, and only gradually calmed down, until finally they lay exhausted, soaked with perspiration.

He kissed her again. That hunger no longer apparent. 'Grace?' he whispered her name.

'Mmm?'

'That was wonderful. Thank you.' He pushed her hair back from her face.

'It was ...something else,' she smiled at him. His hazel eyes looked into hers. She swam in their depths.

'I'm so glad.' His fingers outlined her face.

She pushed herself up. Suddenly self-conscious about her nakedness. 'I'll make some coffee,' she said, aware that it was an inane remark to make at this point.

But he took her hand and pulled her back down beside him. 'I don't want to let you go, even for a few minutes.'

She laughed and snuggled into him.

Their relationship blossomed quickly. Grace didn't analyse it.

Chapter Eighteen

John had been missing for a couple of days. No phone calls. No texts. No emails.

Ruth didn't know what to think and was worried about him.

Meeting Kim meant so much, particularly now. Her sister had everything. A beautiful home. A handsome husband. Two lovely children. The perfect family. And what did she have?

She was still with John, but it didn't seem as if he would ever want the same things she wanted. Or did he even want her now. Perhaps he used the women who worked for them. There were so many of them. He could easily enjoy what they offered. With their wagging hips. Deep cleavages. Full red lips. And he wouldn't have to pay them. He owned them.

But he owned her too. The thought was unpalatable. She was his slave and now he kept her here in this tiny place. In the past, slavery was normal in many parts of the world. It still went on. And perhaps that included her? Would he throw her away like one of his once-worn shirts when he had finished with her? Did he think about her at all when he was away? Make plans for when he returned? What way did his mind work? Perhaps she was only a vague memory of someone he once knew. She thought of their penthouse in Sandyford. Imagined what it was like now. Untidy no doubt. Full of the belongings of others. That white pristine place was no longer. It didn't exist. And the person she had been then didn't exist either. An ache spread through her. A sense of nostalgia for something which had been lost.

Ruth went out to do her scheduled pick-ups and deliveries. The weather was pleasant. She wondered again about leaving John. Closing that door in the squalid apartment for the last time. But she had very little money. Not enough to pay rent on a place for herself. And he owned the car. She couldn't take that.

But to her surprise he was there when she returned.

'John?' she stared at him, shock on her face. 'Where have you been for all this time?' she demanded.

'Business.'

'And you couldn't be bothered to phone me?' There were tears in her eyes.

'There was no time.'

'Not even a text?'

'Ruth, you're a big girl now, don't be acting like a child,' he admonished. 'Would it make a difference if I told you I missed you?'

'I wouldn't believe you.'

'Well, so be it.' He turned from her. 'Things are getting worse,' he was grim.

'In what way?'

'Trying to undermine us.'

She was taken aback, but said nothing.

'I want you to remember you're a very valuable part of the operation. They're never going to suspect you of anything.'

'Could they call here?' she asked, a look of fear on her face.

'Why would they come here, this is our apartment, they've no reason to do that. But I want you to drive the Audi and I'll take yours for a day or two. I'll have the plates changed, give you a new tax disc.'

She stared at him, taken aback.

'You'll be a good cover.'

'A cover?'

'Yes, as I said to you, the Gardaí are pushing close.'

'But they could catch up with me,' she said. Her voice uncertain.

'They're not chasing you.'

'What about my pick-ups. They might be interested in them.'

'They won't be. You've got an unblemished record. No history.'

'I don't really like driving your car.'

'Just for a few days?'

'Maybe I'll just take the bus,' she offered.

'No, you need to be able to make a quick exit from wherever you are.'

'You're scaring me.' His concern about their safety only added to Ruth's own uncertainty.

'Just do as I say.'

Chapter nineteen

'I have a gut feeling about this,' Grace said. 'It was the only operation which offered a countrywide service and we've done a lot of research.'

'It may not be the group who trafficked Elena or the other women.'

'I know that. But they're in the same business, and if we can break them then maybe that will lead on to others.'

'It's very risky,' Peter warned.

'I know, but it's the only way. This one seemed the most sophisticated. Well run. It's not just a couple of pimps doing a bit on the side.'

'We'll put a wire on you.'

'It's only an interview. Imagine I have to go through an interview,' she said, laughing. 'They're obviously very fussy about the hookers they employ.'

'Are you going to look the part?' he grinned.

'Not exactly. Just some *bling*. I'm high-class, you know,' she said with a smile.

'When?'

'Tomorrow.'

Grace stared at herself in the mirror. Usually her curly auburn hair was tied back, but now it hung loose to her shoulders. She wore a black dress. Strapless. Low cut. The only one she possessed. Suede stilettos. Fine tights. Her gold earrings and choker. And to add that flash of colour, a red silk scarf around her shoulders. Over it she wore a black jacket.

There were specific instructions. Grace had to take the taxi to a particular apartment complex in Sandyford. Then to ring a mobile number and a person would give her a code to enter the building. In the underground car park, Peter and some members of the team sat in a couple of unmarked cars and were listening to whatever was going on with Grace through the wire.

She paid the taxi man and climbed out of the car. Aware of him eyeing her up she tried to keep the skirt at a modest length. Through the pedestrian gate then, and up to the main entrance of the block of units. It was high class, with manicured gardens, fountains, pathways and occasional seating for the residents. She made the call and then pressed the number the person had given her on the key pad. The door clicked open. Grace took the lift up to the penthouse. Even in the corridors the decor was luxurious, and her feet in the high-heeled shoes sank into the deep pile carpet. Before ringing the bell she took off the jacket and held it over her arm.

Just on the edge of it all now, her pulse hammered as the door opened and a middle-aged man stood there. He said nothing, simply led the way through into a living room. Like the main building itself, it was beautifully decorated, the colour scheme in off-white tones. Enormous windows surrounded three sides of the room. It was dramatic. With amazing views of the city and the sea in one direction, the mountains in the other. This must have cost a packet in the *Celtic Tiger* days, she thought, although well aware that whoever owned it wouldn't get a third of the price now. Maybe he deserved it. Good enough for him. Then asked herself why she was assuming it was a he? It could easily have been a woman who ran the operation.

The man indicated the couch.

Grace sat into it. Reluctant to perch on the edge of the cushion like a nervous job applicant, she crossed one leg over the other, allowing a fair amount of thigh to become visible.

He sat opposite on the other couch and opened a laptop. Then he went through her personal details, which were fictional. 'You haven't given us your address? Why is that?' he asked.

'My situation is such that I am forced to do this for financial reasons, and my family are unaware. I would expect discretion from you.' She hoped to get away with it, worried that they would follow her to a fictitious place and discover the subterfuge.

He nodded, and went through the other information which Grace had given the woman over the phone, which wasn't much. Then he asked her again about the types of service she was willing to provide and explained the rates which applied. As payment was by commission the encouragement was there to hike up the cost to the client as much as possible. Also there was the freedom to work as many hours as she wanted. But it was essential to book in with central control beforehand. They would then send her to the particular venue, which sometimes could be outside of Dublin.

He closed off the computer.

That seemed to be the end of it.

'It's been good to meet you.' He took her hand. 'We'll be in touch.'

She left.

Some time later, Peter called. 'Where are you?'

'Outside the gates, waiting for a taxi,' Grace replied. Looking straight ahead as she walked a little way down the road. 'You're looking for a middle-aged man in a dark suit. Short. Bald.'

'Right, we're waiting for him to come down, we've a couple of people in front and underneath.' He cut off.

The taxi arrived and she took it into the centre of town. She went into Marks and Spencer and bought a cheap rain coat. In the Ladies she removed most of the make-up and tied up her hair before returning to the office, where she changed into her normal clothes.

The team had reassembled.

'The man you described got into a black Saab, and we have the reg number.' Peter scrolled back on the computer screen.

They stared at the image of the driver of the car.

'That's him,' she murmured. 'Run the photo through our records, and get someone to check the reg.'

'Another man came down a few minutes later, he drove a VW. Although he may have nothing to do with it.' He scrolled down. 'This man was younger. Doesn't look the type.'

'You never know. Check his reg as well.'

'The super wants to see you. Progress report requested.'

'That ring seems to have gone to ground, or they're using different places for their girls. We've surveillance on the apartments we came across but there's nothing happening there now.' Grace brought him up to date, and then told him what had happened in Sandyford.

'You took a hell of a chance. Why was this not passed by me?'

'Didn't think you'd authorise it,' she said. Straight up. Grace believed in saying it like it was even if she got in trouble for her decisions.

He gave her a look. 'Next time you decide to go under cover I expect to be informed.'

'I had backup. And it was only the first step. The next stage will hopefully take me deeper inside.'

'Were you going to mention it?' he was sarcastic.

'Of course, it will be a bigger op.'

'I'll consider it.'

'Thank you, Sir.'

'They're dangerous people. Not to be messed with.'

'I know. But there is one guy we want to pick up. Could be connected or maybe not.'

'I know we wanted results here, but we can't have people taking chances. If this doesn't turn up something soon, then we'll have to leave it for a while. Put one or two people on it but the rest of you will have to be deployed elsewhere. We just don't have the manpower now. Cut backs,' he grimaced.

'Thank you, Sir.' She made an attempt to sound grateful, but was suddenly very worried. This might be a case which could take some time to solve. And if the Super didn't allow it, then she would never find justice for the women and the people running the trafficking operation would be free to continue their evil deeds.

At home, Grace changed and headed out for a run. Although it was quite late, she needed the exercise to ease the tension which had built up inside her. She took a shower on her return, and then cooked a pizza for dinner. The television was turned on for the news and switched off again when it was over. She didn't watch many of the programmes on offer, although enjoyed current affairs occasionally, and half listened as she was reading through her newspapers. It was a couple of hours before the previous day's papers were finished, and then she folded them carefully, and went upstairs in search of somewhere to put them. Today's issues waited to be read next.

As she stood on the landing, Grace felt panicky. There was very little space left up here and if she began to stash them downstairs it might get out of control and it wouldn't be possible to hide her secret from anyone. Her kitchen presses were neat. Cups. Saucers. Plates. Dishes. Pots. Pans. Tea towels folded. The fridge wasn't very full. Just a few basics. Milk. Cheese. Bottled water. Yoghurt. A bowl of fruit stood on the counter. It was a bare, uncluttered space. So different to upstairs. Down here there were so many empty spaces she felt herself being persuaded to consider it.

Upstairs the avenue of space between the tower of newsprint on the landing made it difficult to carry this new pile any further. Tears of frustration filled her eyes. What was she going to do?

The doorbell rang.

Panicked, Grace tried to turn around, but was forced to walk backwards to get to the door at the top of the stairs. She stepped through, but lost her footing and stumbled, the pile of papers sliding down the steps all the way to the end. She rushed to gather them up, but had to stop, run back up and lock the door at the top again when two short rings echoed. It was Mark's signal, although she hadn't expected him to call this evening. He had been here last night.

'Just a sec,' she called out. Left the papers and opened the door. 'Sorry, the place is a mess.'

'What have you been doing?' he said, grinning. 'Sitting on the stairs reading. One paper on each step?'

'It doesn't matter, come on in, will you have a glass of red?' She led the way into the living room.

'Thanks. I walked here. It's a lovely evening and I needed to clear the head.'

'I went for a run along the Dodder, but when I got in after that I just flopped.' She poured a glass, handed it to him and topped up her own.

'Busy day?'

'Yea. There's a lot happening.'

'Come here to me;' he pulled her close. They kissed. Long, slow kisses which sent them towards the couch. Entwined together. With their clothes only half removed they made love urgently.

'Thought about this all day,' he murmured. 'Couldn't wait. Grace, let's move in together,' he suggested suddenly.

To say she was surprised was an understatement. 'It's a bit soon for me.'

He looked at her, his eyes disappointed. 'We're grown up, Gracie darling, surely we know our own minds by now. I love you. And I hope you feel the same although you haven't said those three little words yet. What could be more natural?'

'I want to be with you too, but it's ...just work ...don't know if you could put up with the hours. Sometimes I'm gone all night.'

'I'll tolerate it, at least you'll be coming home to me. The way it is now, I'm worried if you don't reply when I call you.' He kissed her. 'I've been thinking about our houses. We could rent one and live in the other. You decide. I'm easy. I'll live in the back shed just to be near you.'

'That's the problem ...' The words were out before Grace realised. If he knew how she lived then a relationship between them wouldn't survive any length of time. But there was no way to explain.

Chapter Twenty

She was very attractive. A woman with class. And certainly not the normal hooker type John had on his books. He always looked for something different. There were a few on his books and they earned him a great deal of money. For themselves as well. She would be invaluable to him. He had many clients all over the world who looked for the better class of woman and were prepared to pay highly for her services. They all wanted something different. Her green eyes and that wonderful shining reddish hair put her in that category. His business was divided between the average punter and the gold card punters. The person who looked for someone like her was at the higher end. He brought women into this country, but he also sent women to other countries.

He thought about the interview. There was something tantalising about her. He couldn't put his finger on it. But before he sent her to the client, he would dally with her himself. To his surprise, he found that he was attracted to her. It was unusual for him. Most of the women he had on his books were beautiful and very young. But the fear in the young ones didn't appeal to him. He liked the more mature, and especially those who were more experienced but who hadn't been around so much. This one seemed almost vulnerable, and didn't have that veneer of hardness which characterized a lot of the older women he came across. He grinned, looking forward to meeting her face to face.

Chapter Twenty-one

Since meeting Ruth again, Kim had been drawn back into the past. Back to those days when they were young. They had lived in Greystones, Co. Wicklow, and as their parents were keen sailors, the social life of the family revolved around the yacht club. Much of the girls' young lives were spent on the sea.

But tragedy struck when they were in their teens and their father was killed in a car accident. It devastated them. Their mother was never quite the same again. She sold the yacht and became almost a recluse. Only ever seen walking around the village. In and out of the shops. Picking up the things they would need. Her eyes vague. Not seeing anyone really.

Their father had a substantial insurance policy and the family was comfortable. But it meant nothing to their mother, and a few years later she passed away in her sleep, leaving the sisters bereft. They had been in college when she died. In her will she left them the house and money which had accumulated. Then the problems began. They rented a flat in Dublin, and while Kim wanted to keep the house, living there on occasional weekends, loving the place, Ruth had no interest in it. All she wanted was money and insisted on having her share. The rows went on and on. Finally, as Kim couldn't raise a mortgage, she was forced to agree to sell. The sale meant they both received a sizeable inheritance from the estate. Kim invested her share in a house in Ranelagh. Her sister Ruth gave up college and left Ireland. The sisters hadn't met since that time.

One day, Kim and Ruth visited their old home, *Seaview House.*
    'It's still lovely,' Kim smiled.
    'Whoever bought it has kept it in good condition.'

They looked through the wrought iron gates. The extensive gardens were manicured and the flowering beds were colourful. They were glad there was no-one around and that they could gaze without interference on their childhood home.

'Can you remember playing there?' Kim asked.

'Yea,' Ruth murmured. Wistful.

'Remember the summers. Picnics. Parties. All Mam and Dad's friends around,' Kim seemed nostalgic.

'And all our friends from school. We used to trick them. Changing clothes and letting on to be each other. It was such fun,' Ruth giggled.

Later, they went to see their parent's graves. There were no flowers growing there, just a plain gravelled surface beneath the headstone. Black marble with gold leaf lettering. They each brought a bunch of flowers, and stood silently, saying their own private prayers.

'It seems such a long time ago, particularly since Dad died,' Ruth said.

'And poor Mum, she was only waiting to follow him,' Kim added.

'And glad to go in the end.'

'So sad.'

'They were both too young.'

'They never knew their grandchildren,' Kim said.

'I would love to have children,' Ruth murmured.

'Well, why not?'

'It's not part of the plan ...yet.'

'Maybe later on then,' Kim put her arm around Ruth's shoulders. They were hitting it off very well now. She thought. Perhaps it was maturity. They had been so similar in nature when they were young, they sparked off each other regularly. More out with each other than in. Sulking. Arguing. Screaming. Even hitting each other with the nearest implement at times. But they always made up quickly. So sorry for whatever had been said or done. Loving each other again.

As they walked back to the car, suddenly that idea which Kim had in the middle of the night became a possibility. If Ruth agreed, her plan could work ...

Chapter Twenty-two

It was a man who called. Grace didn't recognise his voice.

'Are you in a position to work next Thursday?'

She took a deep breath. 'Yes.'

'It will be in a club where we entertain special clients.'

She waited.

'You will be phoned and given directions.'

'How will we deal with this?' she asked Peter. 'To our advantage?'

'Once you go into that den of vipers God knows what could happen.'

'Raid the place before I'm forced into a position of compromise,' Grace said with a grin.

'We will need authorisation and extra manpower. That could be difficult.'

'I'll see the Super,' she said.

'I'll come with you.'

They met him later.

'I can't agree to this. You're putting yourself in danger again, Grace, anything could happen,' he said.

'If we can break this trafficking ring then it's worth it. Arrest the main men. Get them in for questioning. It's what we've been working towards. And I won't go too far, believe me. If I can get into this place then you never know what we might find,' Grace emphasised.

'I agree with the plan, Sir,' Peter added. 'And she won't be alone.'

'But make sure you get a result or else ...and watch yourself.' He raised a warning finger at her.

'Yes Sir. Thank you.'

She dressed in the low cut black dress again. But this time brightened it up with some paste diamonds earrings, and a pendant. Over the dress she wore a blue satin embroidered jacket, with a large brooch on the lapel. As before, the black six inch heels completed the outfit.

But there was just one more item. She had requested the issue of a small firearm, and now stowed it in an inside pocket which she had sewn into the jacket.

She hurried down the hall and opened the front door to see Mark walking up the drive towards her. Lately, he was in the habit of calling unexpectedly, but she had intended to be gone this evening.

'Well,' he grinned. 'This is good timing. Am I taking you out tonight?'

'Sorry, I'm meeting a few friends ...' she hesitated trying to think of some excuse.

'Must be some do. You're certainly looking good. Can I join you for a drink, or is it confined to a particular group?'

'Yea it is. I'm sorry love.' She closed the door behind her. 'Don't know what time it will be over, it's dinner and stuff, you know.'

'I'll pick you up afterwards, we could go on, you don't have to stay all night, do you?'

'It might be difficult, it's a crowd I know from the old days in Waterford.'

'I'm insanely jealous,' he grimaced. 'How could you dress up like that for them? I haven't seen you in that outfit. But I'm very interested, know what I mean?' He kissed her.

'Mark, stop.' Grace pulled away, afraid he would come too close and notice the bulk of the gun. 'Anyway, we don't go to flash places which would give me the opportunity to wear this. I really don't even like it.'

'How about Saturday, I'll book a table. Somewhere very upmarket. And you can wear that dress. I'm looking forward to it already.'

'Yea, maybe. I'll talk to you. Must go. There's my taxi.' She saw it drawing up behind Mark's car.

'Maybe? You're putting me on the long finger? I feel like an afterthought. A perhaps. You're playing with me, Grace.' He was suddenly serious, pushed his hands into the pockets of casual grey trousers. He stared at her for a moment. 'See you around.' He walked back to his car.

On the journey she felt guilty and upset that Mark was annoyed with her. What awful timing. It just wasn't possible to explain that she was working because of the nature of it. He'd have been furious if he knew. But apart from that, seeing her heading out for the evening had caused a very unusual reaction in him. She wouldn't have thought he was normally a jealous individual, but this seemed to be different. Now a dread that she might have damaged their relationship irreparably began to build up inside her.

The private club was on the ground floor of a hotel in Leeson Street. One of those places where you would find the more exaggerated type of clientele. Peter and a couple of the men on the team wore tuxedos, white scarves, and gloves, and he had a top hat and a cane. Supposedly celebrating some anniversary of Oscar Wilde, they swept up the steps and into the bar. There was undercover support from the Garda team in the street outside and at the back of the building.

As instructed, Grace gave her false name to the security man who stood at the gate, and he personally ushered her down a metal stairs to a plain door which had no identification. He made a phone call and then it was opened.

Inside it was luxurious. A couple of restaurants, and bars which were packed with people. Passing through Grace noticed gambling tables and women on small stages doing striptease for appreciative audiences. She couldn't compete here. What was all this about? Her eyes flashed around as she followed the man through swing doors and into an area at the back which was divided up into booths by blue velour curtains which pooled on the thick carpet. She noted that they were all empty. He ushered her into one of these and closed the curtains. Inside was a chaise longue with a black silk throw draped casually over it, and an armchair opposite. In an ice bucket on a table was a bottle of Champagne, and two glasses beside it. The murmur of many voices drifted in from the main part of the club, and she sat on the edge of the cushioned seat, crossed her legs and tried to look the part, wondering how long she would let it go until she gave Peter the word, a code arranged between them. The wire was hidden in her earrings.

'Hallo?' A soft voice curled around her from somewhere behind. She turned. Switched on a smile. A man came in. Good-looking. Thirties. Dressed expensively in a superbly cut tuxedo. She knew him instantly. It was the guy Peter had photographed in the VW. So he had been involved after all.

He pulled over the drapes, and they were cut off. The sound from outside was muffled. He opened the bottle of Champagne. The cork popped, he filled two glasses with the fizzy liquid, and handed one to her. He raised his glass.

'Cheers.' She clinked her glass against his.

They sipped.

'Thanks for coming in to see us,' he said and sat down beside her. Grace was relieved the gun was hidden on the opposite side of her jacket. He moved closer, his knee almost touching hers, and smiled, white teeth in contrast to smooth tanned skin. 'There are many clients here with different appetites. We like to offer them a selection. It's part of what we do. Our clients must be kept happy. As you can see here, there are many things people like to do in their leisure time. There is one particular man I have in mind. You will be his until he becomes bored. But it's up to you to keep him interested for as long as possible. Clients like to think that we have chosen a woman to suit their needs exactly. It appeals to their ego. And that's everything.' He sipped his Champagne.

Grace nodded, appalled at the scenario he depicted. That itchiness in her hands suddenly returned. It was very uncomfortable. She tried to ignore it.

'I have to mention another aspect of our business here. Confidentiality is paramount. You tell no one what goes on here. And I emphasise *no one*. Otherwise your life could be in danger.'

Chapter Twenty-three

Kim began to plan, and made notes in a small notebook about everything in her life. But she wrote nothing about Andrew a reluctance within her to reveal those intimacies to Ruth. For herself she put down every tiny detail.

What temperature the shower should be. How long she spent there, letting the water cascade over her. Stepping out, did she wrap up in a towel and take her time about it, or quickly dry herself. Did she check on the children the moment she climbed out of bed or wait until later. Did they rush into her bed when they woke up. Each day Kim went through the same routine, and noted her moves. It was like looking at herself in a mirror, learning new things about who she was. Kim saw a side to her own personality which surprised her. A secret unexplained side. There were times when she faltered. Her better nature didn't want to be suspicious of Andrew. To behave like a spy.

The notebook included the name and address of the playschool Lorelai attended and also Jason's primary school. Starting and finishing times. The gym. The name of her trainer. The length of time spent on the treadmill. The exercise bike. The weights. The pool. Running schedule. Accuracy was vital.

Then another section. Shopping Centres. Supermarkets. Food. Clothes. The labels favoured for herself and the kids. The fun places they went together. Their likes and dislikes. Every angle was covered.

Kim didn't know whether this plan would work. It depended on so many things. And her one wish was that by some miracle her suspicions would suddenly fizzle out, and she would discover that things were not at all the way they seemed. Andrew was the wonderful person she had always believed him to be. The man she loved.

But in spite of her misgivings, she continued on with it. Always keeping the notebook with her. Any time something came into her mind it was written down. And so the pages were filled up. Information about their family, mostly about Andrew's parents who were regular visitors to the house. Other friends and acquaintances. Names. Descriptions. Items under headings. Easy to find. She didn't expect her sister would need such information but put it down regardless.

And through this exercise, Kim was forced into a strange decision. One she didn't want to make. But if she was to succeed in her plan, it would be impossible to tell anyone that she had met her sister again.

Chapter Twenty-four

'No one will hear about this. I am doing it for financial reasons, to be clear, it's all about money, we are in a recession,' Grace said. 'Euros. Sterling. Dollars,' she smiled broadly at him, winked, and raised her glass.

'I'm glad to hear that. We should do well together,' he topped up their glasses. Then leaned closer. 'You're very beautiful,' he murmured softly. His fingers caressed her cheek.

Her pulse raced. But it wasn't a sexual response. She sat quite still, and shuddered inwardly.

To her utter shock he pressed his lips on hers and she stayed immobile, and the sensation in her hands swept right through her body. She wondered how far to let this go.

'Maybe we could delay a little before my client takes possession of you.' His fingers moved very quickly to play with the neckline of her dress.

Her skin crawled, and a scream inside wanted out.

'Don't be nervous, I know you haven't done this in some time, but I'll make it easy for you. Run you in, so to speak,' he said smoothly.

She stood up abruptly, yelled *now,* pulled the pistol out and held it against his forehead. 'Inspector Grace McKenzie ...I'm arresting you,' she went through the routine and cautioned him.

'What the hell?' There was an expression of fury on his face.

'Hands up where I can see them,' she ordered.

She stepped back a little and moved the gun out of his reach but held it tight.

There was a commotion in the distance. A sense of relief within her knowing Peter and the team had arrived. 'Get outside,' she said.

He didn't move.

Suddenly something hit her in between the shoulders and she could feel the butt of a gun cut deep into her back.

'Drop it,' someone said from behind. 'Drop it or I'll shoot.' She let the gun fall and raised her arms. Knowing instinctively that this wasn't important enough to take the risk of losing her own life.

The man picked up the ice bucket, bottle of Champagne and glass and disappeared. Almost immediately the gun in her back was removed. She grabbed her own gun again and followed, but could see no one in the immediate area, running from booth to booth. But they were all empty. At the back there were other rooms. A sitting room. Two bedrooms. An office. But no sign of her man.

'Grace?' Peter appeared. 'You OK? Thanks be to God. I was worried about you.'

'Have you got them out there?' she asked, breathless.

'Who?'

'I was with the guy in the VW, remember, but someone else took me from behind so they both ran.'

'Didn't see them.'

'Let me check.' She hurried through, and had a look at the groups of people being held by the team, disappointed when she couldn't see him. 'Have you checked upstairs?'

'They're doing that now. But apparently it seems legit, regular tourists, upmarket.'

'What did you find?'

'Gambling. Striptease. But we can't pull them in for that, this is a private club. How did you get on?'

'It hadn't come to anything. That area was empty. I'd say it would all happen later in the evening, when he had got as much money out of them as he could. It's all about money. He was very specific. And it wouldn't have been just sex, there was a more social side to it where I was concerned apparently. I was allocated one particular client. I'm very curious to know who he was,' Grace replied. 'But where have the men gone? Bastards.' She was angry.

They went into the booth. 'We'll dust for fingerprints. But I don't know if it will be any use, he took the ice bucket, Champagne bottle and his glass. Clever.'

Chapter Twenty-five

John ran through the tunnel with Victor. He had pressed an alarm button inserted into the side of his jacket even as Grace had pulled the gun on him, and Victor had immediately responded.

There had been no conversation between the two men as the concealed door at the back of the club slid open silently. They slipped through, disappearing into the shadows as the door closed again. They hurtled down the steps and into a tunnel below. John always used this exit and entry. Was never seen in the general area of the club. No one knew him as John Byrne. He didn't have a name. His only contact was Victor, his next in line, the only man he trusted.

They reached the end of the tunnel and followed another flight of steps upwards. He checked a monitor set into the wall and pressed a code. An image of a bar flashed on to the screen. It seemed quite normal. Patrons sat around drinking and there was no undue disturbance. He pressed in another code and this time he could see back into the tunnel. It was all clear.

A door slid back and allowed them access to the basement of a Georgian house which had been built in the eighteenth century. Dirt had accumulated on the brick walls, and floors. Unnameable stuff. The waste of people who lived here in the past. Ground down into desiccated protuberances which cut through the wafer thin leather soles of his shoes. Large veils of cobwebs clung to ancient bricks and the air was damp, musty. This place hadn't been used for many years.

He came up into a dimly lit jazz bar further down Leeson Street, and exited the place to mingle with the crowds outside. Victor followed a few minutes later and went in the other direction.

John was furious that he had allowed himself to be taken in by that bitch. He questioned himself over and over. She had been so plausible. But he realised that he had been too interested. There was something about her that had unnerved him. His usual sharp animal senses had been diverted and a weakness exposed. The establishment wanted to destroy him and he had foolishly let his guard down.

Chapter Twenty-six

Grace phoned Mark the following morning. 'I'm sorry about last night,' she said.

He grunted.

'It was work, you know. Not exactly as I described. I lied to you.' She had to come clean.

'Thanks.' He sounded bitter.

'Would you like to come around this evening. I'll pick up something to eat.'

'I don't know.'

'We should talk.'

'Have we anything to talk about?'

She could still hear the anger in his voice.

'I want to,' she insisted, hoping it wasn't too late with him.

'I'll see.'

At their team meeting, Grace pointed to the photo of the man on the board. The same person she had met at the club. 'That's him. Sounded to me like he's the top man.'

'Maybe he is, maybe he isn't,' Peter said.

She was disappointed. There hadn't been much achieved from their raid the previous night. It was a private club run by the hotel, and as such their hands had been tied. There was some cocaine found but these were small amounts for personal use. Staff were the usual guys, some of whom they knew. The dancers were mostly foreign.

The Super wasn't pleased with the lack of results. Grace's head buzzed. All she wanted to do was to get the man who headed up this trafficking ring. She needed to do that for Elena. After all the effort, to achieve nothing was utterly frustrating.

Mark did come around to see her, and seemed more relaxed now. They kissed lightly and he handed her a bottle of wine. It was formal. Their usual response to meeting each other was very different she thought, worried.

He sat down.

She poured from the bottle already open and handed him a glass.

'So it wasn't a group of friends getting together then?' he asked immediately.

'Not exactly,' she had to admit. 'I'm sorry, I didn't tell you the truth.' She lit a cigarette.

'You could have trusted me. I'm not going to blab about it.' He sipped his wine.

Grace leaned up against the counter. 'You wouldn't have understood.' She was reluctant to go into the details of the raid the night before, particularly if there were any further developments in the case.

'Always try me, Grace. I'm not exactly a kid.'

'It's difficult.'

'Come on. I'm not going to divulge State secrets.'

'I was playing a part.'

'What kind of part.'

'I can't say exactly.'

'Here we go again.'

'But I promise that's all it was. You might say I was on stage last night.'

'In the Gaiety or the Olympia,' he enquired, with a grin.

'Much more upmarket than that.'

'Was it a premiere? And were you successful?'

'Don't know.'

'So the papers haven't come in with the reviews yet,' he enquired.

'I was just reading some of them. I look good in the photographs,' she laughed.

'You looked good last night anyway,' he smiled. 'Come here to me.'

She put out the cigarette, walked across the room to the couch, and sat beside him.

He put his arm around her and pulled her close. 'I've missed you. Thought there was someone else in your life. Stiff competition.'

Grace shook her head and with a sense of relief relaxed into him. She had missed him too. It was only twenty-four hours. Although she hadn't committed herself to him, she was aware that it was the closest they had come to losing each other. And it could still happen. She reminded herself.

He stayed that night. They were back to normal. She just had to keep it that way, and not rock the boat. And for that short time he took away that feeling of dread which dogged her these days. How would she deal with what lay upstairs and have a normal relationship with Mark? As they lay on the narrow bed in the study afterwards, bodies entwined, Grace wished that she could give herself to him completely. Take hold of his hand for life, the way he wanted. But always there in the background was the spectre of her obsession.

'Do you want me to dump those newspapers in the green bin for you?' Mark asked, referring to the pile of papers stacked in the hall.

'No,' she spoke sharply. Suddenly worried that he would do exactly that.

He looked at her, puzzled. 'You still have to read them?'

'Yes.'

'What's the point?' He picked one up and looked at the date. 'This is yesterday's and I presume the others go back a few days at least?'

'So what?' Grace tried hard not to snap.

'How will you ever get the time?'

'I mightn't read every word. Maybe just the headlines,' she said defensively.

'Ok,' he laughed. 'Do you want me to read them to you? Then you could be doing something else while I whisper quotes to you.'

'Don't be ridiculous,' she had to smile too.

'It's good to see you laugh. You've been tight lipped lately.' He put his arm around her and pulled her to him. Then he kissed her gently. 'Relax, baby. All that tension does you no good.'

'Losing you for a night didn't help,' she murmured and kissed him back.

'I'll show you how to forget about it.' He pushed the strap of her top down, and his lips touched her shoulder. 'Let's go inside.'

'No can do, I've to work.'

'What time will you be back?'

'I'll text you.'

'I'm going to the rugby match. Will you meet me afterwards? We can have a few drinks with the crowd. I'd like to introduce you to my friends.'

Chapter Twenty-seven

Ruth sat watching television. It was a small flat screen with only the local channels. She had no favourite programmes and just stared at a few minutes of whatever was on the first one she came across, then clicked the remote and went on to the next, looking at snippets. It was like her life. Divided up. Random. She longed for continuity. To know what would happen at least for a couple of weeks ahead, so that she could plan even the most unimportant of things.

As it was, John called the shots. She wondered what he needed from her. They made love if he spent the night or even a few hours. He still told her he loved her but there was a certain monotony in his actions. Let's do it again. Don't take too long about it. He was taciturn. His eyes always somewhere else. Like she was a hooker. It was ironic.

Most of her mornings were spent on the laptop checking emails, arranging appointments and so on. Her pick-ups and deliveries in the afternoon. John's lack of attention to her made it easier to meet Kim. He wasn't there to notice when she went out or returned.

Ruth was more relaxed now when she met Kim. But couldn't talk about her life in detail. She skirted around it. Remembered the past mostly. Always the past. Reminded of those days when they were children. The games they played. Their dolls. Each one a mirror image of the other. They laughed about how they fought over them. She had always been envious of Kim. People said her sister was the cleverer. The best at tennis. The best dancer. The best singer. The best ...

'I'll be away for a few nights,' John said.
  'Where?'
  'London.'

'Can't I come with you, we could see a show, do some shopping?' Ruth asked.

'No, I'll be busy.'

Ruth was disappointed, John could see that. But didn't care. He went to Dalkey. In the basement office, a number of large monitors were positioned around the room and on the computer he now brought up bank statements and other accounts information and stared fixedly at them. Then stock exchange rates of companies around the world flashed on the screens. He had considerable investments.

But it really was getting too hot here in Ireland. He stared at the figures for this country. The business was going well. Up thirty percent on last year. In other countries not quite so much of an increase. He had a paranoia about the Gardaí going through his records so he was the only person who had access to the details of his multiple companies.

Now he wondered about his decision to remove himself to another jurisdiction. Perhaps he should appoint Victor, his next in line, to manage the business. It seemed a shame to close it down when it was so successful. But as the Gardaí were growing ever closer, and if Victor didn't run the operation as smoothly as he did himself, then he could be finished. They could stretch out into the world through Interpol and find him quite easily.

He thought about the inspector. For once, this was personal. A woman had attempted to play him for a fool, then dared to hold a gun on him. Anger surged within him. Those brilliant blue green eyes edged with long dark lashes came into his mind. They had promised so much. His pulse raced suddenly. What was it about Grace McKenzie which could affect him in this way? He couldn't understand it - a man who could have any woman he wanted.

Chapter Twenty-eight

Grace had a meeting with the Super. 'As I mentioned to you before, there have been no real results in this case, so I've decided to cut back the manpower, except for a couple of people who will keep up a certain level of surveillance on those apartments where there has been suspicious activity, and at the addresses of the two men picked up,' he announced.

'We still think that the man, our number one suspect, is at the head of this ring.' Grace pointed to the enlarged photo taken from the car, and an artist's impression of the features of the man she had met at the club which she had given from memory. 'Something must be done about the trafficking of women. We can't let up. There are so many of them. They're depending on us.' She tried to impress her feelings upon him.

'I'm sorry, Grace. You usually get your man, but this time you put your life on the line. It was extremely risky and there was nothing gained. I'm putting you on another case. I don't want to lose one of my best officers.'

'But those women need our help,' she insisted. Thinking particularly of Elena.

'I agree, they do, but we don't have enough evidence to convict any of these men.'

'Please, give us more time, something might come up.'

'No Grace, my decision is made. Now I want you to oversee a financial fraud case. It will be a change, good for you.'

Very disappointed with the Super's decision Grace decided to take a couple of days off, needing to get away from this whole grimy scene. She went home to Waterford, where she had been born and raised. Her two sisters were in Canada, and her only brother in

South Africa. They only came home to visit every few years and she couldn't always get away to see them. Now suddenly, Grace was anxious to see her Mam and Dad.

'It's great to have you back,' her Dad came from behind the counter and hugged her. 'Mary, look who's here,' he shouted. Her mother rushed out and embraced her as well in front of the customers, who gathered around her in welcome.

It was so good to be home. Sit at the big table in the kitchen and share her Mam's lamb stew, apple pie and custard. And talk. Not about her work. But about home. The family. How they were all getting on.

'It's been too long. And you're not looking that well, much too thin.' Her mother eyed her.

'I've been very busy.'

'That job,' her father dismissed it with a wave of his hand. 'I know you've done well, but it's too demanding. When do you ever get a holiday?'

'When do you ever get a holiday?' she laughed at him.

'That's different. We're our own bosses. We choose not to take a holiday. You can't take a holiday.'

'If I get away for a day, that's a holiday.' She ate a spoonful of delicious apple pie. It was so good.

'How long can you stay?' her mother asked, and gave her a second helping of pie without even asking if she wanted it. Just like she would always have done when she was a child.

'Back home in the morning,' she smiled. 'Sorry. Promised Kim and Andrew that we'd go over to a barbecue they're having before they go off on their holidays.'

Grace could see the disappointment in their eyes and felt guilty. Was she the one who hurt them the most? The others couldn't come back that often, they had accepted that. Their youngest daughter was only a few miles away and didn't come back often enough.

The thought of bringing Mark down here occurred to her. They would have liked him and vice versa. Imagined introducing him as her partner. Telling her parents that he was the man with whom she would spend the rest of her life. Maybe have children with him, if it wasn't too late. And he would be part of their family too.

But she couldn't do that.

They walked through the streets of the town after dinner. It was busy. A lot of tourists around. Her Mam and Dad met people they knew. Grace met friends. It was wonderful to come home. Her heart was full. They had a drink in their local pub. Dad had the one creamy headed pint he allowed himself. Her Mam enjoyed a sherry and Grace joined her.

Her parents took part in everything locally. Sang in the choir at all the religious services in the church. Were involved in the musical society productions. The amateur drama group. Their roles were backstage now but in their younger days, they were out there on the stage loving every minute of it. Even Grace herself had trod the boards, and a longing to be part of that world again swept through her, remembering the night at the club which she had laughingly explained away to Mark as being an acting role in some production.

But there was guilt too that she couldn't do enough for her parents. They were getting old now both in their late sixties and she would have loved to invite them up to Dublin for a weekend, but that was something she couldn't do. The demands of the job always the excuse. Luckily for her, the business of running the pharmacy prevented them from taking time off too. So they understood where she was coming from.

'Is there a man in your life yet?' her mother asked as they had supper before going to bed.

'Well ...' she said, smiling.

'Trouble is, I don't know how he would put up with you,' her father grinned.

'You need someone in your life, love, you can't just be a workaholic,' her mother added. 'And don't forget about children, time doesn't stand still.'

'I'm aware of that.'

'Do a bit of soul searching now and then.' Her father sipped his coffee, a pensive look on his face.

'Take the dogs for a walk on the beach in the morning. Let the wind blow the cobwebs away.' Her mother stood up, patted her shoulder, and collected the mugs on a tray.

They were wise, her parents. And it was only now, in her mature years, she realised that.

She took her mother's advice and drove out to Tramore with the dogs early the following morning. This was where they had spent their childhood summers. Running on the beach. Swimming. Building sandcastles. Playing tennis. Saving up their pennies for the rides at the carnival. Occasionally in their teenage years camping overnight with a gang of friends.

Now she walked that same beach. The tide was in. The dogs paddled. On such a good day, there were lots of people enjoying themselves. Swimming, sunbathing, playing with their kids. The same as it ever was. It could have been years ago. Nothing seemed to have changed. There was a stiff breeze off the sea, it whipped around her, dragging her hair this way and that. Followed by the dogs, she ran towards the dunes. But stopped suddenly. Her breathing uneven. She heard a voice call her name and was suddenly afraid. Could sense that feeling on her skin again. Like she was caught in a sandstorm. 'No!' she shouted out loud. Repeating the word again and again. But it was whipped away by the breeze.

Mark pulled up outside Kim and Andrew's house, and Grace climbed out of the car. He took a couple of bags out of the boot, and they walked together around the side where the chat of the crowd, and the excited screams of the kids could be heard.

'Grace, Mark?' Kim spotted them immediately and hurried over. 'Thanks for coming, it's great to see you. And lovely to meet you, Mark. She didn't tell me you were such a *looker,*' she grinned, and kissed them both affectionately.

'She doesn't want to give me a big head no doubt,' he laughed.

Grace put her arm around him.

Kim introduced Mark to Andrew, who stood cooking at the barbeque. 'Come over here and give me a hand, man, these sausages need turning,' he said.

'We've brought a few things.' Mark handed Kim the bags.

'You shouldn't have. That's far too much.' She pulled out two bottles of wine. A cake. Chocolates. Sweets.

'I'll go over and help Andrew.' Mark walked across the patio.

'How are you?' Grace asked.

'Fine,' Kim led the way into the house and put away the wine, and the other gifts in the kitchen.

'You're looking a bit tired. Any particular reason?' Grace asked.

'Organising everything for the holiday I suppose. Fancy a glass of wine or a beer?'

'A beer thanks.'

'What does Mark drink?'

'Just something soft today, he's driving.'

'What will I give him?' She took the beer out of the fridge.

'Whatever you have, he won't mind.'

Kim handed her a beer, and put her arm around her. 'Come out and meet everyone.'

'Where are the kids?'

'Playing with the others around the garden somewhere.'

Andrew and Mark cooked chicken breasts, ribs, steaks, potatoes, and vegetables on the barbecue.

'Believe you're the driver tonight, what would you like to drink?' Kim asked.

'Just something soft, thanks, if you have it.'

'Sure, I'll get it.' She went back into the kitchen.

'I hear you're heading off to Wexford tomorrow?' Mark asked Andrew.

'For a couple of weeks. So hope the weather will hold. We could do with a few days like today, Wexford in the rain is...' Andrew pulled a face. 'And then when we get back the kids are at school again, so that's the end of the so-called summer.'

'Few good days in June I seem to remember.'

'That's about it.'

'Maybe you'll be lucky,' Mark said, as they put the cooked food into big serving dishes and brought them over to where everyone had gathered around the tables.

After they had eaten, Grace played with the kids, kicking a football around the garden, and then she dragged Mark in. It was a pleasant evening and they were all exhausted when Kim finally put Jason and Lorelai to bed. Most of the friends and family left as it grew dark, and the four of them, Kim, Andrew, Grace and Mark sat drinking coffee and chatting on the patio.

'You're based in London, Andrew?' Mark asked.

'Yea, unfortunately. It's tough on Kim and the kids.'

'Ever thought about moving there? Or getting a transfer here?' he asked.

Andrew stared at Mark. 'What made you suggest that?' There was an edge in his voice.

'Nothing really, you must miss Kim and the kids a lot, that's all,' he said, smiling at her.

'Listen, mate, where we live is none of your business. So keep your nose out of our lives,' Andrew snapped.

'Sorry about that, Andrew, shouldn't have said it, out of order,' Mark said.

It was obvious to Grace that Mark was very embarrassed, as she was herself.

'Bloody right,' Andrew grunted.

There was an awkward silence.'

'Mark is Grace's friend, Andrew, so he can say what he wants at any time.' Kim stood up and kissed Mark. 'I'll get more coffee.'

Grace stared at Andrew, surprised at his venom.

'It was a quite an innocent remark, Andrew, surely you can understand that,' Mark explained.

'As I said before, mind your own business.'

'Sure.' Mark stood up. 'Perhaps we should be on our way.' He looked pointedly at Grace.

'Going already, come on, it's early yet.' Kim returned with the percolator. 'Top up for anyone?' She stood waiting, but no-one replied. 'Why don't you stay here, the two of you, then you could have a few drinks?' Kim asked. 'The guest room is there for you.'

'No thanks, Kim,' Grace said, aware that Mark was feeling awkward. 'We'll head on. You've an early start no doubt,' Grace said. 'Thanks for a super evening, we really enjoyed it.'

'And to you for bringing so much, you're always too generous.'

'Goodnight Andrew, and thanks.' Mark held out his hand. But Andrew ignored it. 'Sorry about my remark, it wasn't meant,' he murmured.

'Night Andrew,' Grace kissed him.

Kim walked to the car with them.

'Sorry about Andrew, he's always on edge when he comes home these days, I suppose it's jetlag,' she explained.

'Don't worry, go off and have a great holiday.' Grace hugged her tight.

They sat into the car, and Mark drove.

'I'm sorry about Andrew, he can be a bit testy at times,' she said.

'I crossed a line obviously, he's very sensitive.'

'You can understand that, his job does take him away from home a lot.'

They didn't talk much more until he drew up outside Grace's house. He reached for her and pulled her close. 'Missed you all evening,' he whispered, and kissed her.

'Yea, know what you mean,' Grace murmured.

'We had good fun with those kids, although I found it difficult to keep up with them, such energy.'

'I'll make coffee.' She went into the kitchen and switched on the kettle. 'I didn't really drink any at Kim's. Sit down, love, push those papers on to the floor.'

'I see you're adding to the pile of papers which had built up since last week,' he grinned at her.

'Had no time to read them.'

'You'll be buried by them one of these days.'

She didn't reply, and brought the mugs of coffee over and put them on the low glass table. There was an air of surrender in the way she sat down again.

'Is there something going on, Grace? Have you a problem?' Mark asked, his voice soft.

'What do you mean?' She rounded on him. Suddenly furious.

'I'm worried about the newspapers. You can't let it get out of hand, love. You must throw them away even if you haven't had an opportunity to read a word.'

'You don't understand anything about it,' her retort was sharp.

'I do. It's part of my job. It's an illness. I have patients who suffer from it. A person could be destroyed if it's not caught in time.'

'You're imagining things. Just because you're a psychologist,' she emphasised the words.

'Forget about it. I'm probably over-reacting. I'm sorry, love.' He hugged her.

They sat in silence.

Time passed.

'I'm sorry ...thank you for your concern.' But there was still a trace of anger in her words.

'Gracie, let's forget about this.' He kissed her on the cheek. But she kept her head averted.

'My love, don't push me out into the cold,' he coaxed.

She picked up a pack of cigarettes, and lit one. She sat there, staring into space, smoking with jerky puffs. The fingers of her other hand tapping on the wooden arm of the couch.

'Do you want me to go?' Mark asked.

She didn't reply. But slowly her body moved closer to his, the stiffness easing out of it. Her head on his shoulder. Eyes closed.

Chapter Twenty-nine

Kim, Andrew and the kids packed up and headed for Wexford the day after the barbecue. Andrew's parents, Dolores and Noel were joining them and they set off in tandem. It was a bright sunny morning and they were delighted that the Met Office predicted good weather for a few days. Every year, they spent the first two weeks of August in Rosslare and usually went to the sun earlier in the year. The house they rented was close to the beach and they always met up with friends who were down at this time of the year as well.

Now the holidays stretched ahead and Kim put all her worries out of her head. Looking forward to spending two glorious weeks away with Andrew and the children. Dolores and Noel helped look after the kids and let them get out in the evenings if they wanted. Not that they ever did that very much, most of the friends had kids too so they all got together for barbeques and just had a good time. The weather held and it was idyllic. Andrew was in wonderful form. Kim couldn't believe it.

After they had been there for almost a week, Andrew received a phone call just as they sat down to breakfast on the patio. He went into the house to take it, and Kim wondered who it was from as she served up muesli, scrambled eggs, grilled bacon. Her mother in law carried out the plates, she poured the coffee and sat the kids at the table.

'Who was that, love?' she asked when Andrew reappeared putting the phone back in his pocket.

'It's bad news,' he said, looking glum.

'What do you mean? What's wrong?' She was shocked.

'I've to go back.'

'Where?'

'London. To take a flight to Sydney, stopping off at Singapore. They're understaffed. A couple of pilots have gone down with some illness.'

She said nothing.

'I have to cover for them.'

'But you're on holidays. They can't expect you to up and go. It's too much,' she exploded.

'I've no choice. I suppose I'm lucky to have a job. Can't refuse.'

'I'm so disappointed,' Kim said, tears in her eyes. 'We were having such a good time. Your Mam and Dad too. It's not fair on them, they hardly ever see you.'

'I'm sorry,' he turned to his parents. 'I don't see you enough. Kim is right.'

They smiled with understanding.

'Will you get back?' Kim asked. 'Even for a day or two?'

He shook his head. Put his arm around her shoulders and kissed her.

She looked at him silently.

'Dad, will you carry the boat down to the beach?' Jason jumped up, having eaten only a few spoonfuls of muesli.

'I can't go to the beach today, Jason, I've to go to work.'

'Why?'

Andrew lifted him up in his arms. 'I just have to.'

'Will you be back later?'

'Don't know when.'

'But you promised you'd take me out in the boat,' he wailed.

'Mum will do that instead.'

'I don't want Mum.'

'Well, maybe granddad?'

'No.' He struggled to get down.

'I'm sorry, Jason.'

The child ran over to where the inflatable boat lay with the things for the beach. He grabbed hold of it and began to drag it towards the gate.

His grandfather, Noel, went over. 'Come on, let me carry it for you, Jason.' He lifted it and the two headed off around the house.

'I'd better get going,' Andrew said.

'Already?' Kim was upset. There were tears in her eyes, but she really didn't want to make a big issue of it in front of his mother. He went into the house and she followed. 'Can't you get on to them and try to get someone else to do it?'

'I'm sorry love, I tried. Do you not think I would? I'm not exactly over the moon about having to break off the holiday myself. We were having a great time.' He was already changing out of shorts and tee shirt. 'Throw a few things into a bag for me love.'

'What time are you leaving?' She put in underwear and socks. 'Your work clothes are all ready at home anyway.'

'There's a flight at sixteen thirty-five and they've booked me on that.'

'I can't believe this is happening.' She was very upset.

'Neither can I.' He buttoned up his shirt.

'If one of those guys suddenly recovers, make sure you insist on getting back here. We've another week.'

'Of course I will, love.' He kissed her.

'What about the car?'

'You can use Dad's.'

He was gone. It was the end of the holiday for Kim. But as she watched him drive out of the gate, suddenly that idea she had in the middle of the night came into her mind again.

Chapter Thirty

Grace stared at the bundle of newspapers piled up in the hall. Mark had said those very words she had been unable to utter and zoned in exactly, which wasn't surprising considering his profession. She dreaded the thought that he would find out the true extent of this need which controlled her. He had no idea that it had gone this far. God knows what would happen if he found out what lay upstairs, and that she had sold her soul to it.

She had not been able to read all of the recent papers and now wondered should some of the earlier issues be thrown out. But the thought of that sent spirals of horror through her. That would mean she could miss something in one of the articles. Maybe a little nugget of information which would make a difference to the trafficking case. It was vital that she put away whoever organised the operation, and prevent them from preying on young women. Imprisoning them. Raping them. And submitting them to a life of hell.

But the news was on the internet. A voice in her head reminded. To scroll through it would be much quicker. Why do you need to read old newsprint? Why? These were questions she often asked herself but never managed to find a satisfactory answer. And there was always a case in which she was involved. A vitally important case. And not to read the newspapers could mean she wouldn't find the perpetrators. In her head it was always the reason. And she didn't know why that was.

Grace went upstairs. Unlocked the door and went on to the landing. There was a muffled silence. And no sound at all from outside. She walked along the narrow corridor between the walls of newspapers, running her hands along the ridged edges. Grey white tones occasionally interspersed with shades of dull colour. But then she turned back, inhaled the clear air from the stairwell, and rushed down again. The green bin stood around the side of the house. She picked up the most recent papers and threw them into the almost empty bin.

It was a terrible betrayal.

Chapter Thirty-one

Andrew took an Aer Lingus flight to Heathrow. He had booked it a few weeks previous. His life planned with meticulous precision. He was looking forward to getting away with Sara and the children for a week. They would take the car and drive down to Cornwall, moving from place to place along the coast.

He never took Sara abroad. Used the excuse that because he flew day to day in his job, it would be too much like work to fly anywhere. But the real reason behind that was the fear of meeting people whom he knew through his job, and having to explain the identity of Sara and the children.

While he had felt some guilt at having to disappoint Kim and the children, a sense of excitement filled him now. Always that thrill of getting away with it. His double life.

He let himself in the door. Cheryl ran out to meet him, followed by Sara. He kissed them. 'All packed, and ready for tomorrow?'

'Yea,' Sara hung on tight to him.

He slipped into his other role with remarkable ease. Had trained himself to switch his personality. Remember names with ease. Sara and the children. Her mother, sisters, extended family. Details about their lives. Where they lived. Their work. And so on. An amazing amount of information.

'Looking forward to the holidays?' he smiled.

'Course I am, hope the weather's good.'

'I've ordered it,' he said with a grin.

'Just thinking, why don't we go to the sun some time. Even Spain would be great. Long days on the beach, or the pool, it would be so enjoyable, maybe next year?'

'You know I fly every day, and hate flying on holiday,' he said.

'Well, I'm going to persuade you to travel on a plane with me next year. It will be a first, and you will have all that time to get used to the idea,' she laughed.

'OK, maybe,' he said, with a grin. 'But this time it's Cornwall.'

Chapter Thirty-two

Ruth's first appointment was in a library today. At a computer. Surfing the net. The man sat beside her. She didn't recognise him. It was always someone different. She wondered how many people John had working for him. And how long he would be able to keep going. And how long they would be together. If the Gardaí caught up with him, would she be involved as well and end up having to serve a long jail sentence? The thought of that terrified her.

Questions tumbled around in her head as she clicked the keys looking at a travel site. Views of the Caribbean flashed in front of her. Visions of gleaming white beaches lapped by aquamarine seas, shaded by palm trees. She longed to go somewhere like that. Her wanderlust had abated since coming back from Seville to live with John and in those early months had been utterly happy, content to put down roots at last.

But life hadn't worked out the way she had hoped. With the exception of Sandyford, the apartments they lived in were utility. Beige grey boxes, with huge plates of glass through which she stared out at other beige grey boxes. He discouraged her talking to the people who lived there. And having been so long abroad, she had no friends. Now to her utter joy, she had her sister Kim, and that made all the difference in her life.

Kim and Ruth met in a small cafe in town. They embraced and chatted. Catching up mostly with Kim's news of the family, and what they had all been doing.

'I envy you,' Ruth said softly.

'I envy your independence too at times,' Kim smiled.

'I suppose we're never happy with what we have, there's always something not quite right.'

'Yea,' Kim sipped her coffee and stared pensively through the window.

'Are you OK? You seem a bit down?' Ruth asked, sensing that her sister wasn't her usual bright self.

'I'm all right, it's just ...Andrew.'

'What about him?'

'Things are a bit strained,' Kim admitted.

'I know what you mean. John and I aren't exactly lovebirds at the moment either.'

'I'm sorry, it's tough if your relationship isn't what you hope for.'

'Do you want to talk about it? Sometimes helps.'

At first Kim was hesitant but then told her of the suspicions she had about Andrew. The electricity bill. The fact that he had cut their holiday short and gone back to work.

'Has he changed towards you?' Ruth asked.

Kim nodded.

'Do you still ...' she hesitated. 'Make love?'

'Yes, that's always great, but ...'

'But?'

'I'm probably crazy, but I feel I don't have him. I search all the time, but he's never there when I want him. He only comes home once in two weeks, stays a night, and is gone again. That's not a marriage. It's some sort of a business arrangement.' There were tears in Kim's eyes.

'Why not ask him if something's going on,' Ruth suggested. 'Force it out into the open.'

'Andrew is very smooth, he would persuade me that I wasn't thinking straight. That I might be imagining things. He always brushes over any doubts I have.'

'I wish I could help.'

'Maybe you can,' Kim said.

Ruth looked at her, puzzled.

'Remember how we used to swop when we were young, we were talking about it recently,' she laughed.

Ruth nodded.

'Would you take my place at home for a weekend?'

'What do you mean?' Ruth gasped.

'I need to go somewhere but I don't want anyone to know, so I wondered if you'd cover for me. You know, like we used to.'

'I don't get it.' She had to admit.

'I want you to be me.'

'Swop?' Ruth couldn't believe what she was hearing.

'Yea, just for a couple of nights. Come over to my house and babysit.'

'Where are you going?'

'London - to check out that address on the electricity bill.'

Chapter Thirty-three

A large amount of money had been embezzled in a stockbroking firm and the team went in to find the culprit. But Grace found the investigative work bland. Uninteresting. They would probably find the person who had done it in time. Whoever had enriched himself or herself from the wealth of others. But in her heart of hearts she didn't really care whether she solved the case or not.

She spent her time in the company offices with their computer experts. Some IT equipment had already been taken away and was being examined, but so far they had not found out who had perpetrated the crime. It would mean that they would have to put in the hours. Hard slog. That's what it was all about.

Privately, Grace was still interested in solving the trafficking case of Elena, and the other women. Aware that the man she had met at the club wasn't necessarily the person who had organised it. She thought of how the girl had been so violently treated and was immediately filled with a sense of righteousness. Grace wanted justice for her, but now there was no opportunity to follow through.

Grace invited Mark out for dinner. She still felt guilty about the night he had surprised her going out to that club undercover. Tonight, she had deliberately not worn the black dress. Had in fact thrown it into the recycling bin at the supermarket. Reluctant to be reminded of the time when she had last worn it. So it was a turquoise dress she wore. A simple design with shoe string straps, and matching sandals. And no jewellery at all.

They went to *La Cascina*, one of their favourite restaurants. This evening it was packed with diners. The level of voices rose as they opened the door and they sat up at the bar and ordered a drink while waiting for a table.

'Cheers.' They raised their glasses.

'I love this place,' Grace murmured, gazing around.

'Reminds me of Rome, anywhere in Italy,' Mark smiled. 'And the food is so good.'

'Have you ever been in Sorrento?' she asked.

'I've been in the north, but I'd love to go further south. Now that you're not so busy, any chance of taking off for a week or even two?' he asked.

'I could request it,' she said. 'How about you?'

'I'll have a look at the appointment book.'

They smiled at each other.

They ate their meal leisurely and finished a bottle of red wine. They left the restaurant and continued the evening in a piano bar a few streets away. Someone played jazz and they sat listening.

'This is something else.' Grace leaned her head back on the soft cushions of the couch.

'Love you,' he kissed her. Playing with the thin strap of her dress.

She hummed along to the tune the pianist was playing.

Mark joined in. She giggled. 'You've a great voice. I like to hear you sing.'

'Any time.' He raised his voice a little and leaned closer to her.

A man who was passing by glanced their way. Grace met his eyes. Then he was gone.

'Hey,' she shouted. Leapt up and ran after him.

'Grace?' Mark called after her.

Certain it was the man she had met at the club, she hurried through the packed bar. Could still see his dark head, ushering a fair-haired woman ahead of him.

The doorman closed the door after him.

She reached to open it, but had to wait impatiently until he did it for her. Then was out into the street, to see the lights on a car parked up ahead flash on. She followed, unsteady in her high heels, but by the time she was within a hand's touch, it roared away and disappeared.

'Grace? What on earth?' Mark caught up with her. 'What's wrong?' He stared at her, his expression shocked.

'Thought I ...knew him,' she whispered.

'Who is he?'

'Just someone.'

'Come back inside.'

They went in again and sat down. He put his arm around her shoulders. Grace sipped her glass of wine, but was in shock. It was like she was back in that club when the man's hand had slid across her face, neck, and breasts, lascivious. Suddenly that sensation of itchiness on her hands returned, and within minutes had spread all over her body. A shiver swept through her, and she knew that it had been foolish to let that guy go so far on that night.

'Can I do some work on the trafficking case?' she asked the Super after a few days. 'There's nothing much for me to do on the fraud case. I'm just overseeing it, and hoping the guys will come up with something. I feel useless.'

'Maybe you need to take a bit of time out. You've been working too hard over the last couple of months. And you can't go on like that, it's too much stress.'

'How do you know?'

'I know you well, Grace, and I'm worried about you. Going into those places under cover was very risky.'

'But I want to try and find out who brings these women into the country. I even saw the guy again recently.'

'Did he recognise you?' The Super's voice was sharp.

'I don't know.'

'If he did, you could be in danger. Have you thought about that? He can find you, but you can't find him. This is a dangerous criminal we're dealing with. I'm glad you're off the case.'

'But there's only two men working on it now, and I believe they have uncovered nothing new. And it does seem that the apartments are not being used at present. The club is still up and running. I was hoping we gave them a hell of a fright, but we have to keep up the pressure and not let this become another cold case through lack of manpower which will be resurrected in ten years. We have to find the perpetrator now before the trail goes cold.' She was passionate.

'It does no harm to stand back, get a clearer view. Something may occur to you,' he advised.

'But I haven't got access to the files. Can't you just put me back on the team, we could trawl all the information we've compiled to date and we may see something we didn't notice before.'

'Look, you can't be out there in the forefront of this. This guy knows you. You've seen him face to face. He could put out a contract on you. These people are very dangerous.'

'That's ridiculous. If he pops me off then he'll really be in the soup, we'll be down on top of him. His whole empire could collapse. He's not going to take the chance,' she argued.

'You don't know what you're dealing with here, Grace. Now, take a break, I want you out of sight.'

'All I'm doing is office work. Come in here in the morning, and go home at night. Talk about nine to five. Isn't that enough out of sight?'

'When was the last time you went on a holiday?'

She couldn't answer that.

'I thought so, you can't even remember.'

'It's a couple of years ago, I suppose.'

'It's more than that.'

'I went home for a day recently,' she said, with a grin.

'Big deal. Now this is an order. I don't want to see you for three or four weeks. You're entitled to that much leave, so take it.'

The argument was lost. And it wasn't often Grace was in that position.

Now she really felt at a loose end. Cut off by her boss. Not essential any longer. She didn't go into work for a couple of days, and at home found time heavy on her hands. But she went for a good run each day. Met Kim at the gym. And even managed to cook a decent meal for herself. But most of all she valued the extra time to catch up on her reading. In the early days, she had kept a notebook of articles which were of interest to her, and she actually had looked back if she needed the information. But at this stage locating an old paper was impossible.

Now some of the older issues lay in the green bin, and the awareness that she had a real problem grew stronger and began to undermine her confidence. Tears came to her eyes the moment she even saw the bin, reminded. It was due for collection today and there were some difficult moments before she finally managed to drag it out to the kerb.

'This is our opportunity, don't you see? I've checked the appointments and I can get a locum to cover me.' Mark was enthusiastic. 'Let's have a look at flights, and hotels.' He opened up his phone.

Grace immediately felt under pressure. Wondering how she would manage to stay away for two weeks. How to manage without her newspapers? She could buy some in Italy but that wouldn't be the same.

'Right, how about next week, we'll try Aer Lingus.' He scrolled down.

'Eh ...I'm not sure.'

'Come on, let's take the ball on the hop. It's going to be great this time of the year. We'll fly into Rome and hire a car. Then we'll spend a couple of nights in the area, and then head down to Amalfi and Sorrento.'

She nodded.

'There's a flight out next Wednesday morning ...that should suit. What do you think?'

Grace was caught. Wanting to go. Yet afraid to go. Would Mark find out about her secret? He was astute and had already suggested that she may even be suffering from a condition of some sort. But so caught up in whatever this was, she couldn't live without it now. Suddenly, a longing to go upstairs swept through her. A need to retreat into that closeted space. Where the air was so dry. She felt safe there.

'I'll book,' Mark said.

She wanted to scream *no*. But hadn't the courage. There was absolutely no reason for refusing to go to Italy. None at all. How stupid.

'I have to check if my passport is in date,' she said, weakly.

'Well, go and get it now. Anyway, if it's out of date they'll do something quickly for you. And what's your exact name on the passport? You know how fussy they are about that.'

Grace went upstairs. Sometimes unable to breathe in here and needing to get out. Other times she couldn't breathe outside and needed to get in. She unlocked the door. Closed it behind her and walked on to the landing. Her hands held on to the sides of the wall of newspapers for support. It was comforting. The soft velvet folds were delicious. Her skin tingled. A sexual response. As if Mark was touching her. She pressed her face into the wall. Closed her eyes. Breathed in the aroma of newsprint. Her pulse raced. Palpitations fluttered. It was like glue sniffing. She was on a high.

'Grace?'

She heard Mark call from downstairs.

'You've been ages up there. Still looking for the passport? Want me to give you a hand?' he asked.

She came out through the door at the top of the stairs in a rush and turned the key in the lock. 'It's not up here.'

'Why are you locking the door?' he asked curiously.

'It's automatic. I always do that when I'm up here on my own. Particularly at night. It's just a habit.'

'You know you don't have to be on your own, and need to lock doors. I'll deal with any potential burglars. But I'm surprised you're scared of anything. I always thought you'd be the one protecting me,' he said, with a grin.

'Of course I will,' she reassured. 'Now let me think, I have to find that passport.' She walked down towards where he stood on the stairs.

'Better find it quick, I'm checking for flights.'

'Thanks.' Grace rested against his broad chest. Suddenly needing his warmth. His love. But she hadn't yet said she loved him. It was much too soon for Grace to make such a commitment.

'Hey?' He kissed her.

'I'll have a look downstairs.' She knew exactly where it was, and went directly to the unit where all her personal papers were stored, picked up the passport and glanced at the date.

'Well?' Mark waited.

'It's all right until next year and I'm plain Grace McKenzie.'

'Then we're away?'

She forced a smile.

'I'm going to spoil you.' He kissed her again. 'I'll have a look for a really luxurious hotel. You won't know yourself. So get the holiday duds out.'

On Monday, she went into work. Couldn't have put in the time at home doing nothing more than read the papers, and take physical exercise. It just wasn't enough. Even the fraud case was something.

'What are you doing here?' The Super asked.

'We're leaving on Wednesday, and we'll be away for over two weeks. But I had to come in. Need to wean myself off work. Otherwise I'll have withdrawal symptoms.'

'Keep your head down, and don't go wandering around the city too much, I will feel far better when you're out of the country. I presume you are going somewhere exotic?' he asked, with a grin.

'Italy.'

'That'll do.'

Chapter thirty-four

John was enraged. That inspector had spotted him the other night and he had thought he would never get out of the place with Ruth. What was it with the woman? The Gardaí were obviously still on the look-out for him. How had she known that he would be in that particular place? He couldn't understand. Was he being watched all the time? Were they following him? He had taken back the Audi from Ruth, but then had got rid of that and bought a BMW so they wouldn't know what he was driving.

He was still considering moving to Geneva, and wondered if it was the best place to go. Perhaps it would be more sensible to go further afield. He had a record in England. But had done his time, and got out of the country some years before. His family still lived in Leeds. A wife and two children. But she had divorced him while he was inside over a decade ago. And when he went to see his children after his release from prison, she refused to give him access.

A loner, John could exist without family dies, but he was glad his mother was alive and he visited her occasionally. She was in her sixties now. And unwell. His two brothers looked after her. Both professional men who ran an engineering business. In their eyes he was the black sheep, and they were not interested in keeping in touch with him. Above all, none of them knew the extent of his wealth.

The nature of his business empire meant he couldn't live an outwardly normal life in either Ireland or the UK. For now, living with Ruth some of the time was a cover. No-one suspected her of anything. She was untainted and knew nothing of his background, even of the house in Dalkey. He was very careful about that.

John met with Victor. They sat in his car in a busy car park in the city.

'How are things on the ground?' he asked.

'We're still tight on accommodation, so the turnover is down.'

'Are we operating around the clock?'

'Pretty much.'

'Have you managed to replace all of the properties by now?' he asked.

'Not yet.

They both glanced out through the tinted windows occasionally, always watching for trouble.

'How close are the Gardaí do you think?' Victor asked.

'I don't know, to tell you the truth. The detective who went undercover is our biggest problem. I met her recently. She came after me. She's a determined little bitch.' His lip curled.

'There's word out there that they've taken some of the team off the case,' Victor said.

'Any idea why?'

'They haven't got enough evidence to justify that amount of manpower apparently.'

'In our structure, there are no real names, no addresses, and only mobile phones. I've already changed mine,' John said.

'Me too.'

'I hope we're in the clear,' he muttered, but still he couldn't get Grace McKenzie out of his head.

Chapter Thirty-five

Grace called to see Kim. She hugged her, and handed her a bunch of summer flowers.

'Thanks so much for these, they're lovely, let's go inside.' Kim busied herself filling a vase with water, and arranging them.

'Auntie Grace?' Jason ran down the hall, and threw himself against her.

'How are you, Jason?' She lifted him up.

'Did you bring a police car? Can I see it.' He wriggled down out of her arms and ran to the window. 'It's not there.' He turned to her, the little face disappointed.

'Not today. But I have something else.' She took a chocolate bar out of her pocket.

He reached up for it immediately.

'Have to ask Mum if you can have it now,' Grace said, smiling.

'OK,' Kim agreed.

The paper was torn off, and the bar demolished in minutes.

'Where's Lorelai?' she asked.

'In bed having a sleep, but I'll get her up soon. Come into the kitchen and we'll have a cuppa.'

They chatted over coffee and some of Kim's home baked banana bread, topped with thick butter, amid constant interruptions by Jason.

'How is Andrew?' Grace asked.

'He was back for one night, then gone again.' Kim's reply was non-committal.

'Why is that?'

'Working all the time.'

'Daddy is in his plane,' Jason said, swinging his arm about.

'That's not easy for you,' Grace murmured.

'No.'

'And it's worrying you, isn't it?' Grace was immediately sympathetic.

'It will come down out of the sky ...*wheeee*,' Jason imitated the sound.

Kim sipped her coffee pensively.

'I know Mark asked if you might move to London and Andrew wasn't too keen, but really maybe it's something you should consider.' Grace remembered that Mark received a very aggressive reaction from Andrew when he suggested exactly that.

'What's Daddy doing in London?' Jason asked. His face close to Kim.

'Jason!' Kim raised her voice. He looked at her innocently. 'Go and play with your toys while I'm talking with Grace.'

'Don't want to.' He was sullen.

'Jason,' she warned.

Grace didn't interfere but she wanted to laugh at his expression.

'Do you want to go and sit on the *bold step*?' Kim asked.

He shook his head.

'Then do as I say.'

He sidled away. At the door, he looked back at her.

'Go on, why don't you make up some Lego? And you can show it to us later.'

He disappeared.

'You can really get around him,' Grace said, with a grin.

'It's not easy. He's very stubborn.'

'Now what were we talking about?'

'You asked about moving to London. Andrew's totally against that.'

'Would you like to move?' Grace asked.

'I don't mind. The kids are still young enough. And if we can't sell here, we could rent, and do the same over there. I wouldn't see it as a particularly big thing. I've lived in London before, all I want is for us to be together.'

'But of course, there's Andrew's parents. They're very nice people and it would be hard to leave them here alone, they need support at their age.'

'I'm very fond of them, particularly as my Mam and Dad are gone.'

'Pity you don't have sisters and brothers, it's nice to have family around if you feel a bit stressed.'

Kim nodded.

'I know all our crowd are abroad but still I can talk on the phone or *Skype* if I want, it's good to keep in touch.'

'I'll just get Lorelai.' Kim stood up.

'I'll go with you.'

They went upstairs together and heard Jason follow them a moment later. Lorelai lay fast asleep in bed.

'She's adorable,' Grace murmured. 'The blonde curls, the pretty little face.'

'And she knows it too, even at that age. God knows what she'll be like when she's a teenager.'

'Lorelai, wake up,' Jason yelled.

'They grow up so quickly. When I look at her I feel broody. Maybe I should have had children.' Grace touched Lorelai's hair.

'Why not? What would Mark think about that?'

'He'd love kids. But all he's thinking of at the moment is taking me off to Italy for a holiday.'

'Never know what might happen there,' Kim laughed. 'Anyway, I suppose if you're going to get pregnant you may as well do it soon, it's more difficult the older you are, obviously.'

'Kim, you're getting carried away,' she laughed.

'It would be a complete change, you have to admit that.'

'Lorelai.' Jason thumped on the end of the bed.

'It would be life changing, don't know if I'm prepared,' Grace admitted.

'Let me know if it happens, I'll give you all the advice you want.'

'Thanks,' Grace said, with a smile.

Kim bent down and gently took Lorelai's hand. 'Hi pet, are you going to wake up for us?'

'She must be tired, Jason's shouting hasn't even woken her up. Lorelai, look who's here to see you,' Kim said.

'Hi Lorelai.'

Her eyes opened slowly. 'Auntie Grace,' she smiled and put out her arms.

'How's my baby?' Grace lifted her up.

'I'm not a baby,' she pouted.

'No, you're not, you're a big girl now.'

'I'm three.'

'Come on down,' Kim said. 'And don't forget teddy.'

Grace put the little girl on her feet.

Grace stayed for a couple of hours, glad to spend time with Kim and the children. Obviously, Kim was upset about being apart from Andrew, but Grace couldn't think how she might help. Today, it was in her mind to share her own problems with Kim, but it seemed her friend had enough to contend with herself. Anyway, Grace realised she couldn't have explained to Kim exactly what it was like to have this compulsion to hoard newspapers. Lately, with all the prompting from Mark she had admitted to herself that it was an addiction ...of sorts.

But on arriving home, immediately she rushed upstairs. To open the door. Go into what was left of her bedroom, reassured that all was the same as it had been in the morning. But Grace had a feeling of loss. She would be away for over two long weeks. She wandered through the narrow corridors which had just enough width to fit her shoulders. For safety reasons, she only ever put on the light in the bedroom. So the other areas were always dark. The box bedroom. The back bedroom. Dark as night. Dark as her heart.

Chapter Thirty-six

Ruth went to visit Kim at her home in Rathfarnham one afternoon when the children were with their grandparents.

'I used the money I inherited from Mam to invest in a house and sold that to buy here when we got married,' Kim explained.

'Sensible you.'

'But you followed your heart and had a great life. Sometimes I wonder if I should have travelled the world too before I settled down.'

'But look what you have. Andrew and two wonderful children,' Ruth pointed out, envious.

'I know, I couldn't live without them. But when I worked in London I might have used my time better.'

'You probably think I frittered my money away.' Ruth waited for her sister's reaction.

'I suppose I resented that you forced me to sell the house. I would have liked to keep it. I loved Greystones. It was where we grew up.'

'I'm sorry about that, I was young and greedy,' Ruth admitted.

'You wanted it sold, and I knew that. I wasn't going to fight for ever,' Kim said. 'Let's not talk about it now, it's in the past.'

'So long ago,' Ruth was suddenly full of regret.

They clung together for a moment in silence.

'You said you have an apartment, where is it?' Kim asked.

'We just rent in Clontarf. It's only a small place. Claustrophobic. I hate it.'

'It's enough for two people I'm sure,' Kim said.

'Wish we had somewhere like this, it's lovely.' Ruth looked around in admiration. 'Maybe I will come and stay...'

'You're going to do it?' Kim asked.

'I'd like to. For you. To do something ...to make up for what happened over the house. But your husband couldn't be here. That would be too difficult,' Ruth said.

'Thank you so much. I really appreciate it.' There were tears in Kim's eyes.

'You'll have to train me in.'

'I've been making notes. Of my day. Where things are. What I do. We'll choose a weekend when Andrew's definitely going to be away. I'll organise a flight for Saturday, and come back on Sunday. The kids should be fine with you. They're young.'

Later, Kim took her around the house. Room after room. In her own bedroom, she showed her the wardrobe. 'We're still the same size by the look of you, so everything will fit. All the casual stuff at this side of the wardrobe is what I wear every day. More formal stuff is over here. That black halter neck dress is my favourite for evening wear.'

'I know,' Ruth said.

Kim looked around sharply.

'Remember that first time I saw you in the restaurant?'

She smiled, and nodded. 'I was wearing it then.'

'It's a fabulous dress.'

'Yea, I like it.'

'I had some nice designer stuff,' Ruth thought of the wardrobes of clothes.

'Had?'

'I left them behind.'

'How did that happen?'

'It's a long story.'

'Mine are not all designer, just a few things which I have for years to tell you the truth.'

'I wish I was you,' Ruth said slowly.

'You have your own life. I'm sure you could have exactly what I have if you wanted.'

'I don't know if John wants children.'

'Get around him. I'm sure you know how to do it.' Kim brought her into the children's rooms.

139

Jason's was all reds and blues. Definitely a boy's room. Lorelai's was pink and lilac. With a collection of dolls and teddies, and a big doll's house. Kim showed her the wardrobes of clothes. Told her their preferences. Which colours they liked. The shoes. The jackets. The night wear.

Then Kim took Ruth into the bathroom, and the routine around that.

'It's all noted here. Just don't lose the notebook,' Kim said.

'I won't. I'll have to learn it off by heart.'

'I'll give you my phone and buy another. We'll be able to make contact easily then.' Kim hugged her.

Ruth wasn't even sure why she had agreed. But it was too late to change her mind now.

'We have to move again,' John said.

Ruth stared at him for a few seconds. 'I don't want to.'

'We're going,' he said bluntly.

'No. You can't force me. I couldn't bear to start all over in another place like this.'

'You've got to go with me, what will I do without you, baby?' He moved towards her and kissed her.

'Stay here. It's not that bad. I've made it nice haven't I?' she begged. 'Look around you.'

'It's not about nice ...' he hesitated. He couldn't explain exactly how he felt. She had no idea of the fears which terrorised him these days. For the first time in his life he felt like a hunted animal.

'Hold on for just a few weeks then we'll go somewhere else, please love?' She put her arms around him and clung tight.

'I'm sorry. I wouldn't do it unless I had to,' he softened his approach. He wanted her to come with him. He needed her. 'It's a very different place this time, I promise you.'

'It's just so disruptive. I hate having to pack up all our things again.' There were tears in her eyes.

'Hey babe, don't cry. I promise it will be the last time.'

As before, it was a hurried departure. 'And don't bother with those bits and pieces you always bring with you, they're only dust catchers,' he said.

'I've bought them, they're pretty,' she protested.

'We'll buy more.'

'You always say that, and I can never find them again. These are my things ...'

'We have to go.' He pulled back the curtain a little and peered through the window. There was no sign of unusual activity. Most of the cars parked below belonged to residents. He knew them all. Could even recite the registration numbers. He had that ability with numbers. Could add up in his head in a flash. Divide. Multiply. So sharp, he was way ahead of anyone else he came across in business. It gave him that edge as they fumbled around for figures. Able to snap his fingers and come up with the answer they were searching for in seconds.

'Give me another few minutes.' She searched around the apartment. Looking in presses. Pulling out drawers.

'Hurry.' He lifted the bags out on to the landing and waited at the door. 'I'm off. If you don't come on and follow me, you won't know where you're going.'

'Wait.'

The door banged.

Chapter Thirty-seven

Mark took Grace's hand as they walked through Arrivals at the airport in Rome.

'This is it, love,' he said, smiling, and kissed her. 'Happy?'

She nodded. It had been a supreme effort, but she had managed to leave home. Something she had to do for Mark. To prove in her own mind that she loved him and was willing to make any sacrifice for this man. That was how it should be. You must be prepared to lay down your life for the one you love.

Outside, a swarthy man held up a card which had their names printed on it, and they followed him out to a red open topped sports car which was parked outside. He handed over documents and keys to Mark.

'Your chariot awaits, madame.' Mark held the door open for Grace.

'Wow, this is fantastic,' she sat in. 'What a car, I'll never get used to my Toyota again.'

'Told you I'd spoil you, didn't I?' Mark said, and kissed her. 'Now, let's go. Hope I can get us to the hotel, but we have a navigation system to help us.'

He drove away from the airport. The sun beamed down on them, and Grace's curly hair streamed out in the breeze. She laughed out loud with excitement. Into the crazy traffic in the city, they whizzed along, passing some of the famous landmarks of Rome.

'There's the Colosseum,' she shouted.

'I thought I'd take us on a tour,' Mark said, as they continued on.

'The Forum ...' Grace was thrilled when she spotted another ancient monument. 'And I think that's the Pantheon ...'

'St. Peters over there ...' Mark pointed. 'And that means we're not too far away from the hotel.' He turned a corner.

'I chose this one because it's near to the centre.' Mark helped her out of the car, and handed the key to the porter.

'It's fabulous.' She stared up at the eighteenth century building.

They walked up the steps.

'Is our car gone?' she asked, disappointed as it whisked out of sight.

'No, we have it for the holiday.'

She responded by kissing him. 'Thanks so much, you really are something else, you know that?'

'Come on, let's get our room organised.'

The glass doors were opened by a doorman dressed in the style of the period. 'I think I'll have to get my crinoline out for tonight, and my wig,' Grace quipped.

'You don't need a wig, your hair is beautiful.' Mark ran his hand through her auburn curls. 'But I wouldn't mind seeing you in a crinoline,' he said, laughing.

They went up to the desk and checked in, and then the bellboy took them up in the lift to the third floor. Opened their door and ushered them into the room.

Grace stared around. The decor of the drawing room was in the eighteenth century style also, with a magnificent gold and burgundy carpet, wonderful gold silk drapes, and period furniture. There were flowers on every surface.

Mark tipped the bellboy and he left.

Speechless, Grace wandered through into the bedroom. The most glorious item there being an amazing four poster bed, curtained in the same silk used in the drapes.

'This is out of this world.' She threw herself down on the bed.

Mark opened a bottle of Champagne and poured two glasses. Then he came over to the bed and handed her a glass. 'To a wonderful holiday.'

'Yea,' she smiled.

He leaned across and kissed her slowly.

She put her glass on the bedside table and wound her arms around him. 'This is a wonderful hotel, I've never been anywhere like it before, it's magical.'

'I just want you to enjoy yourself, my love.'

Their lips met. She let herself relax into the softness of the silk covered bed.

He lay beside her. 'I love you, Grace,' he whispered.

'I'll have to get a four poster ...must have a four poster ...' she murmured sensually and opened the buttons on his shirt.

'Take it as ordered.' He loosened the belt of her jeans.

'I want to live in a place like this for the rest of my life.' She spread her arms wide.

'You can have anything you like, once you share it with me.' He tugged her tee shirt off.

She put her hand inside his shirt, and stroked his smooth warm skin.

They kissed again, tasting Champagne on their lips.

She smiled at him, running her fingers through his tight haircut. 'I don't deserve you, I'm not half the person you are.' She leaned closer to him.

'I'm going to enjoy having you all to myself. We'll be together every minute of the day and night, what a prospect.' He cupped her face in his hand and looked into her eyes. 'No going home. No going to work. Just being in some wonderful alternative time zone.'

'Yea, on an alien planet,' she giggled. 'With blue sunsets, purple skies, and pink seas. We'll have discovered the secret of eternal life,' she whispered in his ear. 'And live forever, always young.'

'Eat delicious food, drink Champagne, and make love all day. Over and over. Each time better than the one before. Heaven,' he sighed. 'Stay with me, Gracie, stay with me for always?'

Suddenly, she thought of home. Upstairs. The darkness. Drawing her back. And wondered if she would ever be free of it.

Chapter Thirty-eight

Andrew was due home this evening and Kim set the table in the dining room for dinner. Lit the lamps. Used the best white tablecloth. Silver. Crystal. Anxious to create a romantic ambience.

Even though she still planned to go to London, she hoped that Andrew might tell her himself about the electricity bill and that there would be a perfectly innocuous explanation. Then her fears would suddenly diminish into nothing, and life would be the way it had been a couple of years ago, before things had changed between them. Happy beyond measure, loving every moment of their life together with their children. They had always planned to have three or four, and lately she had wondered if having a new baby would draw them closer together again. A little girl or boy. A sister or brother for Jason and Lorelai. What excitement there would be. Yes, it was time to mention it.

The evening went exactly as planned. They talked of his trip. How was Singapore. Perth. Weather. People he met. Had he stayed in the usual hotels? His answers were unhurried, casual. Everything seemed normal. She hated herself for being suspicious. What had turned her into this person who believed nothing her husband told her any more. Someone consumed with jealousy founded on a chance electricity bill for an unfamiliar address?

Now he was back. Her love. Here. Beside her. She could talk to him. Touch him. And suddenly the suspicions became illogical thoughts. Her mind playing tricks. That night she wore the black negligee he had given her, determined to get his attention. And it worked.

'You're looking wonderful, my love. That's so sexy,' he said, with a grin. 'But it's not going to be on for very long. Come here to me.' He held out his arms.

Kim went to him. So happy all her fears seemed like nothing. She had imagined it.

He kissed her, gentle. His fingers caressed her soft skin and he took the lacy negligee off and flung it on the floor.

They made love. Slowly, sensually.

'I love you, Kim,' he whispered.

'I love you too,' she kissed him again. 'I was wondering ...let's have another baby before the kids grow up. You know we always planned that.'

He stared at her. His body stiffened. Anger flashed across his face. 'What are you on about?'

'I thought it would be lovely to have another child, to complete our family.'

'Another baby, that's crazy. Two's enough in a family. I couldn't afford another, do you want to bankrupt me?'

'But surely a baby won't be that expensive? And two is a small family. We're comfortable enough surely, you've a good job.' She tried to get through to him.

'I've enough children, don't want any more,' he grunted, and lay back on the pillows.

'But I thought you loved kids?' She leaned over him and smiled.

'I do, but what if I lost my job, how would we manage a gaggle of kids?'

'Surely that wouldn't happen, you've been with the company for many years.' She kissed him, and drew heart shapes on his chest with her finger.

'The company could go under overnight, don't you realise that?' he snapped.

'I thought the airline was doing very well, it's one of the most successful,' she persuaded.

'Never count your chickens ...you know that old cliché?'

'I would love another baby,' she said wistfully, and leaned her head on his shoulder.

146

'Kim, get off that hobby horse. I don't want to hear it again. We have our family. It's complete. Done and dusted.' He pushed her off him, sat on the edge of the bed and stared into space. 'I need a drink,' he said, stood up and went downstairs.

Shocked at his reaction, she put on her dressing gown, and followed him.

He stood naked in the kitchen staring out through the window, sipping a whiskey.

'I'm sorry for upsetting you, my love.' She stood beside him and ran her hands down his body. She kissed his back. Embraced him.

He shrugged her off.

'Don't let it upset you. We'll say no more. We're so lucky to have our two beautiful children,' she said.

'You don't appreciate what you have,' he said, and turned to her.

'But I do, my love, of course I do,' she tried to reassure him.

'There are other women who don't have as much as you. Think about that.' His eyes held accusation. 'This house, your car, and on top of that you don't have to work.'

'I'm lucky my mother left me money, and I was able to buy this house almost outright.' She couldn't resist.

He turned away, and poured another drink.

All the following day he had been moody. Out of sorts even with the kids, and most of all, with herself. She couldn't do anything to placate him. Helpless in the face of his anger. She tried to rationalise. It had only been one question. He didn't have to get so angry. They could have discussed it sensibly, like they had done when they were planning Jason and Lorelai.

He left the following morning with nothing resolved. A chasm between them which for her was filled with unanswered questions.

Chapter Thirty-nine

'Wow ...' Ruth walked into the house in Dalkey and stared around her. 'This is something else. You never told me that you had such a beautiful pad.'

'Yea.' He pressed a remote and the doors into a large drawing room opened. 'We'll be here for a few days.'

'Only a few days?' she was disappointed.

She followed him and wandered through the luxurious room to stare out at the sea through the wall of glass. 'It's so beautiful. What a view. I could live here. I'd never want to leave again,' she swung around to him, and smiled.

He didn't reply.

Ruth's diminishing wardrobe had left her without some of the basic items which had been left behind in the various apartments, and thrown out by Victor's men by now. Particularly some of her warmer clothes which she would need now that the weather had grown colder. But even though they were living in this amazing house, John became tighter than ever with money. She almost felt like demanding that he pay her a salary, until finally he gave her enough money to replace some of her clothes. Not designer admittedly, but good enough.

These days, she noticed that he looked tired. There were dark shadows under his eyes. A permanent frown. Lines on his face which hadn't been there before. Strain obvious on the pristine good looks that had attracted her. His designer suits hung loosely on his frame. She longed to do something more for him, but he wouldn't allow it.

'Just be here for me, do the pick-ups and deliveries, that's enough.'

'But there has to be more than that. There was once, when we first met,' she argued. 'I love you. Don't push me away,' she pleaded with him. 'Why don't we take a break somewhere? Recharge your batteries.'

'I don't need to recharge my batteries,' he snapped. 'There's nothing wrong with me.'

'What about all that business with the Gardaí?'

'I don't give a damn about them. Piss artists.'

'They're not still ...watching?'

'We're too clever for that,' he laughed. 'Have them running around after their tails. They'll never catch up with us.'

'I've been nervous doing the pick-ups.'

'Have you noticed anyone following you?' He turned and glared at her.

'No, I haven't.'

'You sure?'

She said no more. Just concentrated on preparing dinner. They didn't go out to eat at Sonaris so much any more. But she didn't mind. Loving the state of the art kitchen, the size of which would make three of any of the apartments she had lived in recently.

John wandered into the kitchen area later. His mood had improved. She felt relieved.

'I might go to see my sister one weekend,' she mentioned. Had been building up to this but knowing his attitude to family her courage had failed her more than once.

'Sister?' he barked.

'We haven't met for a long time, I thought I might just make contact.'

'Where does she live?'

'Rathfarnham.'

'I thought I told you that I don't want family interfering.'

'Interfere with what?'

'We do our thing. We keep it private. That's what I mean.' He stood close to her. Aggressive.

'My sister is not interested I'm sure.'

'Keep her out there. And tell her nothing. Not a whisper. You can invent yourself but don't involve me,' he rasped.

'I'm not going to tell her anything.'

'Bit difficult when she asks you what you've been doing since the last time? How long has it been?'

'You know I was travelling. That covers a lot.'

'Still, I don't want you to mention me, or our business.' He paced about. Agitated.

'You can depend on me. I won't say anything,' she whispered.

He stopped in front of her. Took her face in his hands, and stared into her eyes. Then he kissed her. 'You are the only one I can trust. There is no one else.'

'You don't mind if I go over for a weekend then?' Ruth asked. She hated having to grovel.

'I don't want you to go, I want you here,' he growled.

'It's just a Saturday and a Sunday.'

'No.'

She had to turn back quickly to the cooker as the steaks began to hiss under the grill, so let it go for now, but had every intention of taking it up with him again.

Ruth served dinner, and opened a bottle of wine. Hoping that he would drink a few glasses and his attitude would change. She broached the subject again, but the result was the same. The one thing she had asked for he wouldn't give her. A simple request to visit her only sister. Suddenly for the first time she hated what he had become. And herself too for allowing him to bully her to this extent. All she wanted was some free time and he couldn't even give her that. She felt like a prisoner.

Chapter Forty

Grace and Mark drove out of Rome towards Naples. They particularly wanted to visit Pompeii and stayed overnight at a hotel nearby. It was early in the morning and warm already. Not too busy yet as the tour bus crowds hadn't built up.

She had been very much aware of her impulse to buy the newspapers during the holiday, even in Rome she had to avert her gaze away from news-stands and shops in an effort to stop herself from reaching out to touch them.

'Good idea of yours to drag me out of the bed at this hour,' Grace took Mark's hand.

'I'd much rather have kept you in bed, but you did insist on seeing Pompeii without too many people sharing the place.' He kissed her.

'It's amazing to think people lived here two thousand years ago. They led perfectly normal lives until Vesuvius erupted,' she looked around as they walked slowly through the streets of the city which had been excavated from the lava which had poured down from the mountain all those years ago.

'It's amazing how much is left of the buildings. The houses. Shops. And how the archaeologists can identify exactly which is which.'

'The streets are incredible. I think of the people who walked on these very stones on which we stand now, doing their work, bringing up their families ...' Grace stared along the length of the street, shading her eyes against the bright sunshine with her hand.

'Temples, baths, theatres, villas ...' Mark murmured.

'It's the shapes of the people which disturb me ...' Grace had been moved when they visited the museum.

151

'They invented the technique of pouring liquid plaster into the empty spaces which had been left in the hardened ash ...' Mark had explained as they stood looking at the prone figure of a woman, her head in her hands, which lay in a glass case.

'It's like being in a cemetery,' she said, and shivered.

'And I was going to suggest a visit to Herculaneum tomorrow.'

'It was fascinating but ...I'm not as enthusiastic as you are about archaeological sites. Maybe I don't have the brains to appreciate history.'

He laughed. 'Let's head on to Amalfi then.'

She smiled at him. 'I'm not spoiling your holiday?'

'No, I'll drag you to a few more places before we're finished, don't worry,' he grinned.

'We'll have to barter. You must accompany me in and out of shops and then I might ...'

'Exactly.'

Pompeii had affected Grace. The thought of all those people being suddenly crushed by the lava stones which had rained down on them, and then burned to ashes in unbelievably high temperatures was almost too much to comprehend. Something about the atmosphere, the empty streets, homes, shops, and the bodies of people preserved in the ashes had got to her. She thought of home. How a spark might suddenly cause a conflagration and she suddenly felt sick.

Amalfi was delicious. The hotel Mark had chosen was high on a cliff overlooking the sea just on the outskirts of the town. They walked out on to the terrace, and sat down, gazing out over the sea which shimmered in a heat haze.

'This holiday is one of the few things I've managed to persuade you to do. Maybe we might progress as time goes on,' he teased.

'I'm putty in your hands, you know that,' she purred, cat-like.

'I'll have to soften you up. Need to get you to the right consistency. How about some massage?' He leaned across and put his arm around her.

She giggled.

It was the tenor of their holiday. Fun. Love. And getting to know each other. Mark was gentle. Generous. Kind. And a handsome hunk of a guy. They walked on the beach in the early morning. But that wasn't easy for Grace. The sensation on her hands came and went and she tried to hide her discomfort from Mark. She explained her preference for swimming in the hotel pool and he didn't mind so they rested on the terrace under the umbrella in the afternoons. Once the beach was avoided, she felt better.

So they enjoyed long evenings over dinner at a little restaurant near the cathedral steps. Drank bottles of Chianti. And made love. That most of all. Making love with Mark was what life was all about, she decided. They visited places along the coast. Amori. Positano. Sorrento. Spent evenings up in Ravello, a village above Amalfi. Took a boat to the Isle of Capri. But slowly the time was eaten up, and their departure for Rome was imminent.

Chapter Forty-one

'I want to go to London soon,' Kim said.

'When?' Ruth asked, taken aback as she realised this thing was actually going to happen.

'In a couple of weeks.'

'I don't know if I can do it,' she said hesitantly. Up to this she had laughingly gone along with Kim's suggestion, only half believing. It had been a game. Like something they played when they were children. Teasing their parents. Friends. Teachers. Forced to be in separate classes at school, they even swopped occasionally. No-one knew. But as they grew older Ruth felt a little in Kim's shadow. And didn't have the confidence to do the switches just as easily as her sister seemed to be able to manage.

'It will only be one night,' Kim persuaded.

Ruth said nothing.

'And tomorrow I'm having my hair styled like yours. Short. Spiky. I like it.' Kim stood in front of the mirror, and wound up her shoulder length hair.

'Don't forget the hi-lights.'

'I'm looking forward to the change. It will be so different.' Kim held her hair up on top of her head, and stared at her reflection. 'Come over, look at us.'

Ruth stood behind her.

'It's amazing isn't it?' Kim asked and moved even closer to her.

Ruth nodded.

'Did you ever feel a connection between us when you were away?' Kim asked. 'Like we were sharing a moment?'

'I put you out of my head in the beginning, guilt I suppose,' Ruth admitted. 'Then later I would get a jolt sometimes, like you wanted to remind me that you were still there.'

154

'Yea, I thought of you too. A lot.'

'We shouldn't have wasted all that time.'

'We were young, things happen and then it's too difficult to retrace the steps. I regretted it,' Kim turned around to Ruth. 'But now we're together and I don't ever want to lose you again.' She hugged her. 'Don't let me down Ruth ...' She looked into her eyes. 'I must find out if there's anything up with Andrew, or if it's all in my imagination. Do you think I'm crazy?'

'Maybe both of us are a little crazy,' Ruth said. 'I certainly am. It's been a long time since we've done anything like this. And now I wonder if I can even pull it off?'

'Of course you can,' Kim said, laughing. 'You have my notebook. It has every tiny detail about me. My hobbies. My friends. Everything I do. Day to day. You don't need to know all of these things, but for me it was an interesting exercise. It's strange when you look at your whole life encompassed in one small notebook.' Kim took it out of her handbag. 'This equals one life. Is that all there is?' she mused.

'I don't know if I could fill such a notebook with my life. A few pages at most,' Ruth said slowly, her face sad.

'I don't believe that. You've had an incredible life. Travelled all over the world. Seen so many places. You'll have to tell me about it.'

'Some other time ...' Ruth was hesitant.

'Come on, I'd love to hear the details, all those interesting people you've met,' Kim laughed.

'I've put all that behind me.'

'I'll get you some night over a few drinks,' Kim said. 'Now, I've shown you where everything is, but would you like to go around the house again?'

'Yes please. I'd like to see the children's rooms again.'

'It's only two days, you'll be fine,' Kim assured Ruth. 'And even if I get delayed for an extra day or two just phone the school and say the kids have colds. And even if I'm delayed for longer you know where the kids' schools are, and the teachers' names, and their descriptions. Don't worry too much. Just remember that you're doing me a really big favour.'

'I'm concerned about the kids, they might sense that I'm not you,' Ruth said.

'I hope not,' anxiety flashed across Kim's features.

'I'm scared. If the children realise I'm not you and tell someone, it could be very serious.'

'I know, I've thought of that too. But if it should happen phone me straight away, and in the meantime tell them you're the new babysitter. I'll come back immediately. But most of all keep them occupied. Take them to the zoo. Somewhere they can enjoy themselves. They will love that, and won't take a bit of notice who's shouting at them to be careful, or to come back, and in the evening they'll be so whacked you can put them straight to bed,' Kim explained.

'Sounds simple when you say it. But in my head it's not quite so easy.'

'Come on, don't lose your confidence,' Kim said with a smile.

'I'll try not to.'

'Then it's Saturday week, agreed?'

She nodded.

'It will be lovely for you to have the two kids for a short time, they're great fun. And you can give them back then and go back to your really nice life,' Kim said. 'Now, I'll give you my phone. And then buy another and take it with me so you can contact me. Everyone I know texts so it will be easy for you to reply to them.'

'I'd better go,' Ruth said. 'It's late.'

'And remember there's plenty of cooked food in the freezer, you just have to defrost.' At the kitchen door, Kim took her hand, and looked into her eyes. 'Thank you.'

Ruth lay on the couch watching a repeat of *Pretty Woman* on the wide-screen television when John came in and dropped a kiss on her forehead.

'Hi baby.' He went to the bar, poured a whiskey and waved the bottle towards her. 'Want a drink?'

'No thanks.'

He flopped down on the couch and kicked his shoes off.

'Tough day?' she sat beside him.

'You could say that.' He closed his eyes.

'Missed you.'

He picked up the remote and changed the channel to twenty-four hour news. 'What's happening in the world?' he asked with a low laugh.

'Don't want to know,' she murmured.

'That's what's wrong with you, Ruth, you wear blinkers.'

'I don't,' she retorted. That was an insult, she thought, annoyed with him. But thought he was probably right. If she didn't wear blinkers then she wouldn't be still here, supporting him in this exploitation of women.

He lifted her chin with his finger and kissed her slowly. She didn't want to make love now. But she had no choice. He pulled her down on to the rug.

Chapter Forty-two

Mark packed the bags into the sports car. 'I hate to go home. The last few days always seem to go far faster than the first.'

Grace looked up at the hotel which glimmered in the sunshine. 'We'll have to come back, I love it here.'

'Soon.' He locked the boot, came around and kissed her. 'It's been wonderful, Grace. Just to be together. No-one else around.'

'It's not the end. There's still a couple of days in Rome.' Grace sat into the seat. White leather. So luxurious. She would relish the last of this magic escape.

'And we'll enjoy the drive up, this is a perfect day.'

'Ciao, Luciano, ciao,' they shouted goodbye to the porter who held the gate, and waved, then Mark drove out on to the narrow road. It wound in crazy arcs downhill, the view along the coast and out over the blue sea stunning.

She put her hand on his arm, and squeezed.

He smiled. 'Have to keep the eyes on the road, pet, don't want to run us off the cliff.'

'Keep us safe at all costs. I don't want to look down. Spinning around doesn't do me any good.' She closed her eyes.

He turned on the radio and music blared. A woman sang a traditional Italian tune almost in time with the stabbing of the brakes as Mark took each sharp corner, and roared on to the next one.

'Hey you're enjoying this,' she said.

'I'm seventeen again, it's my first car, and I'm loving it,' he laughed out loud.

'Mark, don't drive so fast, what if another car comes up the road, there isn't room for two of us and certainly not at speed,' Grace cautioned.

158

'Go on with you, *Mrs. Bucket* ...' he said, with a grin.

'Where's sensible Mark gone?'

'He'll reappear when we land at Dublin Airport, in the meantime I'm a teenager, let's go.'

There was a sharp screech of gravel.

'Tell me you love this car?' he shouted.

She had to smile at his exuberance, pushing her hair out of her eyes.

'Don't you feel like a film star?'

'Oh yea, Marilyn Monroe.'

'And I'll be Tony Curtis.'

'Back in the fifties.'

'They drove like this. Crazy. No speed limits in those days.'

'No limits at all,' she repeated. What an idea. No limits. Nothing to curtail. She thought of how her own life was influenced by something which didn't have any material form. The newspapers were a by-product. It was something imperceptible. But could bend and shape her mind. Her own wishes unimportant.

She looked at Mark. His eyes were bright, his hands gripped the steering wheel, as he enjoyed every minute of this experience. He threw himself into life with such verve it made her question herself. He knew what he was about. So sure of everything he did. And wanted to take her with him on a wild adventure, to throw herself into this escapade without fear. Hang on tight. And scream with delight.

Chapter Forty-three

'Switch places with Kim?' John stared at Ruth. 'You're serious about this?'

'Yea, I've promised her that I'll do it.'

'It's mad.'

'We've done it before.'

'And no-one ever copped on?'

She shook her head, and grinned.

'You were kids then.'

'Yea. So?'

'It's dangerous,' he said, with derision.

'Why?'

'It just is. You're putting yourself out there. Anything could happen.'

'We still look amazingly alike. And Kim is sure it will work.'

'It's far too risky drawing attention to yourself like that.' He was agitated.

'I've agreed now.'

'But I need you.'

'I'll be back in a couple of days.'

'What about the pick-ups and deliveries?'

'Surely you can get someone else to do it? I'm not the only person who works for you.'

'But I rely on you.'

'Please, my love?' Ruth begged, suddenly worried.

'No,' he said abruptly.

She was silent. Wondering what next to say. One couldn't argue with him. His attitude would only harden.

'Please?' She kissed him. 'Just this once. Let me do it. It can be my birthday present.'

'No,' he snarled. 'When I say no, I mean no.'

She could see his inflexible side grow stronger. It stretched like a high wall above her. She was a prisoner on the other side of it. 'Why do you refuse me this one thing, it's probably the only time I've asked you for anything?' she spoke gently, hoping to persuade him.

'I don't need to give you a reason.'

'You must have one, just tell me what it is,' she begged.

'What difference would that make, I'll still feel the same,' he retorted.

She thought if she could force him to explain, she could pick holes in his logic. 'Please, John,' she whispered.

He laughed.

She was suddenly annoyed with him.

'Don't laugh at me,' she said.

'You're my little girl, why can't I laugh?'

'I'm not yours.'

'You are, and never forget it.'

Ruth was silent. 'It's next weekend,' she said after a moment.

'I said no. It's too preposterous.'

'Please, I've promised her. It's all arranged. I can't let her down. You must understand that.' She kissed him.

'You didn't tell me it was so soon. I have to make arrangements,' he grumbled.

'Thanks,' she hugged him.

'And what is the address of this place? I want to keep an eye on you.'

Kim let Ruth in the back door. 'Thanks for coming, I thought you might get cold feet.' She kissed her.

'I have cold feet. They're like blocks of ice.'

'Did you have any problems?' Kim asked.

'John wasn't too keen on my coming over,' she admitted.

'I hope some day I'll have a chance to thank him. Let him know how much I appreciate his generosity.'

'Yes …'

They sat and chatted as if nothing unusual was about to happen.

'I don't want to be up too late, I've an early start,' Kim said.

'I hope it goes well for you, and that you don't find out anything,' Ruth said, sympathetically. 'I meant to ask, did you ever see that phone again?'

'I suppose it was a spare one, as Andrew said, I should really have listened to the message, maybe then I would have found out something more, and there may well be a very simple explanation for the electricity bill but I must find out. I must be sure. How does anyone know if a husband is having an affair? Or a wife for that matter. Don't you ever worry about that?'

Ruth stared at Kim. A sick feeling in her stomach.

'The kids are already asleep, so you can take the main bedroom, I'll sleep in the guest room.'

'I'd prefer to sleep in the guest room?' She was suddenly nervous at the thought of being in Kim's bed.

'No, you sleep in our room,' Kim said, laughing. She led the way upstairs. 'Now wear all my clothes, I've shown you where everything is. I'll be heading off in a taxi about five o'clock, so you won't even hear me.'

Ruth followed.

Kim led the way into the children's rooms. First Jason's. They stood in the doorway. The little boy lay in his bed, arms outstretched, a *Superman* duvet dragging on the floor. Kim went over and gently tucked it around him. He moved a little, but then settled again. 'Be careful you don't disturb him when he's sleeping, he often gets up out of bed late at night and you won't get him down again,' Kim whispered.

Next it was Lorelai, who lay under a pink *Princess* duvet, her arms wrapped around a yellow teddy bear. Kim stroked her hair and kissed her. Then she slowly came across the room and closed the door.

'Thanks for doing this,' Kim put her arms around her sister and held her close.

Ruth nodded. Suddenly it was happening. And she couldn't stop it.

To John's surprise he missed Ruth. This was his house. His bolt hole. But unexpectedly it was a cold silent place without her. He shouldn't have let her go. He sipped a wine chosen from his extensive wine cellars, and thought about the other people who lived around here. Entertainers. Bankers. Business people. All multi-millionaires. Billionaires. He was one of them and just as influential. He could have anything he wanted at the click of his fingers. The world was his oyster.

He drank slowly, deep in thought. Ruth didn't have the ability to attempt such a deception by swopping places with her sister. She was gentle. Lacked confidence. The complete opposite of himself. He wondered why she was doing this. Had she offered, or had her sister persuaded her to get involved. What was the reward. Was it just that twin thing. Maybe they were always on the same wavelength. Could they read each other's thoughts. Communicate. It was fascinating. Why couldn't he read other people's thoughts. He was suddenly envious.

Would he get her back. Would she be contaminated by this contact with her sister. With her life. And because of that the curiosity of other people be drawn inevitably towards him. Fear stabbed. He gulped until the glass was empty. Thinking of the unwelcome attention which was coming at him from all sides. The worst being from that inspector.

McKenzie was the one who had lured him out and exposed him. He still expected to see her every time he went out. The sight of any woman with auburn hair made him draw back into the shadows, suddenly fearful. He couldn't understand these feelings. They were not in his nature. He used women. They didn't use him. He would have to get rid of her.

Chapter Forty-four

Grace found it strange to be back in Dublin after being away for over two weeks. For all that time, Mark had been beside her last thing at night, and first thing in the morning. She could put out her hand and touch him and know he was hers whenever she felt the inclination. And there was no need to make an arrangement, set a time, or call him up. She began to realise what it would mean if they lived together. Parting for a day's work, but coming together again, knowing the other would always be there.

Mark carried in her bags and put them in the hall. 'Feel I should bring in my own as well,' he said, and put his arms around her. 'Wouldn't it be wonderful if we were flying out to Italy tomorrow,' he kissed her.
'Yea ...' She felt the same.
'Wish I was staying with you, Grace,' he said.
She didn't reply and kissed him.
He looked down at her expectantly, smiling.
'Mark, you know I couldn't make a big decision just like that.'
'Am I putting you under too much pressure?'
She kissed him again. 'I promise you that I will make up my mind soon.'
'I'll hold you to that,' he said, with a grin.
'Fancy a coffee before you go, although there's no milk there.'
'No thanks, I'll head home.' He stayed at the door.
'I had a wonderful time, Mark, thank you.' She kissed him.

Grace waited until he had driven down the road and only then closed the door. As usual her immediate impulse was to rush upstairs and she took the first couple of steps but then stopped.

What if she didn't go upstairs at all. Never opened that door again. She had been *clean* of its influence for two weeks. She could put it out of her head altogether by never approaching it again. Live down here. Sleep on the bed in the study. Use the downstairs bathroom. The idea was suddenly a possibility. Although there were some disadvantages. All her clothes were upstairs, but she could manage for tomorrow with something she had worn on the holidays. Then she could buy some clothes which would tide her over. No-one would notice.

She made herself that cup of coffee, and sat down to open the post which had piled up in the hall. She always liked this part of coming home. Opening up envelopes with the knife, and pulling out the letters, or bills, or whatever. But there was little of interest.

In the study she made up the bed, then took a shower, keeping herself busy before eventually forcing herself to go to bed. She didn't sleep well, tossed and turned, and woke occasionally during the night, persuading herself that she was missing the warmth of Mark beside her.

Grace went in to work the following morning although it was Saturday. She couldn't have hung about the house, and needed to check what was going on in the office. But Peter was off, as was the Super, so she did some admin and left the office about five which was early for her. On the way home her need to buy the newspapers asserted itself again. She had managed to pass the news-stands in Italy, but knew that the fear of Mark finding out was the reason for that. On her way home, Grace drove into the car park at the supermarket. She had called Mark before leaving the office and he was on his way over, so she had to stock up. Not that there was ever very much in her fridge compared to his. Passing the newsagents, she stopped and stood for a few seconds in a fever of uncertainty. Then she found herself in the doorway. *Get out of here, you don't need a newspaper or anything in here. I need cigarettes*, she argued, two voices screamed in her head. *You have some at home. Packets of them.* She turned abruptly and nearly bumped into a man coming in, but brushed past him and muttered an apology. He nodded vaguely. Grace returned to the car.

She longed for a smoke but couldn't go back into the shop. Sweat studded her forehead. She opened the window and leaned her head against the headrest, and closed her eyes. Her hands clenched together. All the time rubbing against each other trying to get rid of what seemed to be grains of sand which covered her skin. She had identified it now. But couldn't understand the cause.

Suddenly she could hear the sound of a familiar voice.

'Grace? What's wrong?'

She opened her eyes, shocked to see Mark looking at her anxiously.

'Are you feeling OK? You're pale as death.' He opened the door.

She stared at him, trying to comprehend what he was saying. 'Get me a cigarette ...' she begged.

'Gracie, my God you're in bad shape, what is it?' He pressed her forehead with his hand. 'I think we'll have to get you to hospital.' He took out his phone.

'No, no ...just give me a cigarette.'

He spoke to the operator.

'I don't want to go to hospital,' she protested.

'You must be checked out, there's something wrong.'

'I'll be all right in a few minutes. All I need is a smoke.'

'I can't leave you to go into the shop ...look love, they're coming now, so just relax. He put his arm around her shoulders. Her head rested in the crook of his arm.

A wave of nausea swept through her. 'Water?' she whispered.

'Just give me a minute, I've got some in the car?' He settled her in the seat and closed the door of the car while he rushed to his own and then returned with a bottle of water. He opened it and helped her drink from it. Then put some on his handkerchief, holding it on her forehead.

The sound of a siren could be heard in the distance and within minutes the ambulance drew up beside them and the paramedics jumped out.

Chapter Forty-five

Kim landed at Heathrow Airport, and picked up a black jeep with tinted windows which she had booked. Staines wasn't too far from Heathrow and she drove to the hotel where she had reserved a room. She ordered coffee and tried to sleep but there was no chance of that - her mind was in chaos. After a couple of hours she showered, changed, then took the copy of the electricity bill from her leather handbag.

She had brought with her a folder, a name card holder, and printed off questionnaire forms which looked quite professional. Before leaving the room, she stood in front of the full length mirror and stared at her reflection. Then she positioned a dark shoulder-length wig over her short hair.

I don't even know myself. Kim thought. The wig made such a difference. She repositioned it a couple of times until it was exactly right and prayed it wouldn't blow off. That would be a catastrophe. Under her breath she murmured a prayer and closed the door behind her with heart thumping and mouth dry. Waiting for the lift to come up to her floor, she had a sudden inclination to rush back into the room. Turn away from this thing. She felt deceitful, and regretted not being courageous enough to face Andrew at home. He had flown out to Melbourne on Tuesday, coming back through Dubai and eventually to London for the weekend. But he couldn't make it back to Dublin, the break wasn't long enough, he had said.

Kim had looked at *Google Maps* on the laptop and found the small estate of houses in Staines so knew exactly where she was going. She drove out of the city using the satellite navigation system to find her way, her hands gripping the steering wheel tightly with tension. When she found Hazelbrook Close, she continued on and parked in an adjacent street. Glanced at herself in the mirror, refreshed her lipstick and stepped out. Determined to do this.

It was a mature development and the avenues of houses were lined with trees, colourful with autumn leaves. She walked up Hazelbrook Close, choosing to begin about a dozen houses before number sixty-four. At the first one, she rang the bell. There was no reply. She waited a moment and then moved on to the next, and the next. There was no-one in any of them, and Kim became despondent. If there was no one in number sixty-four, what then?

There was a car parked outside the next house. She rang and almost immediately there was the sound of footsteps on a hard surface, and the door opened. A middle-aged woman smiled at her.

'Hallo, I'm from Lotus Consultants and we're conducting a survey in the area. I wonder would you like to answer a few questions? We just need some opinions. And there is a draw for a holiday or a cash prize for anyone who participates.' She was careful to speak with an English accent, and had made up the company name. 'And because there's only a small sample of people, there's a really good chance of winning.' She felt guilty.

'Oh, do put me in the draw,' the woman replied immediately.

'Right, the first question is just about the number of people living here?' Kim asked.

'Myself and my husband.'

Kim noted that on the form.

'And your names?'

'Dorothy and Thomas Benson.'

'Do you have any animals?'

'Cats.'

One of them appeared around the door.

Kim bent to stroke the thick coat, and then stood up again. 'Now another question, how many holidays do you take each year?'

'Usually only one.'

'Where do you like to go?'

'Last year we were in Spain, my daughter has an apartment near Marbella.'

'How lovely.' She noted that as well. 'Would you be away for one week or two.'

'It's always two.'

'If you don't stay with your daughter, what type of accommodation do you choose?'

'Hotel usually, with breakfast and an evening meal. We like that.'

Kim ticked the last box on the page.

After that she had some success. Most of the people who answered the doors were women, although one man angrily banged the door in her face. Slowly she drew closer to sixty four, calling to two more houses, which were both empty, and there it was. A red-bricked two storey house, surrounded by a well tended garden behind a neat privet hedge. There was a small blue car in the driveway.

Chapter Forty-six

Ruth sat up in the bed and stared around the room. Curtains. Bedlinen. Carpet. Furniture. All cream. Too bright. She closed her eyes again. Wanting to escape the place. And wake up in her own bed with John. Or even the expectation that at any moment he might slip in beside her would have been enough. Her mind kept going over and over the plan. Endlessly. She was terrified at the prospect. To live here in this house for a weekend. Look after two strange children. Try to be a mother. To be someone else.

She heard every creak in this house. Every car which drove past. When finally she heard Kim go downstairs, Ruth wanted to rush after her and beg her not to go to London. But she had given her word and couldn't do that.

Ruth showered and dried herself off. She used Kim's body lotion, soap, toothpaste and brush. Then she dressed in her sister's navy track suit, matching tee shirt, and trainers. Used her make-up and sprayed some of her perfume. After having a cup of tea, she wandered around the house familiarising herself with it, nervously examining the various personal items which Kim had mentioned. She didn't think it was possible to carry this off. Her biggest fear that one of the children would guess she wasn't their mother. As Kim had said, it was just after seven when she heard footsteps, took a deep breath and walked out to see Jason on the bottom step of the stairs. But immediately he rushed straight past her and headed for the television room. She followed and stood in the doorway. He rummaged in a box of DVD's, pulled one out, and pushed it into the player. Then he turned on the widescreen television using the remote control, and sat on the ground in front of it, cross legged.

Ruth couldn't believe it. He hadn't taken the slightest notice of her.

She went into the kitchen and poured Rice Crispies into a bowl, added milk, and took them into him. Jason wasn't the best of eaters apparently, so Kim said, but Ruth was to try and get something into him, whatever it was.

'Breakfast, Jason,' she said, and handed him the bowl. Totally engrossed in *Spider Man*, he took it and slurped the contents.

She was relieved, went back into the kitchen and now, feeling hungry herself, made toast and marmalade, and nibbled on that before going up to Lorelai.

She opened the bedroom door and walked across the wooden floor to the bed. The little girl lay under the duvet, still asleep.

'Hi Lorelai?' she whispered. Gently moving the duvet away from her face. The blue eyes opened slowly and focussed on Ruth. This was the acid test. 'Are you going to get up? We're going to the zoo today,' she smiled at her, and received a little smile in return. 'Let's have a bath first.' She helped the child out of the bed and brought her into the bathroom where she sat on the toilet and gazed at her. 'You smell funny, Mum.'

'Do I?' The hairs rose up on the back of Ruth's neck.

'Different.'

'Maybe it's the soap or my perfume,' she murmured. 'I'll let you have some, would you like that?'

The little girl shook her head. She slid off the seat and pulled up her pyjama bottoms. Then she flushed the loo. All this was done slowly. With an air of concentration. Unusual in one so young.

'Let's wash your hands.' Ruth turned on the tap and the little one rubbed soap on them, rinsed and dried them herself.

Now Ruth found herself wondering about things the children might notice. Imagining scenarios which brought her sense of terror to a level she hadn't thought possible. Bathing was next, and Lorelai was quite happy to splash around in the sudsy water playing with the plastic toys which lined the edge of the bath. Her hair was washed and eventually she was persuaded out. Ruth put on her dressing gown and they sat in the bedroom as she dried her hair. A mass of blonde curls which floated around her head in the warm air.

'What would you like to wear today?' Ruth opened the wardrobe.

'That.' Lorelai pointed to a pink top, and matching skirt.

The process didn't take long and she was eventually dressed in the outfit which included leggings, boots, and jacket.

'Let's see what Jason is doing.' Ruth took her hand, but immediately she slipped it out of her grasp. 'Your hand is too hard,' she said. Ruth was taken aback but said nothing.

They went to the TV room where Jason still watched *Spider Man*.

'Jason, let's get ready, we're going to the zoo,' she said, with a smile.

He shook his head.

'Come on, I thought you loved the animals. Let's have a bath and get dressed. We don't want to be late. They could be all at their lunch or having a nap.' She tried to be funny.

'Animals don't have naps,' he retorted, with a dismissive attitude.

'I'm sure some of them do,' she smiled.

'I like the hippos and the keeper throws their dinner to them and they don't sleep, they just swim around all day,' he said, still watching the screen.

'Lorelai is ready, and so am I,' she said, hoping to shift him. Jason was stubborn according to Kim.

'I want to go now,' Lorelai whined.

'Right, Jason, turn off the television and you can look at it when we come back.'

He turned around to glare at her, and then looked back at the screen.

Ruth thought things were beginning to unravel. Would Jason resist her?' She began to feel totally inadequate. Shaking with nerves. 'Come on, Jason,' she encouraged.

'No,' he said.

'If you don't come you won't get any ice cream.' She tried a different tack.

'Ice cream,' Lorelai shouted suddenly.

Jason looked around again. Brown eyes serious under tight cut black hair. 'Promise?'

'Yes.'

Slowly, he pressed the remote and the screen went blank.

All day both children ran her around the zoo, and her doubts about meeting people who knew Kim decreased as time passed. They had to visit every animal enclosure and the wide open safari areas, and seemed to love every minute. She had brought a picnic which Kim had prepared and they enjoyed their sandwiches and orange in the middle of the day. But Ruth was aware that Jason didn't like her. Each time she took his hand, he ran from her. A baleful look in his eyes. He knew she wasn't his mother. But he didn't have the language to explain how he felt. Poor kid. She was sorry for him, and made a supreme effort to appear as relaxed as possible. If she was too uptight, they would react immediately. But underneath all of that, she wanted to get them home soon. Home. Away from people. Out of sight of the world.

Chapter Forty-seven

Kim's heart hammered. Terror stalked as she stood outside number sixty-four. The door was painted white, with a high gloss. The knocker, letter box, and door handle were polished brass. With trepidation she waited for a moment before finally forcing her hand up to press the bell. The door opened. A young woman with long dark hair smiled at her. A little girl about Lorelai's age hung on to the floral mini skirt the woman wore.

'Hallo,' Kim began, her voice a mere croak.

The little girl giggled.

Kim explained that she was doing a survey and the young woman agreed to answer her questions. The child squealed with excitement.

'Go and see if your sister is OK,' the woman said, and the little one rushed away.

'Why don't you step inside?' She held the door.

Kim did so.

'Please sit down.' She indicated the chair at the hall table.

Kim was accustomed to the order of her questions now and immediately began. The woman answered without hesitation until the child returned.

'She's asleep,' she said, and hung on to her mother again.

'That's good. Now will you let me answer the lady's questions. We might win a prize.'

'It's a sun holiday or cash of one thousand pounds,' Kim explained once again.

'A holiday wouldn't be much use to us,' she laughed. 'My partner is a pilot so as he is in the air every day of the week he hates to fly when we go on holiday, it's always somewhere in the UK.'

Kim could feel her pulse race, and almost dropped the pen with fright. 'Where do you like to stay, hotels or in an apartment,' she stuttered.

'It varies, depends on where we are.'

'That's fine.' Kim ticked the box. 'I just need your names.'

'My name is Cheryl,' the little girl chimed in.

'OK, I'll write that down.'

The child giggled again.

'I'm Sara Chatsworth.'

'And your partner?' She forced a smile.

'Andrew Morris.'

Kim's hand was frozen over the form. She stayed in that position for a few seconds, her mind whirling with the knowledge that her suspicions had been correct. Staring down at the form as if she was checking the information. All the time wanting to scream at the woman. You stole my husband. You bitch. But she gathered her wits about her, and quickly stood up. 'I've kept you long enough, thank you for your time,' she whispered.

'I'll show you my Dad.' The little girl said, ran back into one of the other rooms, and returned almost immediately. 'Here he is, and he'll be home later, and the new baby isn't in the photo, she's too small,' the child said, and held up the photo to Kim. 'Mummy said I can stay up until he comes.'

'Maybe ...' The woman ruffled her dark curls.

Chapter Forty-eight

Grace lay on a trolley in A & E. She had been administered oxygen and now felt better. But the medical staff were unable to pinpoint exactly what was wrong. She had been there for a few hours, and felt guilty taking up a trolley as the area was very busy. She wasn't that bad, and just wanted to go home.

'How do you feel now?' Mark asked, anxiously.

'I'm much better. I'm so sorry for giving you such a fright.' She managed a smile and moved the oxygen mask in order to speak more clearly.

'I'm glad I was there. As I was on my way over to you I decided to call into the supermarket to pick up a bottle of wine, and only saw your car by chance.'

'I'd give anything for a cigarette.'

'You can't smoke in here, and anyway maybe it's not such a good idea. The doctors haven't diagnosed what's wrong yet, and you don't know what a smoke could do to you. Try and do without them, please?' He kissed her.

'It's not easy.'

'I know love, but ...'

A doctor came over. He held her wrist and checked her pulse. 'Well, your heart has calmed down, it was all over the place a few hours ago. Your blood pressure was sky high too, so we'll have to keep an eye on you. I'll arrange for a few tests.'

'Have you diagnosed exactly what happened?' Mark asked.

'Not sure, I think it may just have been a panic attack. Are you prone to such attacks,' he asked Grace.

'No.'

'Has it ever happened before? For any reason?'

'No.'

'Well, perhaps it was an isolated occurrence. You're feeling better now?'

She nodded.

'You should go home, and rest up for a few days until you're completely recovered,' he advised.

'I'll make sure of that,' Mark said.

'How's your breathing now?' The doctor removed the mask.

'It's fine, thank you.'

Mark insisted on taking her back to his house. 'I'm looking after you now, don't trust you on your own.'

'Maybe just for tonight. But I'll go back home tomorrow.' She hadn't the strength to argue.

'We'll see. I was very worried about you tonight, so we have to make sure to find out exactly what caused the problem.' He drove slowly. 'You'll have to have the tests he mentioned.'

'I will,' she agreed, although knew that it wouldn't happen. She didn't need someone to tell her what had gone wrong.

'So stay in bed tomorrow, I mean today, it's after one o'clock now.'

'I'll be all right.'

'You need rest, the doctor said. Don't you ever listen?' He was suddenly impatient with her.

Chapter Forty-nine

Kim walked down the driveway of number sixty-four. She was in a state of shock, her heart beat at an uncomfortably fast pace, and she felt like screaming. Her eyes filled with tears and she found it difficult to make her way back to the car almost tripping over the kerbs and grass verges in haste. Then the tears flowed freely, and Kim couldn't get her mind around the fact that Andrew actually had this other family here. Another family. It was incredible. The bastard. She muttered *bastard* out loud more than once. Thinking how blasé he was. So loving. So convincing. Although it explained why he came home so seldom.

She wondered how long the relationship with this woman had been going on? That child was about four years old, although may not have been his. But perhaps the baby was. Kim thought of her suggestion recently that they have another child, and understood now his reluctance. He had four already, it was obvious why he didn't want any more. Anger swept through her. He was spending his time with this woman, and her children. And Jason, Lorelai and herself were neglected. She clenched her fists with fury and wanted to smash his face. If she could only get hold of him.

Remembering then that the woman had said he would be back tonight, she decided to wait to confront him here. If she didn't bother and tackled him when he came home, then he could deny it outright and force her to prove it. And that would be difficult. Here he couldn't get out of it. It was quite clear what was going on. She wiped her eyes. The woman had told her his name. It could not be a coincidence. And she had seen his photo, the one shown to her by the child.

Kim returned to the hotel. She sat in the room feverishly going over the various options open to her. But as the evening stole on, was no nearer a definite plan, and couldn't imagine how she would face him.

About eight o'clock she returned to Hazelbrook Close, and parked the jeep around the corner from number sixty-four. Kim was very nervous now, and stared out of the darkened window but nothing stirred. The street lights were dim, and there were deep shadows under the trees. Various cars drove in and out, but none stopped outside the house. When finally a taxi drove past, she strained her neck in an effort to identify the passenger, but whoever it was sat beside the driver and wasn't visible.

Kim shuddered. Was it Andrew? She watched as the car drove around the corner and slowly pulled up outside number sixty-four. Her breath caught in her throat. Her chest tightened. Tears moistened her eyes again. She started up the jeep, and drove towards the corner. The man climbed out of the taxi. Quickly she threw off the black wig and opened the car door.

'Andrew?' she called.

He stopped in his stride and stared as she climbed out of the car. He walked towards her and she could see an expression of utter shock on his face. 'You bastard,' she muttered, stepped closer and hit him across the face with the palm of her hand. 'How dare you do this to us? How dare you?' She hit him again.

He stepped back and put down his flight bag which he had been carrying. But then he grabbed her hand and held it shaking in mid-air. 'What are you doing here?' he asked.

'I might ask you the same question.' She felt stronger now that they were face to face. Wasn't going to cry. Determined not to lose control. 'I've met Sara and Cheryl,' she said through clenched teeth. 'But I haven't seen the new baby.'

'Don't bring them into this,' he growled.

'Why not. I'm sure she knows about me and Jason and Lorelai? About your family?'

'She knows nothing. Get into that jeep, do you want the whole neighbourhood to hear?' Andrew pushed her backwards.

'I don't care who knows,' she exploded.

179

'Well, I do. Get in.' He grabbed her arm and forced her around to the passenger side of the car. Opened the door and pushed her in. 'Give me the key, we'll get out of here,' he growled.

She took it from her pocket and handed it to him. Deciding if they were going to talk it would be better somewhere else.

He picked up his bag, put it into the back, and then climbed into the driver's seat, started up the engine and drove out of the estate.

She attacked him again. 'You kept that secret very well. What possessed you to do such a thing? It's disgusting. And what about Jason and Lorelai, where do they fit in?' she raged at him.

'Who's looking after them while you're here?'

'Your parents of course. Maybe I should have brought them with me. Let you explain to them that they'll have to fight with these other children for a piece of you.'

'They have as much of me as these kids do,' he muttered.

'Spread yourself around, that your motto?' A wave of emotion flooded through her. She fought back tears.

He didn't answer. Just drove steadily along the main road.

'What are you going to do about this?' she demanded. 'Which family is priority. You have two it seems or maybe there are more than that? Is it three or four by any chance?'

'Don't be ridiculous,' he laughed.

'You think this is funny?'

He raised an arm in a gesture of helplessness. Then slowed down the car to a stop and indicated right.

'Well, are you going to leave her and come back home or are we going to be ditched?' Kim demanded.

He turned down a narrow laneway.

'You're incredible. A bastard if ever there was one. I don't know how I ever married you.'

'You loved me and I loved you. But that was then. Times change.'

'You think I'm going to accept this?' Kim shouted at Andrew.

He was silent.

'I'll make it so difficult you won't know yourself.'

'You will?' He was sarcastic.

'Yes, I'm going straight back to the house now and will tell the woman who thinks she's your partner that I am your wife.'

'Don't you dare,' he growled. Pulled off the laneway and stopped the jeep in the shadow of some trees.

'I'll open such a can of worms you'll be finished for good,' she threatened.

He grabbed her. Caught her arm and pinioned it. He leaned heavily and held her down.

'Get off me.' She struggled underneath him. Fought against him, hitting, punching. But his weight was like a stone, crushing her.

Suddenly she could feel his fingers tight around her neck.

She couldn't breathe.

'Andrew ...' she shouted his name, trying to gulp in air, but the pressure on her neck grew tighter. She felt dizzy. A mist between them. Couldn't see him clearly now. He was fading away. She screamed, mouthed words, but was in some strange dark place. Like in water. Underneath the surface. Drowning.

Chapter Fifty

Completely recovered, Grace returned home the following evening much against Mark's wishes, but couldn't have stayed away any longer. She had tried to go against her impulse to buy the papers, but the need was stronger. When Mark went to shop for dinner she cut around to a local shop and picked up the issues for that day, at last consoled.

Mark arrived back with everything he needed, including a bunch of flowers. 'I notice you bought the papers,' he commented as he peeled potatoes.

'Do you want any help with those?' she offered.

'No, you sit down and relax.'

She leafed through the Sunday Independent.

'What were you working on yesterday, I never got a chance to ask you were in such a state.'

'We've got an arrest in the fraud case.'

'So they managed it without you,' he asked, with a grin.

'Yea,' she replied, and laughed softly.

'What's next?'

'We're looking back at some cold cases, it would be good to get someone for those crimes.'

'It's amazing what can be done with forensics, DNA etc.'

'I get great satisfaction solving an old case. It's so important for the families. They really need closure, even if it's a long time ago, so I'm looking forward to it.'

'You're going to be very busy?'

'I hope so, nine to five doesn't suit me.'

'Are you going to make those appointments suggested by the doctor?' he asked.

Grace didn't reply, knowing she had no intention of doing anything about it.

'Maybe they'll give you one of those twenty-four hour monitors to check your blood pressure, and you may need medication to control it.'

He cooked a delicious meal, and opened a bottle of wine. They sat down to eat.

'You're a great cook, thanks so much,' she said, and meant it.

'I need some mustard,' he stood up and went to one of the presses. 'Where do you usually keep it?'

'It's not there, I've reorganised things,' she said quickly.

But he had already opened the door and stood there staring at the newspapers folded on the shelves. He looked at her. A question in his eyes. 'Strange place to keep them,' he said, with a smile.

'I haven't read them yet so just to get them out of the way while we were away on holiday, I shoved them in there,' she hoped it sounded convincing.

He nodded. 'What's the point of squashing newspapers into kitchen presses?' He opened another door and stared at the contents.

That press was also full of papers.

Chapter Fifty-one

Andrew loosened his hands. Kim's body lay limp on the seat in the car. Her head to one side, face pale, eyes closed. He was breathing heavily, and tried to get control of himself. He wiped the sweat which had gathered on his forehead with his hand, opened the door and glanced around. He stepped out. All was quiet. He couldn't believe that he had actually done this thing. His mind was in chaos.

He stood there for a moment, confused. But knew that he had to make a decision quickly about what to do. Something which was second nature to him. Trained to take a plane up into the air, fly it thousands of miles, and land it gently without the passengers being subjected to the slightest bump or discomfort. Able to deal with any emergency. Save the day. Whatever the circumstances. But this was something very far out of his experience. Fear took hold of him.

He thought of Sara, and knew he would have to explain his absence. He had texted when he landed but now must find an excuse. He wasn't coming home. He took out his phone and sent a message. His explanation that he had to attend an urgent meeting, didn't know how long it would take, so he would stay in the hotel as he had to take a flight to Paris the following morning.

He leaned across and checked Kim's pulse. There was none. And to him it seemed that her skin was already cooling. His heart hammered in his chest. He would have to get rid of the body. She was Kim no longer. He looked at her. Her legs twisted. The dark skirt riding up. Why had she done this crazy thing. She had just wanted to spoil everything for him. It had been working so well. Stupid bitch. He lifted Kim and put her body in the boot, struggled out of his coat and threw it over her.

He drove west away from Staines, but didn't really know where he was going. Constantly watching the speed limit, in case he was stopped by the police. He was looking for a place where he could dump Kim's body.

Eventually, he came to an isolated rural area and he stared out through the windscreen, his eyes darting left and right until at last he came to where some woods overshadowed the road. He slowed down, driving carefully until he spotted a narrow turning, and took it, the jeep bumping over the uneven surface of a narrowing lane which brought him to where the woods deepened and he parked. Cursing the moon which was high in the clear sky above, shining silver.

He walked through the trees, checking the terrain. Eventually coming to a natural slope which was covered with deep undergrowth. He stood looking down into the darkness. This would do.

He hurried back to the jeep. It was quiet. No-one around at this time of night. He removed any items from Kim's handbag which would reveal her identity - credit cards, driving licence, and anything else which had her name on it. He put her phone under his heel and crushed it.

Then he lifted her body, covered with the overcoat, and began to trudge through the woods. Unsteady with the weight, he scraped past the trunks of trees which were covered with damp lichens. It was a struggle to get past overhanging branches, and undergrowth. There was a sudden screech. A whirr of wings. And something big flew just over his head. He lost his balance with a stifled shout. While his mind told him that it was only an owl or something like that, his heart leapt and told him it was some weird beast which only came out at night to catch murderers.

He reached the beginning of the slope, and put Kim on the ground. As he stood there, his mind was suddenly full of regret, and there was an unexpected gentleness in his movements as he let her slither down and crash through the undergrowth and disappear. He threw her handbag after her. The floor of the forest was covered with old leaves, branches, twigs, and he spent time gathering a large pile and flung it down too.

He checked the car and found the wig, disposing of it into the bushes near the track. Then he changed into a pair of jeans he had in his bag, bundled up the uniform and drove to Heathrow, filling the car with petrol on the way. He knew the name of the hire company from a sign in the car. Returned it and the keys, and went to the usual hotel he used. It was five o'clock in the morning at this stage. In the bathroom, he washed down his uniform, removing most of the stains which adhered to the dark fabric. He had a spare uniform in his bag and left it down to reception to have it pressed for the morning. Then he showered, lay on the bed and closed his eyes.

Chapter Fifty-two

Ruth took the children home from the zoo without incident. They were exhausted and after eating some lasagne which Kim had prepared, they were ready for bed. Jason hadn't changed in his attitude, and as soon as he climbed into bed, he turned away from her, burying his face into the pillow. She didn't try to kiss him, and just tucked him up. Lorelai seemed much more amenable towards her.

She was tired and would have given anything for this to be tomorrow night and that Kim would be on her way home. She went into the main bedroom, and stood in the doorway. How would she sleep in that bed. Last night had been too difficult. She lay on the armchair and closed her eyes. This felt all wrong. She was not a mother. Jason and Lorelai were not her children. She was an imposter.

It was uncomfortable lying in the chair. She couldn't sleep, all the time wondering how Kim was doing. At one point, she had to go downstairs, feeling really anxious about her sister and immediately wanted to call or text. But Kim had been very particular about that and asked her to wait until she made contact. Ruth turned on the tap and splashed cold water on her face until slowly she began to feel a little better.

All that night, she sat in the chair, dozing on and off. Next day, although she was exhausted, she took the children to the zoo again as Kim had suggested. As she watched Jason and Lorelai kick a ball together with some other kids, a sense of longing stole over her. What if she had children of her own? How wonderful that would be. But it wasn't on the cards. John had reacted vehemently when she had mentioned having a baby on one occasion. It was a definite *no*. Anyway, the way they lived wasn't conducive to family life.

Moving from place to place wouldn't suit kids, she could see that. But since her relationship with John had changed, perhaps she shouldn't be thinking about having a child with him at all.

Lorelai threw herself on to her lap and she rolled on the grass with her, laughing out loud.

'Mum, I like your new hair.' Lorelai pressed her hand on it.

'I'm glad you do.' They sat with arms around each other.

'Can I go see the giraffes again?'

'Yea, sure.'

The ball bounced across them.

'Goal,' Jason yelled and ran after it. Another boy followed him, and they crashed together and fell on the grass.

She called, but they ignored her. Jason decidedly the stronger of the two and on top of the other child.

'Jason?' She ran over and pulled him off. 'Enough of that, don't be so rough.'

The two boys gazed at her, sullen, and then the other fellow wandered back to his own family.

'We're going to see the giraffes again,' she said.

'I don't want to see them,' Jason said.

'I promised Lorelai. We'll go wherever you want afterwards.'

'I want to go to the hippos first,' he demanded.

'We're going now, Jason, coming?' She wasn't going to give in to him.

'Don't want to.'

'We'll see the hippos later.'

'No,' he yelled, and ran across the green area into the trees.

Quickly, she put Lorelai in the double buggy and followed him. But she couldn't see him and wandered among the trees calling his name eventually coming to the conclusion that she really hadn't a clue where he had gone. Jason was lost. The thought of that filled her with terror. And Kim was due back tonight.

She went to a security man. In a state of panic now. He was very concerned. Asking for a description of the child, his age, what he was wearing, and any other relevant details. Immediately, he made contact with base, and the other security personnel at the zoo.

'I'll take you around in the jeep,' he said. She collapsed the buggy, lifted Lorelai up and sat in beside him. They went in the general area Jason had gone, but couldn't find him. Beyond the green area, it became heavily wooded and there were many places a small boy could hide. Ruth was terribly worried, and Lorelai sensed her concern and cuddled up to her.

'Are there animals in there?' she asked tentatively.

'No, there are some enclosures further on but no animals roaming wild.'

'Could we check the hippos, they're his favourite.'

'Bit of a distance away, but let's do that,' the man smiled.

They drove in the direction but there was no sign of him. What was she going to say to Kim? Ruth wondered. Her sister expected to find her children safely tucked up in their beds tonight, yet had made no contact so far. But Ruth hoped not to hear from her yet. Knowing that she would be unable to hide the worry in her voice in effusive chat about their experience at the zoo.

The security man was reassuring He brought them back to the office, made tea and offered biscuits. She couldn't have eaten a thing although Lorelai shyly accepted a chocolate bar. Ruth became impatient. Anxious to be out there herself looking for him. But she couldn't leave Lorelai on her own, the poor child just didn't know what was happening. Time crawled. The little girl slept in her arms. The security man came in.

'I wonder could you search the hippo area again,' she asked. 'If he was looking for them he might have arrived there by now.'

'That enclosure is a long way from where you were, a little fellow of five would never find it.'

'You don't know him, he's very determined.'

'Right.' He called some of the other searchers on his phone, asking them to concentrate on the hippo enclosure. 'We'll go over that way in the jeep, come on, jump in.'

It only took a few minutes. Ruth held her breath and prayed. Suddenly, there was a shout. They climbed out of the jeep, and a security man brought Jason over. But he didn't want to come to her and hung back.

'Your Mam won't say anything to you, go on now.' The man pushed him in her direction.

She put her arms around him and held tight. He stood, head down, and wouldn't look at her.

Once Ruth was satisfied they were both soundly asleep in their beds, she went downstairs and checked the phone, hoping for a call from Kim. Her flight was due in about ten o'clock and Ruth was looking forward to seeing her, so relieved that this veneer she had carried over the last two days could be shed. She watched the time, and once it had passed the hour called Kim. But the phone didn't ring out, or was there any voicemail. She checked her watch. It was twenty-two fifteen. Perhaps the flight may have been delayed. She stood staring out the window praying that every time a car turned into the road it was Kim's taxi. But no cars pulled up outside the house.

It was after twelve now. Ruth became more anxious. Sent a text, but received no response. Sat staring out the window into the darkness. Sheer exhaustion caused her to crash into sleep once or twice, but something always woke her again, refusing to let her sleep. In the study she opened up the laptop. Stared at the list of flights which had arrived at Dublin Airport, and checked the number with that noted on the piece of paper in her hand. It had arrived on time. Over two hours ago. She went into the kitchen and made a cup of tea. Sat at the table. Maybe Kim had decided to take the coach instead. With all the stops the journey might have been much longer. And then she would still have to get a taxi from the drop off point and that could be difficult. Ruth made another call to Kim but the result was the same and she became more and more worried.

Chapter Fifty-three

Grace kissed Mark goodnight and went back inside. Put away the dishes in the washer, and tidied around. Picked up one of the day's newspapers and highlighted an article about the amount of money to be made by the criminals who ran prostitution. She noted the journalist's name and went on to outline anything else of interest on the page. Time passed. It grew late. She had a shower in the small bathroom, put on her dressing gown and climbed into bed.

She had tried to defeat this thing which dominated her by sleeping down here the first night after the holidays. But as she faced into another night, courage deserted her. She closed her eyes and tried to fall asleep. Counted sheep. Thought of different cases she had worked on. Imagined some of the places Mark and herself had visited in Italy. Thought of anything except what was upstairs, but it didn't work. She had to get up again.

She made coffee. Smoked a cigarette. Tried hard to say no. But couldn't. You're such a weakling, she accused herself, went back to bed and lay there. Eventually she checked the time on her phone. It was just after three.

She gathered the papers which she had stored in the kitchen presses. And those which were bought yesterday and today which she had read, and took them as far as the stairs. Then slowly walked up. Took out the key and opened the door. She switched on the light in the bedroom and the bare bulb glimmered. Then made a few trips up and down until all the papers were shifted. Adding them to the pile on her bed. Then she lay down, and slept almost instantly. For the first time since Grace had come home she slept well, even if it was only for a few hours.

The following morning she was refreshed. Her hands gently stroked the papers over her, and then she pushed them aside and got out of bed. Some had fallen on the floor and she left them there and re-made the bed with the sheets and duvet, and then rearranged the newspapers on top like a bedspread.

Chapter Fifty-four

As morning approached, and Kim hadn't arrived, Ruth decided that there had to be some delay. It was a difficult thing her sister planned to do in London and perhaps there had been some unexpected events which prevented Kim from coming home. But she had left Ruth in charge, placed those two precious children in her hands and expected them to be cared for as she would herself.

Ruth wondered how she was going to cope. She was very nervous and had become even more agitated through lack of sleep. This was a school day. And while Kim had said to make the excuse that Jason and Lorelai had colds, Ruth thought that might cause more problems with the kids, so she went through Kim's notebook. Noted the details of the various teachers, and other parents. Their names and descriptions.

The children got up as usual. Were bathed. Dressed. And ate breakfast. They went through their routine, but Ruth was aware that Jason continued to be cautious of her, and every time she met his eyes, she felt sick inside. Lorelai seemed quite used to her now, although she still wouldn't hold her hand.

Ruth strapped them into the car seats. And drove first to Jason's school. Faced with an immediate quandary. Reluctant to leave Lorelai in the car while she brought Jason in, Ruth just managed to persuade him to stand close to her as she took the little girl out of the seat.

'Lorelai's not at my school,' he said, pulling away from her.

'No, we'll both come in with you and then we'll go to Lorelai's school.'

'I can go in on my own. You don't come with me.'

'OK,' she agreed, aware that she had to give him some leeway.

'Hi Kim?' One of the other mothers climbed out of her car and waved. Immediately, Ruth began to panic unsure of the woman's name. Short dark hair. Blue car. Tried to visualise the notebook. Then it came to her. Mary. She was almost sure. But didn't mention the name just in case it was wrong.

'How're you?' she feigned a casual approach.

'Fine thanks.' They walked towards the school entrance. Her boy and Jason immediately running ahead. The two women waved at the children, and turned back together, Ruth holding Lorelai's hand.

'We're going to organise that fundraiser soon, and want to arrange a meeting. I'll let you know the date,' the woman said.

'Yea, sure,' Ruth replied, with a smile.

'I'll text you, and see if it suits. But it will be in a couple of week's time, it's hard to get everyone together on the same night.'

'Thanks, I'd better get Lorelai to playschool, see you.' Ruth went back to the car. Shaken by her encounter with this friend of Kim's, but relieved she had managed to get through it.

Dropping Lorelai off was easier, she waved at a few people but wasn't forced into conversation. Her phone rang. She prayed that it was her sister, but the number which came up on the readout wasn't Kim's.

'Where are you?' John asked.

'I'm still here.'

'What time will you be back?'

'I'm not sure.'

'Why not?' Irritation edged his voice.

'My sister hasn't come back,' she spoke in a low tone.

'What? I was depending on you to do the pick up today as usual, and I need you here to make the appointments. I've had to get someone else to take over your work.'

'Can't they just continue,' she said sweetly. 'For today?' Her pulse raced.

'No, they can't. They have their own work to do.'

'Well, hopefully my sister will be back soon, but I can't leave until she arrives, I must look after the children.'

'What about the father?'

'He's away.'

'This is too much,' he groaned.

'I'm sorry, my love.'

'It's not good enough.'

'I'll phone as soon as she arrives, then I'll be straight home, I promise.'

He cut off.

She sighed. This was becoming more difficult. What if Kim was further delayed? And where was she, anyway?

Chapter Fifty-five

Andrew flew into Dublin Airport and went into the city. Reluctant to go to a local dry cleaners to have his uniform cleaned, he tried to think of where there was a dry cleaners in town and then remembered one at the end of Georges Street. When he had left it in, he felt much better. He had jokingly said to the girl behind the counter that he was at a party in a house which had an indoor pool and as everyone was a bit under the weather with drink there was a lot of messing about with water, and he had almost slipped in.

He took a taxi home, and hurried up the driveway. He had done a lot of thinking since Saturday night, and had decided that when he went home and found that Kim was missing he would report it to the Gardaí. He could talk with Grace perhaps. She might help.

Above all, he would say that he had no idea where she had gone. He had left last week and flown to Melbourne, via Dubai. He rehearsed the story. He had come back and she wasn't there. She had asked his parents to look after the kids and gone off somewhere. He would be distraught. Suggesting possible ideas why she might have wanted to go away. Did she just decide to head off for a few days to be on her own? Maybe she needed some space. Or was it another man? People disappear all the time. And no-one knows why they go. He decided that any of those scenarios were possible.

And his story would be perfectly feasible. His alibi was watertight. He went over it again. And was satisfied that he had covered everything.

There was no car in the driveway. Andrew wasn't sure what arrangement Kim had made with his parents, as they normally used their own car which had child seats, if they dropped the kids to school. Kim must have taken their own car to the airport. Fuck. How would he get it? They usually used the Bewleys car park. But he would need the code number. Damn. Opening the front door the alarm whined. He punched in the code and went straight to the laptop in the study to check. But there was no information about where Kim might have left the car. Nothing at all. He was without a car. Unable to go anywhere. And couldn't afford to hire one. His financial situation was stretched. Not that either of the women in his life were aware of that. Andrew managed a very tight ship. There was no mortgage on the house in Dublin, and he just rented in London, but still running two homes and families was tough on a pilot's salary.

Lately, he had wondered if perhaps he might live permanently in London with his partner, Sara. He loved her. But he loved Kim too in his way, and enjoyed the excitement of the secrecy. How he managed to walk such a tight line between the two families elated him. It often crossed his mind that this could be done a third time. But his financial situation didn't allow so he played around whenever he got the opportunity.

But who would look after Jason and Lorelai now? That was something he hadn't considered. He wondered if he could afford to pay an au pair and doubted that. But then realised that as Kim had gone there would be a few more euro floating, so it should cover the cost. He had destroyed her credit card, licence and the other items he found in her bag, but knew that he couldn't withdraw any money out of her account. He stood in the bedroom. Stared at the bed. And suddenly regretted that he would never make love to Kim again.

He heard a key in the front door, and went downstairs into the hall. Jason and Lorelai ran towards him. He bent down and hugged them both. Then he stood up and stared at the woman who stood in the doorway. 'Kim?'

Chapter Fifty-six

'You're looking good,' Peter commented.

'Thanks,' Grace said, smiling.

'You enjoyed Italy obviously?'

'Yea.'

She threw herself into work, so glad to be back at the coal face, involved in just the type of case which got her adrenalin flowing. Then she could forget about what lay at home.

There were a number of cold cases which still lay unsolved in the files. The team went through the evidence which had been collected at the time. Finally, the one chosen was the unsolved murder of a man in North County Dublin over twenty years previously.

Now it was painstaking work trying to fit all the pieces together like in a jigsaw. To think outside of the box, and find an angle which the Gardaí had missed at the time. Elena came into her mind. There were still a couple of officers working on the trafficking case, but there was nothing new to date. Perhaps some other Garda would be looking at such a case twenty years down the line. If she had only been given the opportunity to do some more work then maybe the team might have come up with something. They had been close. That man at the club was connected. Without a doubt.

Being busy took her mind off herself. Grace had only recently admitted in her heart that this obsession to store the newspapers was a serious problem. It had probably been at Mark's insistence, but Grace was still certain she could handle it.

The team put all the photographs and other details on the board.

'People had knowledge of this. He was a small time criminal, and was involved with a number of others who worked the north inner city.' Grace pointed to the area on the map. 'There were a number of tit for tat murders, and while we had an idea of who might be responsible at the time we couldn't get the evidence we needed to convict.'

'We pulled in this Dave fellow the last time. He was a member of a gang, but we haven't heard of him in a long time,' Peter said.

'Let's bring him in.'

'The address would need to be checked.'

'We'll put surveillance on it.'

'Right, let's split up the team. Keep a twenty-four hour watch,' Grace instructed.

She sat in the car with Peter outside the house on South Circular Road. They had the information that the man they wanted to interview called here to see his parents most evenings. About seven, a large car drew up, stopped outside, and a man went into the house.

Grace tensed. 'Do you think it might be?'

'Can't tell.' Peter leaned forward.

'We'll wait.'

They kept watch. Their patience was rewarded when at last he came out. Illuminated by the light of a street lamp.

'It's him, isn't it?' Grace asked.

Peter glanced at the photograph in his hand. 'His hair is a bit thin on top but really he hasn't changed that much.'

The man got into his car, and drove away.

Grace followed immediately. There was some traffic and she felt certain he wouldn't know he was being tailed. He drove across the river towards Clontarf and turned on to Vernon Avenue. The car lights were visible up ahead. It turned into a cul de sac. They grinned at each other with satisfaction, and saw the car pull into a short driveway. Its lights were extinguished. They waited a few minutes before they drove along and noted the details of the house and the car.

Back at the station they checked their information.

'He's been doing well, that's an expensive car,' Grace murmured. 'Wonder is he still involved in drugs? Check it up. Mortgage. Loans etc.'

'Let's get a warrant.'

'He was brought in on this case in ninety-three and interrogated, but we couldn't hold him.'

'Slippery character.'

The following morning, very early, the team raided the house, and arrested him. They began the interrogation later. But this Dave fellow was clever. He knew about the law and kept his mouth shut. He gave them no information. And he could afford one of the best solicitors around. Whatever he was doing it paid very well.

'We've got nothing from him, but we'll pull in the rest of the people involved at the time,' she said.

'It's a long list,' Peter warned.

'Someone will talk. It could be guilt. Revenge. Fear. Lots of reasons.'

'We hope.'

'We'll get a break,' she said, with a grin.

'Wish I had your determination.'

She thought about that. Somewhat cynically.

Since she had moved back upstairs again, she didn't know how she would keep Mark from discovering what lay up there. It was as if she had another lover.

Chapter Fifty-seven

'Dave's been picked up,' Victor reported.

'What for?' John asked.

'Don't know.'

'Fuck.'

'I'll keep you up to date,' he said.

John was worried. Why was one of his top men arrested? That inspector had to be behind it. Was she trying to get to him in a roundabout way? He felt even more vulnerable. Was there someone in his organisation who had snitched?

Lately, he had been shifting money. Buying shares, selling shares, and transferring it out of the country through a contact in New York. The money he made was laundered through various small businesses which he owned.

He called Victor back later. 'Any news?'

'We've got someone on the inside. They're questioning Dave about a murder twenty years ago.'

He was relieved. Dave hadn't been in trouble with the Gardaí since he had known him. How could they have pinpointed the man for something that long ago? He was furious. Hating the fact that they could stretch out into his complex web and disturb the equilibrium.

'I need to know something. This is just between you and me, Victor. It's to go no further. Your life depends on it. Get it?' John spoke quietly. An inherent threat in his words.

'Yea?'

'I want you to get me an address.'

John went into the hall. With a remote control a section of wood panelling slid open to reveal a lift. He went down into the basement and opened a heavy steel door. In that room was an armoury. An amazing collection of knives. Hand guns of every description. Rifles. Shotguns. Machine guns. Now he examined the smaller hand guns. Chose one, ammunition and also a silencer. He always carried a gun. Then he checked the knives. Anxious to carry something with an extremely sharp blade.

In the boathouse which had access to the sea, there was a swift sleek vessel moored. It bobbed up and down in the water. On board, John started the engine and it turned over smoothly. The containers of fuel were checked in the store room, and he was satisfied there was enough for the journey. Slowly, a plan was forming in his mind. He thought about it all the time. Day. Night. Perfecting every detail.

The bell on the gate rang. His hair rose on the back of his neck, and he checked the monitor which showed a view of the outside of the house. To his relief he saw the housekeeper. He had forgotten he had called her yesterday. He pressed the access code. The gates and front door opened and the Slovakian woman came in. He closed the door behind her, and she went straight into the kitchen and began to work. Cooked meals which were kept in the freezer for his use whenever he wanted. Cleaned. Scrubbed. Polished. Brushed. She had never seen him, and didn't know who he was. Her wages were always put in the drawer of the hall table.

John questioned his reaction to the doorbell. He was becoming paranoid and would have to get control over himself. If not, then he would lose his grip on everything. He rang Ruth. The call went on to voice mail. He was angry. To his surprise he missed her and wanted her back. She was one of the few people in whom he had complete trust. This thing with the sister had him puzzled. Was it true at all? Maybe she was living with the man in that house, and made up the story about having a sister. An identical twin sister? He began to doubt it.

A text came through on his phone. A cryptic message. The name in code. Instantly he knew who it was and deleted it.

John met Dave in a packed pub late at night. First he ordered a whiskey at the bar and made his way over to the back of the place where the man sat hunched over a pint.

'How did the Gardaí get to you?' he asked him immediately.

'They were going on about a murder twenty years ago. I was questioned at the time.'

'What was the name of the guy who was killed?'

'Sean O'Dwyer.'

'Were you involved?'

'It wasn't me.'

'But you knew about it?'

'Yea.'

'Do they have evidence on you?'

'Don't know.'

'They've let you go, whatever they have is insufficient to press charges unless they're sending a file to the DPP.'

'I hope not.'

'Who interviewed you?'

'A man and a woman.'

John stared at him. 'Red hair?'

'Yea.'

'Fuck.' He gulped the whiskey.

'Is there something about her?'

'No. But I want you to keep your head down,' he rasped.

Dave stared at him, his mouth slack. 'What?'

'Spend a few days out of the country. Go wherever you want. Enjoy the sun. I'll let you know when it's safe to return.'

Dave tightened his thin lips. 'I can't just disappear,' he said.

'You'll do as I say.'

'But what about the family?'

'Say you're doing some business deal.'

'You don't know my wife.' He raised his eyebrows.

'To hell with your wife.' John hadn't thought it was possible for this to happen. The Gardaí were picking people from his organisation. It was like they were trying to destabilize the whole structure. Was his financial empire going to collapse? Could they communicate with Interpol and freeze his bank accounts? His investments? Would he be left with nothing? 'I sense there's more in this than just a regular Garda investigation,' he said slowly. 'All of us are under her microscope.'

Dave looked at him.

'Who?'

'The inspector.'

'You know her?' Dave asked.

'Can't say I know her, but we've crossed paths.'

'Tough cookie.'

Victor had given him the address. It was in Ranelagh. He went around there one night. The house was at the end of a terrace. He parked a few doors away. But it was a couple of hours before a car turned into the driveway and stopped. He straightened up. Stared through the tinted glass in the windscreen. He watched the woman get out of the car, and walk up to the door. In the light which splayed from the hall he could see her red hair.

It became a habit with him. To wait near this house and watch. He used Ruth's car sometimes. He loved to follow her for some distance when she went for a run. There was a man in her life although he didn't live with her. They went out occasionally. He was enjoying the voyeuristic element of knowing where she lived. This was a very different person when she took off the dark work clothes. The night he had met her at his club in Leeson Street she had looked extremely glamorous. Now with a little less glitter she was positively chic. He vowed he would get in there easily and do what he wanted.

Chapter Fifty-eight

Grace received a call from her mother shocked to hear that her Dad wasn't well and he was coming up to Dublin to see a consultant. Her parents, Liam and Mary, were full of energy and always worked hard, but to her they seemed the same as they had been years ago. She had never thought they would die, reluctant to even go there. And although it wasn't possible for her to get home so often, that last time she was in Waterford they were in top form.

She took a few hours off and was there waiting at the railway station when the train pulled in and wandered along the length of the carriages looking for them. Finally rewarded when she saw her mother help her father down the steps. His face was pale, and his breathing uneven. She was taken aback, and tucked his arm in hers and slowly they made their way out of the station to the car.

Grace sat with her mother in the waiting room. She should have been at work, but had rung Peter explaining about the delay. Her parents couldn't be left alone to deal with everything.

'Dad seems quite ill,' she said to her mother.

'He had a bit of a turn last week.'

'Dad knows everyone else's health problems in the chemist, hears about them on a daily basis, but thinks he is immune,' Grace said softly.

'We should have retired years ago, I'm sixty-eight, and he's seventy next birthday.'

'You could employ more staff, and just supervise,' Grace suggested.

'The business wouldn't sustain it, with the recession it's hard to make a profit. We just take enough out of it to live, but if we have to employ fully qualified staff it would be difficult.'

'Maybe it's time to retire altogether?'

'I wouldn't mind, but your father ...' she paused. 'I don't think he could survive.'

'He might be forced,' Grace warned.

'That's what I'm concerned about.'

The consultant called them into the office. Her father was looking worried. Grace took his hand and squeezed it. The consultant wanted him to have some tests, but they would have to be carried out immediately. He suggested they go through A & E, which was the quickest way into the system.

Her Dad wasn't happy.

'Couldn't I have the tests in Waterford?' he asked.

'No, I'd prefer to keep you up here,' the consultant said.

'But what about the pharmacy?' he turned to her mother.

'I'll go back this evening, we'll manage,' she patted his hand.

'I'll be with you, Dad, don't worry. The tests are just to make sure there's nothing up, routine,' Grace reassured.

'We'll get someone to bring you down.' The consultant made a phone call.

'Mary, you be careful going back on your own,' Liam said to his wife.

'Of course I will. I promise not to talk to any strange men,' she grinned at Grace.

'That's not what I meant,' he grumbled.

'I know love,' she said, smiling. 'But let's lighten up a little, you'll be home tomorrow probably.'

He grimaced.

It took some time, but eventually a porter arrived pushing a wheelchair.

'I'm not sitting in that,' her father exploded.

The man shrugged. 'It is the doctor's instructions.'

'I'm not an invalid,' he grumbled.

206

'It's a long walk, Sir.'

'I'm well able.'

The man stood looking at him.

'There's no point in tiring yourself out, John. I'll push it if you prefer,' Mary offered.

'You're not much better than I am.' He shot her a look of derision.

She raised her eyes.

'Now Dad, let's be sensible. You don't want to make yourself any worse. So I think it's better to take the wheelchair, and be as comfortable as you can. If you get yourself all in a rush from the effort, it could falsify the results. You don't want that to happen, do you?' Grace said.

'Suppose not,' he nodded, and gave in.

They followed the porter to the A & E which was quite a distance. It was almost too much for her mother, she thought.

Grace took Mary to the train and returned to the hospital and sat beside her father. He slept soundly all night. Although trying to stay awake, sleep overcame her more than once. But she awoke sharply when any noise penetrated, and immediately went outside to have a cigarette. The night was cold, and the sharp air cleared her head. There were other people standing around having a smoke, but she didn't talk to them and kept to herself. Hugging her black jacket around her, she stared into the night, and pulled deeply on the cigarette. Dragging the smoke down into her lungs and exhaling. Dragging. Exhaling. The cigarette only half smoked when she put it out and lit another.

Grace longed to be at home in her own bed. Secure in that place. And carried one of the newspapers she had bought earlier. Rolled flatly, it was held close to her cheek, that feeling of velvet softness from the paper and aroma of ink always comforting.

The following morning, Grace's Dad seemed slightly improved. But he was very reluctant to stay in the hospital and was anxious to go back home, particularly worried about his wife managing the pharmacy on her own.

'Can't I just come up and down for tests?' he asked, petulant.

'It's much better to stay here for a short while and have them all carried out, Mam will manage fine. And the assistants will help, she only has to do the prescriptions.'

He snorted.

A nurse came in. 'We're taking you down now, Mr. McKenzie.'

He glowered.

'I'll have to go home to change, and I've to work then,' Grace said. 'But I'll see you later.' She kissed him.

Tears suddenly moistened his eyes, and he took her hand and squeezed it. 'Thanks for staying with me, and sorry for being such a grump.'

'Don't worry, love.' She kissed him again.

'Let's bring in the rest of the people involved in this case. It will take a lot of time, but it's worth it,' she said to Peter. 'Someone is going to drop a hint about an old friend. After all this time, people become careless, particularly criminals. And none of them want to do a long stretch at this stage in their lives.'

'Quite a number of the gang are dead, the feud continued for some years and they killed each other off. There are a couple of others still in prison.' Peter looked through his notes.

'Let's try and locate anyone else connected, and then we'll talk to the two in prison.'

She found it hard to concentrate. Her mind with her father at the hospital, very worried about his condition. But she tried to push it to one side, and threw herself into work for the rest of the day, but rang the hospital in the afternoon to check on her father's progress, and was told he was still in A & E and awaiting results of the tests. After five she rushed over, and found him on the same trolley but now he was in the corridor.

'Dad, how are you feeling?' She touched his hand.

His eyes opened. 'Like I've been through the wringer. Pulled, pushed and prodded all day.'

'You poor thing. Did they give you anything to eat?'

'Toast and tea,' he grimaced.

'Can I get you a sandwich?'

208

'No, I'm not hungry.'

'I talked to Mam and she's doing fine. So you needn't worry about her. Did they give you any idea about the results of the tests?'

'The doctor will be around later they said,' he sighed.

'Fancy another cup of tea or coffee? I'm getting one.'

He shook his head.

Grace bought the papers as usual, a coffee, and headed back to her father. When she arrived, he was in a cubicle and the consultant was there. Her father didn't look pleased. The results of the tests were not good. He needed a triple by-pass. She was shocked.

'You're sure?' Liam asked.

'Yes.' the consultant nodded.

'When do you need to operate?' Grace asked.

'Straight away.'

Her heart sank. She patted her father's shoulder.

'We'll get you a bed, and schedule you for surgery as soon as possible.' He hurried off.

'Just as well you came up to be checked, you might have had a major heart attack,' she said.

'I'll be out of action for weeks probably,' he groaned.

'And then you'll be much better. You haven't been well, admit that. Even though you told no one.'

He didn't say anything.

'I'll go out and phone Mam.'

Mary immediately saw the benefit of doing the surgery immediately, always the more practical of her parents. But was concerned that she wasn't able to be by her husband's side, and had to stay in Waterford to run the business. Grace assured her that she would be there for her father, and her Mam could make a day trip to see him.

But there was something else which was worrying Grace. What if her mother wanted to stay with her overnight?'

Chapter Fifty-nine

Andrew's heart thudded. He couldn't believe his eyes, and felt the blood drain from his head. He closed his eyes just for a second, thinking that this was a hallucination. Then opened them again. She was still there.

'Hi Andrew, how was your flight?' Kim moved towards him, smiling.

He forced himself to act normally but was unable to understand what this was. He kissed her in his usual fashion. Slightly off hand. But was afraid to touch her. Had he imagined what had happened in London? Was it all a dream? Maybe that's what it was. Perhaps someone had spiked his drink?

'Would you like some lunch, we're just about to have pizza, but I could cook you a pasta, if you prefer?' She walked ahead of him into the kitchen.

'Come on Dad, have pizza.' Jason hung out of his trousers.

'Dad.' Lorelai reached for his hand. 'Have you presents?'

He shook his head, realising that he had forgotten. 'Sorry kids.' He followed them to the table. 'Next time.'

'Sit down, lunch will be ready in a minute.' She worked at the counter. Mixing a salad. Slicing pizza and garlic bread. She put the plates on the table. 'What will you have to drink?'

'Coke,' shouted Jason.

'Yes, yes,' Lorelai joined in.

'No Coke, it's milk for you two,' Ruth said.

'Dad, we want Coke, tell her to give us Coke,' Jason demanded.

'If Mum says no, that's it,' Andrew said. 'I'll have a glass of wine.' He went to take a bottle of red wine from the press. 'You?' He waved it towards her.

'No thanks,' she smiled.

'I want Coke, I'm not going to do what she says,' Jason shouted.

'You have to do what Mum tells you,' Andrew said.

'No,' he grumbled.

'Jason.' There was a warning in Andrew's voice.

He knocked over the glass of milk on the table. It spread through the checked tablecloth.

Ruth rushed for a cloth to mop it up.

'Go to your room,' Andrew ordered.

'No. I won't.'

He stood over the small child, and marched him out of the kitchen.

Ruth removed dishes on the table, wiped down the surface, and put on a fresh tablecloth.

Andrew returned. 'Let him cool his heels for a while.' He ate some pizza, but really it almost choked him. Was there something wrong with him? Was he losing his mind? Maybe go to see a doctor. A psychologist. Someone like Mark. But he couldn't tell anyone about this. If it had all been a dream of some sort then were Sara and the kids even real?

He went up to check on Jason, and told the child to go back downstairs. Then he hurried into the bedroom and made a call. 'Sara?'

'How are you, darling? Where are you?'

For a second he had to think of his schedule to get it right. 'Paris.'

'I'm envious,' she whispered softly. 'Will you be home tonight?' she asked.

'No, I'm off to Dubai from here and then on to New Zealand.'

'Pity, when will I see you?'

'Can't be sure, but I'll text.'

'I miss you.'

'You too, love.'

He cut off. Relieved that he hadn't gone totally mad, and at least that part of his life wasn't imagined. The events of Saturday night came into his mind. Images of Kim flashed past. Her face. Her body. Like in an old black and white movie.

They had dinner together after the children had gone to bed.

'That was really delicious,' he said, smiling.

'Thanks, I'm glad you liked it.'

'I'm not home often enough to enjoy your cooking,' he admitted. Surprised at himself saying such a thing. He remembered the rows they had had on that subject recently.

She nodded.

'It's hard. The rosters are difficult these days.'

'You go into the television room and relax,' she suggested. 'I'll just put the dishes in the washer.'

'It doesn't look like there's much to do.' He stood up from the table and followed her into the kitchen.

'Won't take me a minute.'

'Don't be long.' He waved his glass. 'Anyway, this place is spotless, you must have been cleaning all weekend.'

They sat on the couch. He flicked through the newspaper. Crazily he wondered if she was a spirit, and his hand would move through her body as if it was smoke. She was looking at the television screen. He recognised her clothes. Hair. She had had it cut short recently and he liked the style. Make-up was the same, just a touch, nothing too heavy. Hands were thin, the fingernails cut short. Normal. It was Kim. Had to be. And if that was the case then he was going mad.

There wasn't that much left in the bottle, and he poured the last glass of wine. He raised it. 'To us.'

She touched his glass with hers.

He leaned forward and kissed her. A slow sensual kiss this time. Her lips were warm and moist. But unusually she held back. Sensing a shyness in her, excitement spiralled through him. It was like she was someone new. One of the women he met in various places. But his mind insisted that this had to be Kim.

His hand cupped her face for a few seconds. Suddenly he wanted her. His need was electric. He took her hand. 'Let's go to bed.' He was aware of a slight tremble reverberating through her, and that only added to his excitement as he led the way upstairs to their room. She insisted on checking on the children first, and then,

212

almost reluctantly, he thought, followed him inside. He closed the door. Stood in front of her and gently began to undo the buttons in her blouse. Slowly. One by one.

'No Andrew,' she whispered, and held the edges of her blouse together.

He stared at her. Puzzled. He was ready for her now.

'I'm tired ...'

'What does that mean?'

'I didn't sleep much last night,' she hesitated. 'I think I may be coming down with something.'

'Come on, you don't look sick,' he laughed.

'I feel ...'

'Kim, don't mess with me.' He leaned to kiss her.

'Not now, Andrew.' She pulled away from him.

'But I'm only here for tonight,' he complained, peevish.

'I have to go to the bathroom,' she rushed away from him.

'Kim?' he ran after her, but she closed the door in his face.

He sat on the bed. This wasn't the Kim he knew. The realisation suddenly hit him. The events in London had actually happened. His mind wasn't playing tricks. He had killed his wife.

Chapter Sixty

Grace waited for the phone call from the hospital to say that her father had come out of surgery. He would be in intensive care after that and she was ready to go over as soon as the word came through. She sat at her desk, going through the details held in old files and trying to see something which had been missed. Sighing, she leaned her forehead on her hand, so preoccupied with her father and mother. The rest of the family had been on the phone regularly over the past couple of days, but Grace hadn't felt any of them needed to rush home just yet.

It was later that evening when her father was brought into the ICU. Grace talked with the consultant, who was pleased with the surgery. It was a success. She sat by her father's bedside. But he wasn't aware of her presence still groggy from the anaesthetic. Mark had come over, and he waited outside. She took a break. He bought her a cup of coffee from the dispensing machine. It was awful. But she drank it anyway. It was hot and helped a little.

He put his arm around her, and kissed her.

She leaned into him, and had a sudden urge to cry. To let it all pour out. But she managed to get control over her emotions, and went back into ICU. Her father was on a drip and attached to various monitors. And only awoke occasionally, staring at her as if he didn't know her.

'I should stay with him,' she said to Mark.

'There's no need, you'll be exhausted. The staff will look after him.'

'No, I want to.'

'Then I'll stay as well.'

'You don't have to, there's no point in that. Go home to bed.'

'I'd prefer to be with you.'

She shook her head.

'Please? I'd like to.' He kissed her.

'What about work, you'll be shattered.'

'I'll survive. We've had many a late night, didn't kill us,' he grinned.

She hadn't the strength to argue.

Grace was glad Mark was there. Someone to talk to on and off during the long hours. They lay on the seats in the waiting room and managed to sleep some of the time. She went into her father during the night, and just sat by the bed, although he probably didn't know. It was just ...if anything happened she wanted to be on hand, immediately.

They went home at six in the morning, and she showered and changed. Put in a couple of hours at work, and then collected her mother from the train and took her to the hospital. Mary had arranged for a locum to cover the work at the pharmacy and now felt more relaxed about staying with her husband.

But Grace was worried. Before leaving the house this morning, she had taken out fresh linen, pillows, and a duvet. She stood on the landing, aware that her mother couldn't sleep up here. God help her, but Mary would have to sleep in the study. Grace wondered how to explain her lack of bedrooms in the house and why there wasn't a spare. And worst of all, why was upstairs locked off? There was a sense of dread in the pit of her stomach. Her mind a ferment. After a while she decided to explain that upstairs was a junk room, full of her own stuff. And that it had been a flat when the previous owners had been here. She hoped her mother would accept that. While her Mam and Dad had visited her occasionally, they had never needed to spend a night, as they always stayed with Aunt Sissy who had died the previous year.

And there was another thing. Her parents had not met Mark, or any of the other men she knew over the years. She had a distinct aversion to introducing him. And couldn't bear the thought of the questions which would follow about any plans they might have. But she couldn't avoid it, as Mark called around to the hospital at lunchtime, and for the first time he was introduced to her mother. It gave Grace the chance to go back to the office and he looked after Mary, saying he wasn't busy. After they had left her father in the good care of the nurses that evening, Mark took them to dinner.

In a way it was good to have him along. Grace would have found it difficult to make small talk with her mother and keep up a bright optimistic attitude. But Mark and Mary chatted so much her own detachment wasn't even noticed by either of them.

He came back to the house with them. Grace fussed. Very nervous. She tried to make things perfect for her mother, and regretted not being in a position to give her a lovely bedroom, and welcome her properly into her home. And if Mary found out what was upstairs, her reaction would be too horrendous to contemplate.

'I hope you don't mind sleeping down here, but upstairs is ...I never really unpacked since I moved here. No time ...I suppose,' she said vaguely.

'But you're ten years in this house?' her mother looked astonished.

'I've been busy,' Grace was unable to meet her glance.

A silence yawned between them. She was aware of Mark standing by the counter.

'Not to worry, I'm so tired I'd sleep on the floor,' Mary smiled, sitting down. 'But I don't have to go into the hospital so early in the morning, they won't want me around, so then I'll tidy the rooms upstairs for you. You know I'm a very early riser.'

'Thank you, Mam, but there's no way I'll let you go up there, it's chaos.' She kissed her mother.

'I'll have it done in no time. Let's have a look up there now and you can explain how you want things, won't take a minute. You have downstairs so perfect, I'm sure it's not as bad as you think.' Mary got up again and walked towards the hall.

'No Mam ...' Grace hurried after her mother. 'Come back, sit down.' She ushered her into the living room again and had to make a supreme effort to be gentle with her, although in truth she wanted to scream.

216

'All right, show me tomorrow. I have to do something with my time, you know I'm not one to sit around doing nothing.'

'I'll make coffee,' Mark offered, and switched on the kettle. Then opened the press and took out mugs. 'We'll need sugar ...' he murmured and opened another door.

'It's here,' she took it from a press on the other side, and put it on the coffee table.

'Switching again?' he asked, with a grin.

'I like a bit of variety.' Her reply was too sharp. But she was glad the papers had been shifted upstairs.

She sat down beside her mother, and tried to calm herself. That had been a close call, and a sense of panic swept through her, reminding of that day recently in the newsagents. She couldn't afford for the same thing to happen again.

Mark handed each a mug of coffee.

Grace took a couple of deep breaths. Ran her fingers through her hair, able to feel the dampness of perspiration on her scalp. It took a while before her pulse steadied. 'Dad seems to be doing OK,' she said softly.

'But he is very weak,' her mother said.

'He'll improve. Day by day. You'll see.'

'I hope so.' Tears filled Mary's eyes.

Grace put her arm around her mother.

They sat there without speaking for a time.

'That was good coffee, even though I say it myself.' Mark finished his and stood up. 'I'll head off now, leave you to get a decent night's sleep. It was good to meet you, Mary.' He held out his hand.

She took it and smiled.

Grace went out to the door with him.

He took her in his arms, and kissed her. 'Look after yourself, love, I'm sure your Dad will be much better soon. I'll call around to the hospital tomorrow evening.' He looked down at her, a smile in his eyes. 'And don't worry so ...'

The anxiety within her subsided a little. But she knew well that he understood what was going on with her. He had it exactly. Guilt was very near the surface of her mind now that the people she loved most had gathered closer to her, and increased the risk of her secret being discovered.

Chapter Sixty-one

Andrew had his arms around her. Ruth felt guilty being so close to her sister's husband. She didn't know this man. He was a stranger to her although she lay beside him all night long, very much aware of his body at various times. Tears filled her eyes. How would she explain that to her sister?

She didn't want to move, reluctant to wake him. Then he would surely realise that she wasn't Kim. Last night he had a few glasses of wine, and that would have explained how he might not have known whether she was Kim or not. There were bound to be some differences between them. Without any make up. Being just herself. Unadorned. He was sure to notice that she wasn't Kim.

But where was Kim? She had been away three days now. Ruth tried to find excuses for her absence, reminding herself that Kim had said her search could take longer than a weekend. Perhaps the house had been difficult to find and that was the reason she had not returned. But why hadn't she called to explain? Or sent a text? Perhaps something had happened to her?

On the other hand, if her sister was missing Ruth knew that she should report that fact to the Gardaí. But if she did, her own life would be exposed. They would find out about her so-called career. And if John became aware of that he would …

She decided to hold tight. Act the part. Although didn't know how long she could keep it up. Jason was suspicious of her. Lorelai was the complete opposite and behaved as if she was her mother. Her bright face full of joy at the smallest thing. For Ruth, the thought of someone loving her that much blew her away. Everyone she had ever known since leaving home had wanted a piece of her. They took as much as they could until finally they disappeared out of her life, and she was left alone. A woman of simple needs who just wanted to be loved. Now here was a child who seemed to love her unconditionally. She had even held her hand today. Maybe it wasn't so hard, after all.

Ruth crept out of the bed and went to the bathroom door, looking back at Andrew who still slept, and wondering was he really involved with another woman. If so, he carried it off very smoothly.

He opened his eyes and stared at her.

Caught in his gaze she felt exposed.

He smiled. 'Come back to bed.'

'The children,' she murmured.

'There's plenty of time,' he said, and patted the bed beside him. 'Are you feeling better?'

'Not so good,' she smiled, and went to take a shower.

'I have to leave about twelve today,' Andrew groaned.

'Where are you going?'

'Capetown.'

'How long will you be away?' she asked.

'I'd hope to be back at the weekend. Why don't you ask Grace and Mark over for dinner on Saturday, just make it provisional, you can confirm it when I know the schedule exactly. I had a bit of a barney with him the last time they were here and I want to make up for that.'

'I wonder ...' she hesitated. 'If you could give me some money?'

He stared at her for a few seconds. 'Yea, yea, sure.' He put his hand into his pocket and pulled out his wallet. 'You're lucky I went to the ATM at the airport yesterday. 'Three hundred do?' He counted out the notes. 'Here's five, should keep you going.'

Ruth dropped the kids to school, and came back quickly without going to the gym as Kim did most days. It would have been too difficult to pass herself off as her sister in that situation, so she had decided to feign a pulled muscle if anyone asked. Andrew stood up from the table as soon as he saw her.

'How are you feeling?' he asked.

'Not great.' She sat at the table.

'No gym today?' he asked.

Frantically she tried to think of something to say to this man, but could think of nothing.

'You're very quiet,' he said.

She shrugged.

'Perhaps you should call to see the doctor.'

'No, I'm sure it will pass.'

'Are you happy, Kim?' he asked, taking her hand. 'I've neglected you, I know that. But I promise that things will be different from now on. And I'll see more of the kids too, they don't deserve this.'

She nodded. A shout swept through her. What sort of an idiot are you? I'm not Kim. How could you think that I'm her. I'm Ruth. Are you really that stupid? But she kept her mouth shut. He was leaving shortly so by the time he returned Kim would be back.

After school, she picked up the children and took them to the park. Sitting on a bench watching them on the swings, there was a text. She pulled the phone out of her pocket and pressed the screen. She didn't recognise the number but it could still have been Kim. She prayed it was.

Hi Kim, are you at home, on our way over. See you soon. Love. Dolores.

It was from Andrew's mother. Ruth began to shake. This wasn't what she had expected. Not part of the plan. Tears filled her eyes.

Lorelai ran over. 'Mum, push me on the swing. I want to go higher.' She took hold of her jacket and pulled.

Ruth nodded, and followed the child, standing behind and sending the swing a little higher.

'Higher,' Lorelai demanded, excited.

Ruth didn't know what to do about the text, but eventually replied.

At the park.
When home?

She was confused, they weren't planning to go anywhere else, and the kids would be hungry and tired too.

Half an hour.

Dolores and Noel knocked on the door shortly after Ruth arrived home, and there was great excitement from the kids when they saw them. They were a nice couple. Both of them embracing her and the children warmly.

'How are you?' Dolores smiled. 'You look a little pale.'

'I'm fine, thanks. Although I didn't sleep well. You missed Andrew, he only left a few hours ago,' she hoped to take their attention away from herself.

'I know, we talked to him on the phone,' Dolores said.

'You should make sure you get the full eight hours, girl.' Noel put his arm around her. Then he lifted Jason up on his shoulder.

'Me too, me too,' Lorelai screamed.

'You'll get your turn later,' he smiled down at her.

They walked into the kitchen, and Dolores took Lorelai up on her lap.

'So he's gone to the sun,' Noel said.

'Capetown.' Ruth made tea.

'Is that man ever home?' Dolores asked. 'How do you put up with him?'

'I'd prefer if he was home more often but ...' she shrugged.

'He enjoys his job, all he ever wanted to do,' Noel said, trying to balance the boy who now struggled to get down.

'He's happy, and that's the main thing I suppose,' Dolores added.

'And he has a job which is even more important.' Noel put Jason on his feet.

Ruth poured tea and sliced a fruit log. She managed to behave normally for the rest of the afternoon, and didn't think that Andrew's parents noticed that she wasn't Kim, glad that the kids allowed little chance of making any adult conversation. When finally they left, she was glad to see the back of them, although was grateful for their more than generous offers of help should she need it.

But the day wasn't over yet. Later that evening Ruth received two more texts from friends of Kim. One from an Emma who wanted to meet at the gym and have coffee afterwards. She declined and explained about the pulled muscle. Another from Trish who wanted Kim to join a bridge club with a few other friends. She put her off as well, and made a note of the names just to bring Kim up to date when she returned.

Then the final shock as she sat watching television that night. The house was quiet. She stared out the window, praying that Kim would come back home soon. Tears dribbled down her cheeks. Where are you? She cried. Then a text came through. She stared at the screen. Praying it would be her. But it wasn't.

Are you alone?

Yes. She texted a reply.

I'm at side of house open patio door.

Ruth's heart sank.

A sharp noise took her attention to the window which looked over the side garden, darkly shadowed.

John stood outside, and she could immediately see that he was angry. His very stance told her that.

She unlocked the patio door, and slid it open. 'You can't be coming around to this house, what if Andrew was here?'

'Is he?'

'No, he left today.'

'How long will he be away?'

Probably for a week or more. He doesn't get home that often.'

'I want to know how long this is going to continue?' he demanded.

'Sshh ...' she put her finger against her lips. 'The kids are asleep.'

'I want you back.'

'My sister hasn't returned yet.'

'Has she been in touch with you to explain why?'

She shook her head.

'Then how long does she expect you to stay here minding her kids?'

'I don't know.'

'This is ridiculous. I need you. You're part of the business. The person covering you is bloody incompetent.'

'Would you like a drink?' she asked, in an effort to placate him.

'No.'

'Coffee?'

'Well, OK, I'll have a cup.' He was surly.

'Sit down.' She went into the kitchen.

He shrugged out of his navy overcoat and flung it across the arm of the couch. Then he followed her. 'Maybe you could operate from here,' he said.

'What do you mean?'

'This place is a good cover. No one would suspect,' he grinned.

'I can't do that.' She was shocked.

'You'll do as I say,' he snapped.

'I can't, Andrew would discover what we're up to.'

'I'll bring over the laptop, you can hide it somewhere.'

'No, please, don't make me do it. I'll be back soon, I promise,' she begged him.

'You haven't a clue when you'll be back, could be weeks, could be months. In the meantime I have to survive without you. I wonder have you told me the truth. Perhaps you've just shacked up with this pilot? And the story about the sister is just a cover, that it?' He moved behind her quickly, took hold of her hair and twisted.

Ruth grimaced in pain. 'No, that's not it, I want to come home, it's true about my sister.'

'Bullshit.'

'I'd never lie to you. Let go, you're hurting.'

'No?' He tightened his grip.

She shook her head.

'Maybe I'll come around and interview the husband. This Andrew character. What does he think about you being here?'

'He thinks I'm Kim,' she whispered.

'How is that possible?'

'She didn't expect to be gone more than the weekend.'

'So you're playing the part of his wife?'

She was silent.

'In every way?'

'No, I said I had a headache last night, and he was gone today, back to London.'

'You weren't even enticed, just a little?' he smiled. But the smile didn't reach his eyes.

She shook her head.

'What are you going to say next time. Will you have some other complaint?'

'It won't happen. Kim will be home by then.'

'She'd better.' He pulled her towards him. His fingers pressing deep into her shoulder. 'Now I'm warning you, if you keep this up, it will get much more painful.'

When he had left, Ruth sat down, feeling hurt. How could he be so rough with her? She had often overheard him on the phone and his attitude towards certain people was very aggressive. But she had never thought he would actually behave in that way towards her.

Chapter Sixty-two

Grace's father recovered well. Her mother came up and down to see him, and continued to sleep in the study. She still went on about helping to clean out the upstairs, and Grace found that very hard. Anxiety dogged her days now.

She went into work early and spent the evenings at the hospital with her father. Surprised that she could organise her life so well. Even Mark commented on that. But having quiet evenings at the hospital gave her too much time in which to think. Dark empty spaces in which she foundered, terrified.

Mark had met her father now and it was good to have him visiting when her mother was back in Waterford and Grace was working. She was grateful to him. And knew she didn't appreciate his kindness, generosity and how much love he had in him. There had been other guys along the way, but none of them had the stamina to keep up with her. A few weeks was the max. There had even been a fiancé when she was in her twenties. A wedding was arranged. A honeymoon. A dress. But at the last minute she backed out and felt very guilty about that. Her fiancé was furious and never spoke to her again. But it was the general upset to everyone she most regretted. Still, she couldn't have married anyone at that point in her life. If the wedding had gone ahead God only knows where she would be now.

'I like Mark,' her mother said.

'So do I,' Grace said, smiling.

'Why don't you get married, love? It's about time you settled down.'

She shrugged.

'He is such a nice person.' Mary leaned back in the armchair and sipped her glass of white wine. "You know, I had all you children by the time I was your age.'

'I don't think children will be on the cards.'

'Why not?' Mary asked sharply. 'Anyway, you don't have to wait until you get married, have a baby straight away. It seems to make no difference to anyone these days.'

Grace shook her head.

'Don't let that man get away. He's too good. And seems to understand you very well. Do you realise we've hardly ever met any of the men in your life and I'd say there were quite a few over the years.' Mary held the glass out.

'More wine?' Grace asked.

'Why not?' Her mother smiled.

Grace went across to the fridge, and took the bottle out. Just then her attention was drawn by something outside the front window. Downstairs was open plan and she could see straight through the venetian blind which wasn't fully closed. There was a street light there and it reflected on the shining body work of a car which moved very slowly across her gate.

'Tell me something, Grace, why do you keep the door at the top of the stairs locked?' Mary asked.

Chapter Sixty-three

Andrew was preoccupied. He knew now that he had murdered Kim and that it hadn't been a hallucination. He had done a terrible thing, and had to make a real effort to hide the fear of being discovered from his co-pilot and staff at work. The woman who had taken Kim's place had to be her sister. She told him she had a sister and that they had been estranged for many years. But there was nothing about being a twin. It was amazing how alike the two of them were. Identical almost. This situation blew him away. He needed an alibi, and he had it. Just like that. His wife was still there. No-one would guess that anything had happened to her.

But what of this woman? What was her motive? How long was she going to stay, he wondered. Had she any life of her own?

Kim had arranged it. That was obvious. Suspicious of him, she travelled to London and asked her sister to take her place. To set a trap for him. Clever. He thought. Bloody clever. Didn't know she had it in her.

He returned to his partner Sara, and the children in Staines.

'It's been too long,' she said bluntly.

'I'm sorry, love,' he said with a deep inward sigh. She was annoyed, he could see that.

'Two weeks, and then you turn up. How long will you stay this time?' she demanded.

'I've a flight tomorrow afternoon ...' he muttered.

'I don't know if I can tolerate it for much longer. I really don't have a partner. My children have no father.'

He said nothing.

'Have you any ideas about improving our life?' she asked.

He shook his head.

'Do you love me?'

'Yes, I do, but my work is difficult.'

'It's not conducive to a real relationship between two people,' she emphasised.

'I've tried.'

'Not very hard.'

He didn't want to promise anything more. Not now. 'Let's go to bed.' It was always his way out of awkward situations with women. He reached down and kissed her.

'You really know how to get around me.' She returned his kiss with a smile.

'Good, we'll feel better in the morning.'

She turned off the light, put her arm around him and they slowly walked up the stairs, laughing.

'Sshh ...' she said, her finger to her lips.

He went to the half open bedroom door, and stood looking at the child in the small bed, and the baby in the cot.

'Maybe we should think of moving to a bigger house. The kids have so much stuff. And Cheryl will need her own bedroom soon,' Sara whispered.

He didn't reply. There was no way he could afford to do that.

'And it would be nice to live in a better area ...'

He opened their own door. Hoping that Sara wasn't going to keep this up. He had no intention of moving. Couldn't have afforded it. As it was, he just barely managed to cover the costs of this house. He put his arms around her, and kissed her. Shut her up for now. Otherwise she would keep on and on. That's the way she was. Normally, it didn't bother him too much. He could usually do what she wanted. But this was bigger. This was difficult. This he wasn't going to do.

They took off their clothes and lay close together.

'I love you, Andrew,' she kissed him. 'And I want you home more often. Get on another roster. The shorter trips. And bring us with you when you go long haul. What about that? My mother agrees with me. She can't understand it.'

'What is it with you women, you're all the same, nag, nag, nag, never satisfied with what you've got?' he snarled.

She stared at him. 'But Andrew ...'

He had a sudden recollection of hearing himself say something similar to Kim not so long ago.

Chapter Sixty-four

Ruth became more and more tense. She was certain something had happened to Kim. Was it an accident? Had someone hurt her? Her mind went around in crazy circles. She couldn't eat properly, and hadn't had a good night's sleep since coming to this house.

Dolores and Noel came over. The children were delighted to see their grandparents, but Ruth was claustrophobic, nervous, and felt she needed to get out of here. To just walk away. Without any explanation to these people and children who seemed to think she was theirs. Her own personality was submerged. Suddenly she felt faint. 'I don't feel well,' she said.

They were immediately concerned.

'Can I get you something?' Dolores asked.

'I'll just have some water.'

Noel poured and handed her a glass.

'I thought you looked pale yesterday, you must be coming down with the flu. We have a few friends who have been quite ill. It seems to be a dreadful dose. Why don't you go to bed for a while. It will do you good.' Dolores put a hand on hers.

'I'm all right.' She sipped the water, and felt a little better.

'We'll stay and look after the children, so you can rest and not have to worry about them.'

'No, it's OK, I'm not that bad.'

'But we'd love to stay. It's no problem at all.'

Noel went into the garden. 'Hey kids, we're staying for the evening.'

The two rushed towards him.

'Maybe you should just lie on the couch. What were you planning to cook? I'll make dinner.'

'No thanks, I'm feeling better already.'

231

'Let me help then.'

'It's a casserole, I only have to put it in the oven.'

'Well, if you wish ...' Dolores gave in.

They were there for hours. Doing her head in. After dinner and the children had been put to bed she hoped that they would leave, but no, they insisted on staying. They settled down on the couches in the television room and switched on their favourite television programmes.

'You don't mind if we look at *Coronation Street?*' Dolores asked. 'We hate to miss it.'

'Dolores loves *Corrie*,' Noel said, with a grin.

'He loves it just as much, except he won't admit it.'

They teased each other.

Noel took up the remote control and switched the programme on.

Ruth was tense, and didn't know how she would put up with them for the evening.

To her relief they finally went home just after ten o'clock. She turned the lights off, lay on the couch and closed her eyes, praying that John wouldn't come around tonight. But the phone beeped about an hour later, and she went around to the patio door to find him standing outside. For a moment she stood there. Wondered if she should just ignore him. Pretend that Andrew had come home. But changed her mind after a few seconds and opened the door, reluctant to antagonise him.

'Are you ready to go home?' he barked as soon as he stepped inside.

She shook her head.

'That sister of yours is not back yet?' he growled.

'No.'

'Fuck. I don't believe that you have a sister. You're playing some game.' He backed her up against the wall.

She was suddenly scared of him.

'I have a sister, and I'm not playing a game,' she blurted.

'Who is this?' He picked up a framed photo from the mantelpiece. His fingers pressed against the glass, the knuckles white. 'With you.'

She turned back. 'That's Kim and a friend of hers.'

'That's you.'

'It's not, I told you we're identical twins.'

He peered at it. 'Who's the friend? Do you know her name?'

'I'm not sure ...'

'Come on?'

'I can't remember. Wait ...that's Grace. She's a Garda.'

'How very interesting,' he said slowly. 'Have you met her?'

'No.'

'Amazing,' he muttered.

'What do you mean?'

'I've come across her before.'

'When?'

'Never you mind,' he snapped. 'And be careful of what you say if you do meet her,' he warned. 'Don't open your mouth about us.'

'I won't.'

'Few jars, girl chat, never know what you might say.'

'She's not a friend of mine.'

'But you have to act the part, don't you?' He grabbed her wrist and twisted.

'John, why are you doing this?' she cried out in pain.

'To get it through your thick head that if you ever say anything to anyone about us, you will be ...' he stared at her fixedly.

'Do you think I'm mad?' She pulled away from him. But he didn't let go.

Tears sprang into her eyes. She was so stressed out with tiredness and tension it was difficult to deal with this.

He stared at her for a few seconds. Then let go of her, picked up his coat, marched across the room and out the patio door.

She sat down on the arm of the couch, rubbing her wrist, and let the tears come then. What was she going to do?

Chapter Sixty-five

Grace was in the act of closing the slats of the venetian blind when she heard her mother's question, and swung around quite unable to speak, her body in shock.

'I don't know what's up there, but do you have to hide it?' Mary continued, but her voice was gentle.

Grace didn't reply, just walked back to where her mother sat and poured another glass of wine for them both. Pulled another cigarette from a pack, lit it and took a deep pull.

The doorbell rang.

Grace was puzzled as to who it might be at this time. It was after eleven. And then the thought struck her that it might be the person in that car.

'Aren't you going to answer?' Mary asked.

'Sure.' She put down her glass.

The doorbell rang again. A double ring.

And then she knew who it was, and hurried out with a great sense of relief.

'Hey, thought you had gone to bed without me.' Mark put his arms around her and pulled her close to him.

'Didn't expect you this late,' she whispered.

'I was delayed in the office this evening but I called around to your father and sat with him for a bit. He was asleep, but I stayed for a while anyway.'

'Thanks so much, you're a darling.' She kissed him. 'Did you see a car outside?'

'There were a few.'

'But none outside this house?'

'No. Why? Are you expecting someone else? Should I scarper out the back door, and disappear?' he laughed.

She put her arm around him and they walked down the hall together. 'We opened a bottle of wine. Come in and have a glass.'

'No thanks, I won't stay long.'

He chatted for a while. Mary was in particularly good humour.

'I'll go, don't want to keep you up,' Mark said.

'Are you suggesting I'm flagging?' Mary asked. 'I'm full of energy.'

'There's no stopping her,' Grace said, with a smile.

'One of these days I might even be allowed into the locked rooms upstairs,' she directed her remark at Grace.

'Sounds like there's going to be a row here, I'll get out of your way then,' Mark laughed.

They stood together in the hall. 'I've missed you, Grace.' He kissed her.

'I've missed you too.' She leaned against him.

'Let's go upstairs later, will you unlock the door for me?' he whispered.

She giggled.

'Does your mother think we still hold hands like two kids?' he grinned.

'I don't know what she thinks. But I'll have to get back to her.' She opened the front door.

'I'm not letting you go.' He kept kissing her.

'Stop, Mark,' Grace couldn't help laughing.

'Let's go out at the weekend, have dinner, I just want to have you to myself for a few hours,' he asked.

'I don't know if I'll have time, love.'

He groaned.

'Go on, you'll have to go.' She held the door open.

'I'm being thrown out now. What did I do? Just tell me, please?' he begged, melodramatic.

'Get on with you, I'll see you tomorrow some time.'

After her mother had gone to bed, Grace smoked her last cigarette, and then took a shower. Upstairs she lay on the bed and stared around her at the towers of paper. Smoothed the surface of those sheets of newsprint on top of her duvet, and breathed in that

235

particular aroma which filled this part of the house. It gave her a high for a few minutes. But then her eyes filled with tears. How would she ever live without this?

Grace met with the team working with her on the cold case. 'Any joy on the list of people we interviewed at the time?'

'No.' The man stared at the screen and tapped quickly on the keyboard.

'We can't bring that guy in again unless we have something.'

'No.'

'What about the other suspects'?'

'We're trying to locate them.'

She sat at her desk. Looked at her own screen. The details of the man named Dave whom they had arrested. Everything about him. Family. Home. Personal details. Past record. She searched. From when he was a young boy picked up for shoplifting. And then released. Out on the street again. Arrested for criminal damage. Time spent in prison. A longer stretch. In and out of the revolving door. Until he was in his mid-twenties. Then unexpectedly he disappeared out of sight. And now years later he had reappeared without explanation. But he was just a name. A description. He gave nothing away. No matter how hard she looked. He was flat, one dimensional. A cardboard cut out.

Before Grace left for home she called in on the two members of the team who were still working on the trafficking case.

'I know I'm not on the case, but have you made any progress?' she asked. Aware that they didn't have to tell her anything.

'No, we still have surveillance on the houses and apartments but there has been no progress, although we're building up a dossier.' He went back to the file he was perusing.

'No sign of that guy I met at the club?'

'No.'

Grace stood at the desk, waiting, wondering, and felt suddenly superfluous. What was her role in the Gardaí now? She looked around the room. It was so familiar. But her assignment was not completed here. She fingered the edge of the wooden desk. It was smooth. How many days and nights she had sat here going through the facts they had amassed, looking for that tiny piece of information which would send her mind into another trajectory.

She wanted to look through the files again. Search through the gaps between the words. For something which had been missed. Imagined using a magnifying glass to enlarge everything. The letters of the report would be huge then. Big enough to walk around. The world between them a new place where everything was bright and clear. There the people they were looking for would be found. Those who had trafficked women and held them against their will. To be raped. Over and over. She shivered suddenly. Once again knowing how it must have been for them. For Elena. Sweat broke out on her forehead. Terror swept through and her body stiffened. A scream swirled in her mind. Stop. Tears gathered in her eyes. She rushed out of the office.

Peter met her. 'How's it going?'

She passed him in a rush.

'Grace?' He looked after her.

She went into one of the cubicles in the ladies room, and was violently ill.

At home, Grace went inside, turned off the alarm, and ran fast up the stairs. Unlocked the door, swung on to the landing and lay against the wall of newspapers, getting her breath. Here she felt safe. Her fingers gripped the ridges. Her face buried in their softness. After a while she went into the bedroom, threw herself on the bed and lay there staring into the darkness. A question banged in her head. Why was she ill? It was like that last time when Mark had found her and she had been brought to hospital. But she had never suffered in such a way before. And what about that sensation on her body? Like being at the beach and forgetting to shower afterwards. Tormented by the grains of sand which remained caught in the crevices of her skin. She wondered about going to her doctor and having a check-up. But how to explain what was going on in her life? There was no answer to that question.

237

Chapter Sixty-six

As if by telepathy, Grace phoned the following morning. 'Kim, I haven't seen you in ages, if I called in an hour would you be there?' she asked.

Ruth tried to sound enthusiastic. If she had to meet any more people who knew Kim she would scream. Dolores and Noel were bad enough, now it was Grace. She knew that Kim was very fond of her and that made it even more difficult. Quickly, she leafed through the pages of the notebook until she came to Grace's name, and read down the details to refresh her memory. And after the threats by John last night, she didn't know how she would even talk to the woman. Kim, where are you? She whispered. It was the fifth day now and Ruth simply couldn't see how she was going to continue with this charade.

'It's so good to see you.' Grace threw her arms around her, and hugged tight. 'How are you? And Jason and Lorelai?'

'Great thanks, come on in.' Ruth led the way into the kitchen, trying frantically to think of how Kim would have responded to her friend. 'Coffee?'

'Lovely.' She sat down, and put a box on the table. 'Some sweets for the kids.'

'Thank you.'

Ruth made it and poured. Put out some cookies, and the butter dish on the table.

'They look delicious, you're such a good cook,' Grace said, smiling.

'You know I enjoy it,' she murmured, taking a deep breath. 'What's been happening in your life?'

'It's been hectic, Dad's in hospital. He had a bypass.'

'How is he doing?'

'Making progress thanks be to God, Mam was really worried about him, we all were naturally.'

'I'm glad to hear he's recovering,' she said gently. 'And Mark, he's good?'

'You know Mark ...' Grace smiled.

'He's a nice guy.'

There was a strained silence for a few seconds. Ruth had to admit Grace was beautiful with that rich auburn hair tied back in a bunch. Her skin pale and creamy. Her green eyes luminous. A sudden longing came over Ruth, and she had an impulse to tell Grace everything and ask her for advice. She seemed such a nice person.

As Kim hadn't come home, Ruth had even wondered about employing a private detective to find her. But she had very little money in her bank account. John only ever gave her cash and even then any purchase had to be sanctioned by himself. Kim had given her two hundred euro but that had almost gone at the weekend. Now she had the five hundred Andrew gave her but that was already diminishing. There was plenty of food and cooked dishes in the freezer so she should manage to stretch out the money. But what to do as time wore on, that was her main worry. So anxious now she found it hard to hide it from the children.

'Have you been to the gym,' Grace asked. 'I just haven't had the time lately, I'm going to be so unfit.'

'I've strained a ligament, so haven't even managed a decent run. I miss the exercise.'

'We're a pair of crocks,' Grace said, laughing.

'Yea,' Ruth smiled.

'It's a pity it's so early, I won't see Jason. How is he?' Grace asked.

'Fine.'

'And Lorelai? Surely she's home from playschool by now?'

'She was tired and I put her down for a nap.'

'I'll go up,' She pushed back her chair. 'Just give her a kiss.'

Ruth was taken aback. She hadn't realised how familiar the other woman was with the children and the house.

Grace was out of the kitchen and up the stairs before Ruth was able to say anything.

She followed her into Lorelai's bedroom. The little girl lay asleep under her lilac duvet. Grace sat on the edge of the bed.

'She's such a pet, I think she's actually grown a lot since I saw her last. Her face isn't as pudgy.'

The child's eyes opened slowly, and for a moment she stared up. Then, with a cry, she threw her arms around Grace. They hugged each other.

Ruth had an inexplicable pang of jealousy.

'Thank you for waking up, my love, I thought I was going to miss seeing you.'

'My new doll cries tears, Daddy brought her back to me from *Merica*.' She slipped out of the bed and ran from the bedroom, followed by the two women. In the playroom Grace was shown everything. All her favourite toys were trotted out for approval.

'I'm going to take you home with me,' Grace laughed. 'Will you come?'

The little girl nodded. And then looked at Ruth who stood in the doorway watching. She felt under scrutiny. 'Would you like some lunch?' she asked.

'No.'

'Come on, just some salad, and chicken. It will be nice.'

'No.' She shook her head. 'Want to play with Auntie Grace.'

'I'm sorry, but I have to go, must get back to work.' Grace picked Lorelai up and swung her around.

'Don't go. Don't go,' she cried.

'I'll come again soon.'

'Please?' the child begged.

'Of course she will,' Ruth took Lorelai's hand, and together they walked to the door with Grace. 'It's been really nice seeing you, come over for dinner soon, and bring Mark, maybe Saturday evening? Andrew suggested it, he's hoping to be free.'

Ruth felt she had managed all right in the end.

'Thanks so much, but I'll have to come back to you, we're not sure what's happening with Dad.'

240

John couldn't get Grace out of his head. He had wanted her that night at the club and thought he would have her all to himself until she pulled the gun on him. That had taken his breath away. How could this have happened? What chink in his armour had allowed her in. Watching from outside. For God knows how long. Setting him up over weeks no doubt. Waiting to pounce. But he would have his revenge. For that night when she had taken control of him. No one did that. Least of all a woman.

He went around to the house in Rathfarnham again. 'What are you going to do?' he demanded of Ruth. He was getting very tired of this.

'I don't know,' she said hesitantly.

'You're going to stay on here and look after her kids and her husband, while she is off with her new man?'

Ruth didn't reply.

'It's bizarre. Do you realise that? You've subsumed your life completely and picked up hers. You have no personality now. You're a different person.'

'No, I'm still the same.'

'What about us?'

He didn't really care about whether there was an *us*. He just wanted to make her feel uncomfortable. He was still suspicious there was no sister at all and that he had been dumped. It angered him. But for the moment he was content to let things be. It suited his plans. He wasn't thinking beyond that. 'I miss you.' He pulled her towards him on the couch.

She resisted. 'I can't, the kids.'

'Come on, I'm longing for you.'

'They might come down.'

'Lock the door.'

'There's no key. Please my love, don't make me?' she begged him.

'Forget about them.' He kissed her. Sliding closer. Pushing her under him. 'You can't resist me, you know that.' He tore open the buttons on the silk shirt she wore.

'No, no …please?' She burst into tears.

'No, no? That's not very loving. What's got into you? Is it this Andrew character, your new husband?'

'Of course not, I told you.'

'Then what is it? Why have you changed?'

'It will be different when I go home. We'll be back to normal. This is just temporary, you know that.'

He closed her mouth with his, and cut off the sound of her voice protesting. Her breath was warm and drew him in. He ignored her cries.

John called a meeting with Victor. They met in Dalkey. They went through the cash receipts for the last month. The money laundering system. Arrangements for transporting the girls around the country. The level of business. Numbers of clients. Types. The whole structure of the business.

'Our costs for property has increased. Diesel has gone up,' John said. 'Margins have dropped.'

'Should we begin using those apartments again, the ones we thought the Gardaí had sussed?' Victor asked.

'No.' John shook his head. 'Take no chances there.'

'There's something else,' Victor murmured.

'What?' He raised his head sharply.

'Remember that murder case. Dave was involved. The Gardaí questioned him. Now they're bringing in more people. Trawling through everyone.'

'Are any of them on our payroll?'

'Not that I know of, but we don't know the background of all of the people we employ, so the net could spread wider.'

'Find out who else is on their list. We'll have to watch it and be ready. Can't afford to have them get too close to us. Could be dangerous.' John was concerned. 'Let me know if anything happens. We need to be ahead of them all of the time.'

He parked at the end of the cul de sac, and waited to see if she came out of the house to go for a run. But an older woman visited with her recently. Probably her mother, he surmised. And she didn't run as often. Occasionally the man went with her. If that happened his plans were thrown into disarray.

But tonight she was alone and he could feast his eyes on her. He followed. Although it was dark he could see her figure up ahead. Her arms swung athletically. Her hips moved. Her hair was tied back and bounced. She wore a white tee shirt and black track suit bottoms. Reaching the Dodder she took the pathway along by the river. He was taking a chance. She might recognize him. But he kept his head down. Just another person out for an evening jog. It was quiet. There was no-one else around. He knew in that place he could have taken her. Dragged her off the path. But really it was the enjoyment of the chase he relished and he had no intention of confronting her just yet. He would wait and bide his time.

Chapter Sixty-seven

Grace's Dad was transferred to a nursing home for a few days, and now it was even more difficult to keep him happy. He wanted to be home in Waterford. Back at the pharmacy. And resented this enforced imprisonment, which was how he saw it. 'But Dad, it's for your own good.' Grace tried to placate him.

'Liam, it's only for a couple of weeks, then you'll be back home, fit as a fiddle.' Her mother added.

He grunted. Sitting there hunched up in an armchair.

'Now, you have to follow the instructions of the consultant,' Mary said.

John's face was a picture of discontent.

'And I'll come in to see you as often as I can,' Grace added, her eyes meeting those of her mother. 'Bet you'll enjoy that.'

He grimaced.

'If you don't want to see me, then maybe I won't bother,' Grace grinned.

He turned to look at her. Obviously disappointed. 'Please come, I didn't mean to be churlish, it's just, I was longing to get home.'

'You're on the way to full recovery, every day you should feel better, when you come back you'll be able to do everything you used to do, although the consultant did say you have to cut back the hours.'

'He said that to me too.' Liam was gloomy.

'Just leave the pharmacy at six o'clock in the evening and don't go in until eleven, we can work it between us,' Mary suggested.

'But there's always so much to be done after we close, checking stock, ordering, balancing the books, and no one else can do it,' he pointed out.

244

'We'll have to look at that, and restructure,' Mary said, smiling. 'After a while you won't know yourself.'

He was silent.

They sat there with him until he had to go to the dining room for tea.

'We'll see you tomorrow.' Mary embraced her husband. 'Take care.'

'I will, don't worry, go on with you now.' He waved at them in an offhand way.

Grace went home now more worried about her father than when he was in the hospital.

'He's always more cranky when he's getting better, so I wouldn't worry too much,' Mary reassured.

'You know your man well,' Grace observed.

'Should think so, after nearly fifty years,' her mother retorted.

Later, they met Mark at a new restaurant in Temple Bar.

'You know, I'm really enjoying myself. Although I don't like saying that and your poor Dad so ill,' Mary said, with a smile. 'Better not tell him.'

'It's been lovely for us to see so much of you.' Grace covered her hand.

'I'll have to head back on Monday, and hopefully Liam will be discharged in a day or two,' Mary said.

'I'll drive you down if you like,' Mark offered.

'Not at all, I have my free travel, why would you be wasting petrol?'

Grace listened to her mother and Mark chat. They were firm friends now and she was glad of that. But as she had to fend off Mary's curiosity about the fact that upstairs was locked off, she was almost happy to see her mother return home to Waterford.

But Grace's recent visit to Kim had left her with a sense of disquiet. She couldn't quite put her finger on it, but there was something up with her friend and Grace was worried. She dropped in to see Kim again one morning.

'I had a call in the area,' Grace explained when she opened the door.

'It's lovely to see you, come on in,' she welcomed her in.

'I thought you might have been at the gym, has that injury healed?' Grace grinned.

'No.'

'Why not take a few sessions of acupuncture. It should help. I know how much you enjoy the gym. It's one of those things that keeps you going, gets all the adrenalin shooting around your system,' Grace encouraged.

She nodded, uncertainly. And flashed her a look.

To Grace it seemed almost like panic.

'I'm hoping to get back to it soon,' she said.

'Same here. I particularly miss running every day. If I can manage a couple of days I'm lucky.'

There was a strained silence between them.

'Are you feeling all right? You don't seem to be yourself lately,' Grace asked with a smile. 'I worry about you.'

'No, I'm fine. A bit tired maybe, the kids ...'

'Are there any problems, Kim? You know you can tell me anything. We've talked through enough things over the years,' she said, smiling.

'No ...but thanks ...' There were tears in Kim's eyes.

'Are you sure?' Grace took her hand.

She nodded.

'Thanks for inviting us on Saturday, I'll let you know as soon as I can, but everything's still up in the air. Dad should be discharged this week so I'll text you. Is that OK?'

'Thanks, I look forward to seeing you both ...' Kim said.

Chapter Sixty-eight

This time Andrew arrived home with presents for all of them. The kids went wild. He put his arm around her and pulled her close the minute he saw her. 'How've you been?' His eyes met hers, warm, teasing. He kissed her. It was like he was confirming that he owned her.

'Dad, it's a ship, great, thanks.' Jason was already spreading the Lego pieces on the floor.

'Do you like my doll?' Lorelai held up the pretty pig tailed doll for inspection.

'She's beautiful,' Ruth stroked the fair head.

'Shouldn't you be in bed, it's late?' he asked the kids.

They ignored him.

'I left them up just to see you,' she said.

'Come on now, up to bed, get your heads down on the pillows.' Andrew lifted Lorelai on to his shoulders and took her upstairs. She screamed with excitement.

'I want a piggy back,' Jason followed, pulling at Andrew.

'Wait down here,' he promised.

The child waited anxiously until he reappeared and took him upstairs on his back too.

Ruth bathed Lorelai and put her to bed. Sitting down on the edge of the bed beside her to read a page of her favourite book which was all about farmyard animals. Andrew took care of Jason and eventually all was quiet. They went downstairs again.

'Did you like your present?' He put his arm around her.

'Thanks, they're beautiful.' She touched the gold earrings he had brought her.

'Let's open a bottle,' he said, and took out two glasses and a bottle of wine. He handed her one, and raised his. 'To us,' he said, and reached to kiss her again.

They sat on the couch. She didn't drink and was very quiet. Couldn't actually think of anything to say, and let him talk on about problems he had during the week. A situation which could have proved dangerous with one of the other flights. She listened, dreading the moment when he would suggest going upstairs to bed.

'Did you see the parents during the week?' he asked.

'Yes. They called most days.'

'Did you invite Grace and Mark over?'

'Yes, but she's not sure about tomorrow, her father is ill.'

'Call her in the morning, if they can't make it then we'll head out on our own, the parents will babysit.'

She topped up his wine. Hoping that he might drink too much and fall asleep the moment he got into bed. But while he finished the bottle off, it didn't seem to have any affect on him.

It was after twelve eventually when they went up. She was frantic at this stage, and couldn't believe that he still thought she was his wife. There had to so many inconsistencies on her part.

Kim was missing a whole week now, and she still hadn't called or texted. Ruth's mind went around in circles as she tried to find an excuse not to have sex with Andrew. This whole thing was getting to her now. She would have a breakdown, trying to play the part. She had to chat with Kim's friends as she took the kids to and from school. Phone calls and texts came through regularly and demanded replies that made sense. She was especially nervous with Grace, having to be so careful of what she said. On top of that there was John's increasing anger towards her. And having to keep Andrew at bay. Ruth still prayed that Kim would contact her desperately conscious of her promise to hold it together for her sister if she didn't return as planned.

The moment they were inside the bedroom door, Andrew put his arms around her.

'I'm sorry, Andrew, but I've a terrible headache, I have to sleep.' She pulled away from him.

'What's this?' He asked, quite obviously irritated.

'It just came on. I feel quite ill actually.' She pressed a hand on her forehead.

'I'll make you feel better,' he teased, and kissed her. 'Come on, don't be a spoilsport. You know how much you love it.' He began to pull off the pink top she wore.

'No, I'm sorry.' She moved towards the bathroom door.

'What's up?' Annoyance crossed his face.

'I told you, I've a bad headache.'

'That's a right excuse,' he laughed, sarcastic.

'It's true.'

He stood looking at her. Silent.

She went into the bathroom, brushed her teeth and undressed, coming out a few minutes later wearing Kim's nightwear. He was sitting on the edge of the bed, naked.

She climbed into the bed and turned off the lamp on her side.

He got in beside her. 'Feel any better?'

'No, it's pretty bad. I took a tablet.'

'Go to sleep then.' He switched off the lamp on the bedside locker and the room darkened.

Ruth lay there, very much aware that he was angry with her. But she couldn't have had sex with him. She just couldn't.

The following morning, he was already up when Ruth awoke.

Downstairs she found him watching cartoons with Jason.

'Anyone for breakfast, what would you like?' She tried to be relaxed and normal.

'We've had ours,' Andrew said.

She made a cup of tea and toast for herself, and tidied around the kitchen. Then she showered, dressed and got Lorelai up. She wondered what they usually did on a Saturday if Andrew was home. He probably had his own plans. She had taken a casserole out of the freezer the day before, and decided to heat that for dinner. But if Grace and Mark came she would have to make something special. There were less prepared dishes in the freezer now. She looked in the fridge, making a note of the things they needed to buy. Milk. Juice. Fruit. Bread. Yoghurt. Biscuits. Eggs. The list got longer. She still had some money left and hoped there would be enough.

Andrew came into the kitchen. He said nothing and she could see immediately that he was still annoyed with her over last night.

He flicked on the kettle, and made a mug of instant coffee.

'Andrew? I wonder could you give me some more money ...' she hesitated. 'I need to buy food if Grace and Mark are coming to dinner, but we need a few basic things anyway. I've made a list.' She held it out to him.

He pulled out his wallet.

Ruth was silent. She simply didn't know what to say. She hated having to ask for money. As much as she detested asking John. The phone rang. She picked it up. Her pulse raced. Always hopeful that it was a call from Kim.

'Are we still on for tonight?' It was Grace.

'Yes, sure. Love to see you.' She forced enthusiasm.

'What time?'

'About eight?'

'Look forward to it.'

'So they're coming?' Andrew asked.

She nodded.

'You'll definitely need some extra money then.' He counted out two hundred euro. 'Is that enough?'

'Yea, thank you.'

'Cook something nice,' he moved closer and kissed her. 'How's the headache?'

Chapter Sixty-nine

'Kim is doing things differently now. It's like looking at someone in a mirror. Lefts become rights. Coordination is wrong. I can't understand it,' Grace said to Mark. 'Have you any idea of what I mean?'

'Is she unwell?'

'I asked her that.'

'And what did she say?'

'Apparently there's nothing amiss. Anyway, we're going over tonight for dinner, so you'll be able to see if I'm imagining all of this.'

Andrew opened the door. Chatting amicably, he ushered them in and poured drinks. Even apologised to Mark immediately about his attitude on the previous occasion they were over. He was in a jovial mood and to Grace, he seemed much happier than he had been in recent times. Leaving the men talking she went to find Kim who was in the kitchen preparing dinner.

'Hi there, it's great to see you.' Grace went over to where she was closing the oven door.

'Just checking on the lamb,' she said.

'How are you?' Grace asked.

'I'm good, thanks.' She picked up a wooden spoon and began to stir something in a pot.

'What are you cooking?'

'Sauce.'

'Smells delicious. You shouldn't have gone to so much trouble, something simple would have done us,' Grace said from where she now sat at the table.

'Hope you'll enjoy it.'

'We must have you back, I'm terrible, never returning the compliment,' she admitted with a sense of guilt.

'Right, that's perfect.' Kim poured the sauce into a sauce boat, and put it into the top oven to keep it warm. Immediately, she went to the sink and scrubbed out the pot.

Grace was struck by the tidiness of the kitchen. No dirty pots or pans to be seen, only the basic cutlery on the chopping board which would be needed. She laughed inside. Kim had changed in that respect anyway. Normally, once the pots were used they were piled up on the draining board and washed later. She said nothing.

'I think we're ready to serve,' Kim said. She went to the fridge and took out the starters which she put on a tray and carried into the dining room.

'Let me help you with that,' Andrew rushed towards her, took it from her hands, and set it on the table.

'Thanks,' Ruth said.

'What else can I do?' he asked.

'There's bread warming in the top oven, if you could?'

'No prob,' he said and disappeared into the kitchen.

Grace met Mark's eyes, and she stared at him pointedly for a few seconds. Whatever was going on around here it had affected Andrew as well. He was a totally changed person. The old Andrew hardly ever helped around the house.

'Right, let's eat,' Andrew served the food, and sat down himself. Then he raised his glass. 'To Kim,' he smiled at her, reached over and kissed her.

It was a pleasant evening. But for Grace it had a surreal quality. She didn't know these people any more, and found herself watching Kim in particular. Making a mental note of those idiosyncrasies she had noticed. How she held her knife and fork differently. Ate very quickly, in contrast to before. Drank more. Both of them did. And there were other things too. Andrew insisted on clearing the table. Again, this was unusual. These were small insignificant things which Grace almost didn't want to think about, and accused herself of being ridiculous. But she followed Kim into the kitchen and watched her put the dishes into the washer just before she served the dessert. She never did that, Grace said to herself. Usually they left the clearing up to the following day and laughed about it.

'Do you think I'm crazy?' she asked Mark as they drove home.

'Crazy?' he laughed. 'No, just a little unhinged betimes.'

'Go on, you're not taking me seriously.'

'I'll try.'

'It worries me. I think this woman is not the same Kim I know.'

'Impossible.'

'Did you notice the changes?'

'Not really. Then I don't know Kim as well as you do, and I probably never saw the things in her that contrast.'

'What about Andrew?' she pressed. 'He was so very friendly, and I was surprised at his apology.'

'No harm in that. Just wanted to clear the air between us no doubt.'

'But he was all over Kim. Like they've only just met. So peculiar.'

'Maybe they've just made up, fallen in love again.'

'No, it's more than that, much more,' Grace insisted, vehement.

'You're being an inspector. Leave that behind you in work.' He put his hand on her thigh with gentle pressure.

'I can't do that. I am what I am. And stop that, you're such a tease.'

'I'm just building up. I want you to be aching for me by the time I get you home,' he said, grinning.

'Remember I could have you up for careless driving. You might gain penalty points. Be heavily fined,' she warned.

'You'd do that to me?' He pulled a face. 'Your one and only?'

'I'll let you off this time. Just as a special favour.'

'The thought of that has certainly cooled my ardour.'

She laughed. 'When I get you home, I'll set a match to you and then you'll be all fired up again.'

'Can't wait.'

Grace and Mark didn't delay once they had arrived at her house. Mary had gone home, and Grace had been to see her father earlier in the day. He was in good form, and really looking forward to going home to Waterford.

She kissed Mark's lips slowly.

'I love you.' His hands traced the shape of her neck and shoulders.

'Mmmm ...' she moaned, loving the touch of him.

'I've missed you, my darling, you don't know how much.' He moved closer, his arms around her.

'I'm sorry, but with my mother here I couldn't relax,' her voice tailed off and she forgot about Mary as he moved closer to her and they moulded together, sweeping into a rhythm which took her into a magic place of love. She let herself go with him. His movements increasing in tempo as he brought them to a climax eventually exploding in delicious orgasm. They enjoyed this special time of ultimate communication. So in tune, it reinforced her love and she knew deep down that Mark was the only person with whom she wanted to spend the rest of her life.

'Let's move in together, Gracie, I need you.'

She was silent.

'Say when.' He kissed her.

'Soon,' she murmured.

'Promise?'

Chapter Seventy

Andrew flew into London and went to Staines. Sara had arranged for her mother to babysit and they went out for dinner.

On the surface everything was normal. But as time passed he became more and more anxious. Very worried that the next time he arrived home the woman who had taken Kim's place would be gone and he would have to deal with everything. Flashbacks sent him into the horror of that night. What if someone had seen him and reported him to the police? What if they had found Kim's body and were already looking for a man of his description?

He drank more than usual. Mixing shorts and wine.

'Just as well we didn't bring the car,' Sara laughed.

'You saying I'm drunk?' He was belligerent.

'No, just a little tipsy. But you've had much more than you usually drink. Anyway, tonight you're fun. Different. I like that side of you.' She leaned forward and kissed him.

'You like me?' he asked.

'Of course I do, I love you. That's the ultimate. I know I've been crabby lately but forgive me for that, it's because I love you so much.'

'You don't know me at all,' he stated bluntly.

'What do you mean? You're my partner. I know every bit of you,' she murmured, teasing. 'Every part of you. Come on, let's go home.'

He called for the bill, and paid it.

She took his arm and they left the place.

They went to bed but Andrew was unable to make love, and feigned sleep. His mind was in turmoil. He had murdered Kim. The events were replayed over and over. It was worse than any nightmare. In the morning, he got up immediately and began to pack his bag. He had to get back to Dublin.

'I thought you didn't have to go until tomorrow?' Sara was incensed.

'I made a mistake.'

'What? But we were going to take the kids out today, I promised Cheryl.'

'I'm sorry.' He was tight-lipped.

'Is that all you can say?'

He shrugged.

She burst into tears.

'For God's sake ...' He couldn't deal with this now. 'Next time we'll go somewhere with the kids, I promise.'

'That's all you say. Next time. With you it never happens. You're totally selfish. I don't know how I put up with you.'

'I have to get to the airport.' He went downstairs.

'You have kids here. What about them? Do you even care?'

'Of course I care.'

'What's going to become of us?' she screamed at him.

'I don't know,' he said and opened the door. Took out his phone and called a taxi.

He would take the first flight back to Dublin. His mind was a crazy whirl of uncertainty. He had to see Kim. And when he kissed her this horror would leave him. He could persuade himself that nothing had happened to her. He hadn't hurt her. She was still alive. His wife and mother of Jason and Lorelai. At home.

Chapter Seventy-one

Still curious as to what was going on with Kim, Grace called again one evening.

'How are the kids?' Grace asked, took off her coat and hung it over the back of a chair in the hall. Kim picked it up and put it in the cloakroom.

'I'm just about to put Jason in the bath, and Lorelai is already asleep. Do you want to make yourself a coffee, I shouldn't be long.' Kim ran up the stairs.

'Thanks I will. I'll make a cup for you as well.'

'I'd prefer tea, thanks.' Her voice drifted down from the landing.

Kim never drank tea, Grace thought, and here was this tidy thing again. Putting her coat in the cloakroom wasn't something Kim would ever do. Always too excited about seeing her to even notice where her coat had been thrown. And she would have brought her up to see the children immediately. They would have had fun with Jason in the bath, and certainly Kim wouldn't have left her downstairs alone. Grace wondered about that, went into the kitchen, put on the kettle, and took two mugs out of the press. She looked around and noticed Kim's handbag on the counter. It had been her Christmas gift last year. A black leather.

Reluctant to invade Kim's privacy, she hesitated for a moment, but then guiltily she went to the bag and opened it. Everything was in perfect order. A wallet was in one of the side pockets. Hairbrush at the end, with a small cosmetic bag. A bottle of perfume. Tissues in a holder. Immediately Grace decided that this wasn't Kim's handbag. She took out the wallet, listening all the time for footsteps on the stairs. She opened it. There was some loose coin in the purse. A small amount of money in notes of various denominations. All in appropriate sections. Photos of the children. Andrew. A family group at a barbeque in the garden, even herself and Mark included.

She heard Kim coming then. Quickly put the wallet back in the bag and reached for the tea bags, and coffee tin.

'I'm sorry for keeping you waiting, but Jason didn't want to go to bed.' Kim appeared.

'He can be a little monkey,' Grace said, pouring hot water over a tea bag. 'But he's a pet.'

'He is, they both are. Thanks for making the coffee.'

'I thought it was tea for you?' Grace asked.

'No, I always drink coffee.'

'But I ...' she was sure that Kim had said she would have tea, but immediately made a second coffee.

Grace did almost all of the talking. Mostly about the past and the things they had done. But Kim's replies were uncertain. Some events she didn't seem to recall, and only remembered them at a prompt from Grace, who continued to notice contrasts in her personality. As she listened to her speak she came to the definite conclusion that this woman was not Kim. The things she noticed about her were slight, but nevertheless all added up to the fact that this person had taken her friend's place. And Kim didn't meet her eyes as she spoke. They were everywhere else. Grace attempted to hold her glance, but a shadow came between them. A look of fear in those blue eyes.

As she drove away from the house, Grace decided to request one of her team to look into the background of Kim and her family.

258

Chapter Seventy-two

John sat in his car and watched the house. His face was pale in the shadows. Dark eyes stared through the windscreen. Teeth gripped his lower lip. Fingers twisted around the binoculars in his lap. Grace McKenzie had gone in earlier and turned on the light. Now he raised the binoculars and could see the shadow of her figure through the venetian blind which was not fully closed. He stayed there. A voyeur. Imagining what she was doing inside. It was after ten o'clock. She had been delayed at work, he guessed. He imagined she was waiting for him. Longing for him to arrive, a bottle of wine open.

The suspense was killing him. He wanted to go in at that very moment. But held himself back. This woman had many sides. He had only seen one but there were more. He was certain of that. There was a sudden shout from somewhere. A small car drove past. He tensed. Felt exposed. Had he been noticed? He looked around to stare into the shadows. Was anyone lurking there? But after a moment he relaxed back into the seat. The streets were narrow and here in this cul de sac only an occasional car came in and parked. Dark clothed people walked to their homes. Heads bowed. The night was damp, and a misty rain had begun to fall, visible in the dim yellow light which splayed down from the nearest lamp. His imaginings took him into that house. He would appear out of the dark. Take her by surprise. Then possess her. Suddenly a car drew up and pulled into a space not far beyond. He waited, breath held, to see who it was, relieved when the person went into a neighbouring house.

Sometimes he was there until the small hours. His mind and body with her when she went upstairs. But he was never quite sure where she slept. The lights were switched off downstairs, but no lights went on upstairs. Assuming she slept in a bedroom at the back of the house, he was prepared to stay there, growing closer all the time to when he would finally get in, and take her to himself.

He went back to Dalkey. Had dinner and sipped a glass of port. Afterwards he looked out over the sea. It was dark now. Only the waves, white tipped, breaking against the beach in the moonlight. Winter stretched ahead. Long grim days of rain and wind. He sighed. It was the one thing he hated about Ireland. He thought of the homes he had all over the world. In particular his place in the Caribbean. On the island of St. Lucia. A white colonial style house overlooking the beach built originally by the governor of the island in the early nineteenth century. He hadn't been back in a couple of years and now yearned for the gentle breezes off the aquamarine sea, the sigh of the palms, the waves lapping on to the white sand.

With the authorities on his heels he wondered how long he had in Ireland. His organisation was slick, and ran like a machine in the hands of reliable people who wouldn't have dared turn against him. He was at the helm. But no one knew who he was. Name changed. Looks changed. His present identity was not held on records held by governments, or police in any jurisdiction. He could run his business from anywhere, and now the only thing which kept him here was that woman, Grace. He couldn't understand himself. He could have any woman he wanted. He had mingled with famous people over the years. Beautiful actresses. Immensely rich heiresses. And here he was spending his time thinking about a cop. Following her around like a panting dog.

'Another of our men has been picked up,' Victor reported.

'Who?' John asked, angry.

'One of the drivers.'

'They're getting at us. Bit by bit ...eating away at us,' he snarled.

'None of our men have opened their mouths.'

'They're weakening the organisation.'

'They'll never do that. We're far too tight.'

'What makes you so sure?'

'We're too big, too strong. They'll only make a few dents,' Victor laughed.

'Yea.' He wished he could be as confident. 'Want a drink?'

He poured a whiskey for Victor and handed him the glass. Then he poured another for himself. 'I'm considering re-locating.'

'Boss?' The other man was surprised.

'The time is right for getting out.'

'Why?'

'Gardaí are too close.'

'What about the operation?' Victor asked.

'When I take my money out, then it won't survive.'

'I could run it.'

'You won't.'

'Why not?'

'It will be wound down, Victor. I'll pay you off. Make it worth your while.'

'But we do well, let me handle it here and take the risks. You could still make a profit.'

John looked at him. Suddenly he wondered if he should consider Victor's suggestion.

Chapter Seventy-three

Grace's father was well enough to be discharged from the nursing home. She picked him up and they drove to Waterford.

'It's great to be going home.' He sat back, a wide grin on his face. 'Thought I'd never make it as far as this.'

'I knew you would. You've got what it takes,' she laughed.

'And all thanks to you,' he said.

'No need for that, Dad.'

'Mam can't stop talking about how good you've been to us.'

'What else would I do? Have to look after you,' she smiled, pleased.

'You went out of your way.'

'I'd do it anytime.'

'Thanks love, I just wanted to say how much we appreciate you, and your young man too. He's a nice person, that Mark. You're lucky to have met him. Are you going to settle down together?'

'That could be some time away, Dad,' she laughed. 'I've already had this conversation with Mam.' Grace didn't say any more and they lapsed into silence.

She concentrated on her driving. Watched the road signs. Feeling suddenly nervous. Her heart raced. Palpitations throbbed in her chest. She prayed that it wasn't one of those panic attacks. Couldn't deal with it here. She turned off a roundabout. 'Almost there now,' she said, forcing an air of normality.

'That's great.'

She could hear the happiness in her father's voice.

A sign up ahead pointed to the road she should take. But beside it was also a sign for Tramore. Her heart raced even faster. She gripped the steering wheel, aware that the feeling in her hands had returned. But she couldn't do anything about it while driving. Even though there was nothing there, the impulse to remove it was very strong.

Mary welcomed her husband and daughter with open arms. Lunch was on the table almost immediately and after that Liam went to bed for a nap. It took a great deal of effort for Grace to compose herself and she hoped her mother wouldn't notice and ask questions.

'Your Dad seems all right, doesn't he? Surprisingly good really,' Mary said.

'He's fine, although it will take him some time to make a full recovery.'

'And he wants to go back to work immediately, but I'm not keen on that.'

'The doctor will tell him how much he can do.'

'He can come in and out. Sit and chat to people maybe,' her mother suggested.

'It will be hard to keep him down. He's stubborn,' Grace said.

'Like you.'

Her mother was right. She was a mirror image of her father.

'Are you staying tonight?' Mary asked, already working at the kitchen counter.

'No, I can't, must get back.'

'What a pity.'

'I'm sorry, I've work to do.'

'Can't you even wait until Dad gets up, he'll be really disappointed if you're not here.'

Grace glanced at her watch. She thought she would never get away. The sensation in her hands growing ever stronger.

To her relief, her father got up within an hour, and seemed fine. Immediately anxious to get back to normal, he suggested they take a short walk. Her mother agreed. But Grace demurred.

'I'm sorry, but I have to be on my way. But you two go ahead.'

Her father was disappointed, she could see that.

'You'll try and get down again soon, won't you?' her mother asked.

'Yes, of course.' She put her arms around her father, and hugged him. 'You look after yourself and don't do too much.'

'I won't, I'm just happy to be home,' he said, with a wide smile.

'He'll do what he's told, won't you love?' Mary covered his hand with hers.

'Your mother will make sure of that,' he said, grinning.

'Then I won't worry too much about you.'

'I just want all of us to go out to Tramore and walk that beach like we've always done,' her father said. 'Then I'll know I'm better.'

'And we will, all of us.'

As she drove away, Grace felt she was on the run. Darkness on her heels. Escaping from that place she loved most of all in the world. But the nearer she got to Dublin, the greater the sense of relief within her.

Chapter Seventy-four

Ruth gradually sensed that Grace did not believe that she was Kim, and had spent hours reading the notebook her sister had prepared for her, looking for insignificant details which she might have missed in order to prove to Grace that she was Kim.

But where was she? Ruth's mind was caught in a crazy spin of worry about her, and she was coming to the conclusion that it was time to report her sister missing. And take that chance that she would be exposed herself.

Suddenly, the front door opened, and she rushed out into the hall, surprised to see Andrew putting his bag down.

'Flight delayed, I got back for an overnight,' he said.

She stared at him, horrified.

'I've missed you.' He reached for her.

It was becoming more and more difficult to accept his embrace. Now she had an immediate antipathy towards him, and shivered in his arms. He held her tight.

'Where are the kids?'

'They're just having their lunch.'

He walked into the kitchen, his arm still around her shoulders. The kids screamed as soon as they saw him and rushed at him. He hugged them, laughing.

She felt more at ease now that he was busy with Jason and Lorelai, and had taken his attention away from her. She busied herself clearing up. If she could stay occupied then he might not take too much notice of her.

'Why don't you go to the park with Daddy?' she suggested.

'Yes, yes,' they shouted.

'Right, let's go then. All of us …' he looked at Ruth.

'I've things to do.'

'Come on,' he smiled at her.

Ruth shook her head. 'I'll have tea ready for you when you get back.' She went into the cloakroom, took out the kids' jackets and put them on.

'See you …'

It was then Ruth decided that she would have it out with Andrew tonight. Bring it all out into the open and talk about Kim and the fact that she was missing. For the millionth time she called Kim on the phone, but it still seemed to be out of charge. She made the decision, and was surprised at herself, but felt the better of it. Yes, after dinner when the kids had gone to bed. When he was relaxed. But then a sudden wave of emotion attacked. She would miss Jason and Lorelai, and couldn't imagine how life would be if she never saw them again. Torn in two, tears moistened her eyes.

As usual they had a glass of wine. Ruth wondered when she would say what was in her heart, but found it hard to build up the courage. Maybe it would be better to leave it until the morning, she thought. No, Andrew would be gone by then, it had to be tonight.

But in the end, she didn't have to say anything to him, as suddenly Andrew turned to her and looked deep into her eyes. 'You are my Kim?' he said, his voice intense. 'Tell me that you are.'

Ruth stared at him.

'Kim?' he repeated.

'You know I'm not,' she whispered.

'You are Kim,' he insisted.

'Let us be honest with each other. Please?'

'What do you mean?'

'Where is Kim?' she asked.

'You are Kim.'

'I am her identical twin sister. My name is Ruth.'

He stared at her. His mouth slightly open.

'Kim and I arranged this between us. She was suspicious of you and went to London. And she was due back the following day. But she never came back. How could she just drop out of sight? Do you know anything about it?' Ruth demanded.

266

'She's done a bunk. Gone off with some guy,' he grunted.

'Kim would never do that. What about the electricity bill she found? It was in your name at an address in Staines, I can show it to you?'

'That was all in her imagination.' His face twisted. 'She's a stupid bitch.'

She was shocked at his reaction.

'It doesn't matter about her. You're the only one that counts now.' He put his arms around her.

'But we have to find Kim,' she insisted.

'I don't want her back.'

'What do you mean?'

'We were over.'

'But surely she wouldn't leave the children, she adored them.'

'Stop talking about her,' he snapped.

'Stop calling me Kim, I'm not her,' she burst out.

'And you'll have to stay Kim, my wife,' he insisted.

'I don't want to be Kim. My name is Ruth.'

'You'll have to be her. That's the only way this can work.' He stood up, threatening.

'What can work?'

'You, me and the kids. This is our family.'

'You never thought I was Kim, did you?' she asked.

'No.'

'And you let me go on ...even tried to persuade me to sleep with you.'

'If you were playing the part you may as well have given it everything,' he grinned.

'It didn't include sex, it was just supposed to be two nights, me and the kids, I was the babysitter not ...'

'Maybe Kim was giving you to me. A going away present.' He sat down beside her again and ran his fingers through her hair affectionately.

'Don't be ridiculous.' She gave him a scathing look. 'Kim wouldn't use me like that. Anyway I have my own life, I'm not giving that up to look after you. I love the children, I wouldn't mind caring for them but certainly not for you.'

'Why is it so ridiculous? Would it surprise you that I feel more for you than I ever did for your sister?'

'That's nonsense, you don't know who I am.'

'Believe me, it's true.' Slowly he encircled her body with his arms and pulled her close.

'Take your hands off me.' Ruth struggled to get away from him. 'Did you do something to Kim?' she shouted. 'Have you hurt her?'

'Me?'

'Yes, you. She's been hurt. I know it. I feel it here.' She pressed her hand against her chest. There were tears in her eyes.

'Of course I didn't,' he blustered. 'How could you suspect me of that?'

'Then where is she?'

'I told you, she dumped me. Happens every day in life. Look around you.'

'Then if that's true why can't you accept it? Why do you have to live a lie? Just get someone in to mind the kids.'

'When I came back and found you here, I was shocked. But then you seemed to fit in so well, I thought you and I might work.'

'You're crazy.'

'Go along with it for a while, please Ruth, for me?'

'No way. It's difficult enough as it is. Trying to be someone else isn't easy.'

'I'll pay you,' he said.

She stared at him, astonished.

'Think about it. I'm flying to Melbourne and onwards from there, but I'll be back next week. You can let me know then. I'll make it worth your while. How's your own financial situation?'

'I don't need your money,' she snapped.

'No-one turns down money,' he said with a grin.

'Money doesn't mean that much to me, and certainly not if I have to betray my sister. What if she comes back?'

'She won't be back,' he muttered.

'How are you so certain?'

'I knew there was something going on. I'm away too much, it was easy for her.'

Ruth said nothing. Had Kim deceived her? Admittedly they hadn't met for many years, but she still felt her sister would not have left Andrew without taking Jason and Lorelai with her.

Chapter Seventy-five

Grace received the details of Kim's family. Where they lived. Dates of birth. Her parents' marriage. Their deaths. The hospital where their children were born. Plural. She was shocked. Kim had never mentioned having a sister. And naturally Grace hadn't been curious about her life. It was none of her business.

But this was something else. Kim had a twin sister.

All her suspicions jumbled about in her mind and reformed into a fact. A concrete piece of information. She read through the report more carefully now. Calmer. Her perception of what this meant becoming ever clearer.

This woman who lived with Andrew now wasn't the Kim she knew at all. Although they looked almost identical, there were differences between the two sisters. The more she had seen this other woman the greater her belief that she was not that lovely Kim of whom she had been so fond.

But where was the real Kim?

Her immediate reaction was to go over to the house. But she didn't allow that impulse to take control. She had to think logically about this. There were official Garda procedures to be followed now.

In the morning, she talked with Peter.

'I'll have to confront her,' Grace said finally.

'Need to be very careful there. We don't know what's going on,' he warned. 'Could be a domestic situation and if you interfere ...'

'Before I talk with her, perhaps I'll visit again and see if I can pick up anything else.'

'You'll have to have cover, you can't go alone,' Peter warned.

'I won't draw any attention to myself, it will just be a normal visit,' she insisted.

'But if this woman suspects anything, you could be walking into danger.'

'Lately I've been calling on spec at different times. There's no reason for her to notice anything odd about that.'

'I'll cover you from a distance then. A couple of roads away.'

'No, don't.'

'How will we keep track of her movements?'

'I'll do that. Starting right now.'

'If the Super hears you're doing this alone, there could be trouble.'

'Look, say nothing for the moment, this woman thinks she is my friend. I know her day to day routine. I don't have to follow her everywhere. But I can check in and out at various times and see if there's anything unusual. No one else can do that.'

'I was hoping you'd all be home.' Grace kissed Kim. In her mind she called her Ruth now, although she had no proof as yet. 'How are you? And Jason and Lorelai? I've brought a few sweets for them.' She handed her a box.

'Thanks.' Kim didn't meet her eyes, and simply ushered her inside the house. No kiss or hug.

Grace noticed that immediately. More sensitive now to her every move.

'Where are the kids?'

'In the playroom.' Without asking, Kim poured juice and handed her a glass.

'They're very quiet. I don't hear a thing.' Grace looked around.

'Lego and dolls,' she smiled. 'It keeps them occupied.'

'Can I go in?'

'I'll bring them out.'

As she waited, Grace watched.

'Auntie Grace,' the kids shouted, and ran towards her.

'Look at Peggy,' Lorelai shoved a long haired doll into her arms.

'She's beautiful, I love her already.' Grace hugged the doll.

'Auntie Grace, I've made a spaceship, it's huge.' Jason dragged at her.

'Later, Jason, Grace and I are talking.'

'I want to talk to Auntie Grace,' he yelled out loud.

'Jason, behave.'

'I won't.' He was stubborn. 'Come in and see my spaceship.' He pulled at Grace's jacket.

'I'll go with them,' she smiled and went into the playroom. Unable to watch Kim, her concentration taken by Jason's explanation of how his spaceship was made, and Lorelai passing doll after doll and other toys to her for approval.

'Grace, will you stay for tea? We're just having scrambled eggs.' Kim asked.

'Sounds lovely.'

The kids grinned and tucked into their meal.

Grace sat down.

It was pleasant. The kids seemed quite happy. Although she could see that Jason wasn't inclined to do anything Kim said, and was much more truculent than he had been in the past. Grace noticed that Kim was quite lenient and let the kids away with far more than she would have done in the past. Today Grace found it hard to keep the conversation going. Kim's reticence confirmed her suspicions and she waited now for an opportunity to catch her out.

It came when the kids rushed into the playroom to get something else to show her and Kim began to clear away the table.

'Can I give you a hand?' Grace asked, picking up some of the dishes.

Kim didn't seem to hear her and went out into the utility.

Then Grace took her chance, and called after her. 'Ruth?'

She turned back sharply.

The air hung with questions.

'That is your name, isn't it?' Grace asked, her voice soft, following her through.

She didn't reply.

'Tell me why you are here taking Kim's place? I've known for a while that you are not Kim. I'll admit you are identical to her. It's

272

extraordinary. But there are small differences between you …' she paused. 'Can you just tell me why?'

Tears flooded the other woman's eyes.

The doorbell rang.

They stared at each other in silence.

'I'd better get it,' she said awkwardly.

Grace looked after her. It was bad timing and her chance of finding out more about this woman had suddenly gone.

It was Dolores and Noel, Andrew's parents, and there were hugs all around. Grace hadn't seen them for a while and was glad of the opportunity. Curious to see how they reacted to Kim. But they immediately wanted to see the kids and even Grace wouldn't have noticed anything strange about Kim in the excitement.

'Would you meet me in the morning and we can have a chat?' Grace asked as she left.

Ruth was silent.

'About eleven, that suit you?'

'Yes,' she whispered.

'Do you want to choose somewhere?'

'It doesn't matter.'

'How about that place in Rathfarnham, it's called *Coffee* something, I can't remember the name exactly, but it's in the middle of the village.'

Chapter Seventy-six

The following night John went to Rathfarnham again. He phoned Ruth rather than texted, and forced a soft approach.

'Is the pilot here?'

'No.'

'I'm outside, can I see you?'

There was no response.

'Please?' He hated this begging thing. But he had to keep an eye on her. She could be a loose cannon, and he wanted to make sure he kept her under his control at all costs. He walked out of the shadows to the patio door.

She slid open the door, and he went in. Immediately putting his arms around her and kissing her. 'You taste so good.'

She let him kiss her, but there was an air of reticence about her. He didn't like that.

'How about a drink?' he smiled.

'Sit down. I'll get you a whiskey.' She went into the dining room. He followed her. Watchful. She poured it, and handed it to him.

'What about yourself?'

'I don't want anything.'

'Surely you won't let me drink alone, so unsociable. Come on. Where's the girl I used to know. You love a gin and tonic. Have one now,' he cajoled.

She poured a small amount of whiskey, and they went back to the lounge.

'I have to say I'm getting to like the new you. The clothes are different. Maybe you're more like your sister now. Maybe that's why I like you better,' he laughed.

She didn't reply.

'Cheers.' He raised his glass and sipped. 'What about your sister's friend, the inspector, have you got together for a chinwag yet?' he said, with a grin.

'No.'

'Didn't reminisce about the past?' He drew nearer to her.

She moved away.

'None of that stuff about remembering the nights you spent in town, the crowd, the fun? You're sure about that?'

She shook her head.

'I want you to tell me when she comes here and every word that passes between you,' he demanded.

'Why are you so interested in her?' Ruth asked.

'She's the one who ...' he muttered.

'Who what?'

'Never you mind about that. Has your sister been in touch with you recently?'

'No.'

'Fuck. What a stupid bitch. Or maybe a very clever one. Another drink?'

She went to get the bottle from the dining room, and refilled his glass.

He drank quickly. Leaned towards her. His mouth caressing hers. His hands wandering all over her body. 'Let's go to bed.' He wanted her now.

'The children might wake.'

'We'll be quiet,' he grinned.

'I don't want to go up. Not there ...'

'But I do,' he insisted.

Jason appeared, sleepy-eyed, in the doorway.

'Are you all right?' she went towards him, concerned.

'Who's he?' he pointed at John.

'A friend.'

'He's a burglar,' he shouted. 'Ring the police.'

'Fuck,' John swore, and took a swipe at the little boy who cowered away from him. He was taken aback. Bloody little shit. He thought.

'How could you?' Ruth took Jason back to bed.

John swallowed the rest of his drink. He was angry with himself for letting a small child upset him like that.

Ruth came back.

'I'm going. But I'll be back tomorrow night. Make sure that brat isn't hanging around. I'll belt him one properly. You know I have no time for kids.'

'You'll belt him one? You nearly did that tonight,' she said.

'Yes. And you too if you don't come home soon.'

Chapter Seventy-seven

Mark kissed her. 'There's been something on my mind lately ...' he said slowly.

Grace looked at him quizzically.

'I've held back but it has to be said.'

'That sounds a bit ...threatening,' she said.

'I don't mean it to be.'

'What is it?' She went in at the deep end. Aggressive. Suddenly knowing exactly what he was going to say.

'It's about ...' Mark began. 'The newspapers.'

She lit a cigarette.

'I know you didn't want me to know, but I guessed there was something ...'

'It's your job,' she said, unable to resist allowing a hint of sarcasm to creep into her voice:

'That's not the reason.'

'I've lived long enough here, haven't done myself any harm,' she countered.

'There are many dangers.'

'Oh yea?' She exhaled cigarette smoke. It drifted slowly upwards.

'I've heard of a man who was suffocated. Another who was burned to death.'

'I'm only buying a few papers,' she retorted. 'Don't be ridiculous.'

'I haven't got statistics, but ...'

'You haven't got anything.'

'That doesn't take away from the fact that you're living dangerously. Taking risks. Every day.'

'Mark, you're talking to me like I was a six year old.' She stood up and walked away from him.

'I'm sorry, but someone has to say it.'

'It's none of your business.' She turned on him, furious.

'Grace, I love you. I want to help. You can't continue to live like this.'

'Why not?'

'Because,' he hesitated, 'If it's not sorted, it will cause too many problems down the line.'

'So you're going to dump me, that it? Stop reading papers or else?'

'I told you I love you. I want to spend the rest of my life with you. But not with a third person between us.'

'The jealous lover. Can't stand the competition?' she quipped, with a laugh.

'I can't live with a hoarder, no-one can, surely you can understand that, Grace?'

'So you've put a tag on it now. I'm a hoarder,' she was really annoyed.

'Well, that's exactly what it is.'

'That's just a generalisation,' she flashed.

'I've seen it.'

'So you're the expert?'

'Look why don't I introduce you to someone I know ...he's very good and may be able to help you.'

'You haven't a clue. You have to be in the situation to understand, not just talk textbook. Theories.'

'I have been able to help some of my patients.'

'And how do you do that? Go and live with them?'

'Some drugs have been tried.'

'There's no drugs which can help. I've read up on it.'

'Then it's something you have to deal with yourself. Perhaps get therapy. Maybe look at hypnotism which could take you into the past and examine some of the things which happened in your childhood. It may go back as far as that.'

'Fancy doing that yourself. Dangling a chain in front of my eyes. You'll give me instructions . Go to sleep now ...relax ...close your eyes. Then you'll get me to behave like a chicken or do other crazy things. And with a click of your fingers I'll wake up and won't even remember what I've been doing.'

'If I thought it would help, I'd certainly have you behaving like a chicken,' he laughed out loud.

'It's not funny,' she snapped.

'The very idea of you squawking like a chicken is,' he grinned.

'You're making a fool of me.'

'No, Grace, love,' He stood up, put his arms around her and pulled her close to him. 'I'm sorry, I shouldn't have said anything, I've upset you.'

'You have,' she snapped.

'But you'll have to address this soon.'

'You can't get off your hobby horse, can you?'

He raised his hands in a helpless gesture. 'Maybe I can't, where you're concerned.'

'You don't know what it's like,' she retorted.

'I do,' he insisted.

'You haven't a clue.'

He left then, an ominous silence between them. She banged the door after him.

The following morning, Grace was very upset about the row with Mark. Her anger was spent now but she knew that unless she made some move to deal with the problem in her life Mark was gone. It was quite clear. A voicemail came through. It was him. An apology. Mark never harboured anger, and it was one of his better traits. But she didn't respond. What to say? *Thanks and I'll see you this evening?* Then start all over again until the next time? She sent a text. *Thanks. G.*

Grace was in the coffee shop first, and as she sat there wondered about Andrew's role in all of this. Did he even know Ruth was playing the part of Kim. He must. He had been married to the woman for years and had to know every nuance of her personality. How could Ruth persuade him that she was Kim? When they made love. In the darkness of the night. It was not possible.

279

Along with her concern for Kim's whereabouts was the increasing worry she had about the children. A strange woman was looking after them, but she purported to be their mother and Jason and Lorelai seemed to accept it. Admittedly she was their aunt but still there were a lot of questions in Grace's mind.

She opened up a notebook. Wrote down the names of all the people involved and stared at the information, hoping for a sudden flash of inspiration which would give her some answers.

Ruth came in, her umbrella battered by the rain and wind. She put it in the container at the door and came over, unbuttoning the short red jacket she wore. She seemed anxious, her face white and pinched.

Grace ordered a latte, and tea for Ruth, and tried to make this casual. 'Thanks for coming,' she smiled. 'I appreciate it.'

Ruth didn't reply.

'Are you going to tell me why you have taken your sister's place?' Grace asked.

'Is this on the record?' she whispered.

'No, of course not. To begin with this is between you and me.'

Ruth went on then to tell Grace why Kim had asked her to take her place, and what had happened.

The waitress came over with their order. Grace waited while Ruth poured a cup.

'And you say that it's been over two weeks since Kim went to London?' Grace asked.

Ruth nodded.

'Do you know if she found out what was going on with Andrew?'

'I didn't hear from her since she left.'

'Strange.'

'I'm really worried now. I was relieved when you realised that I wasn't Kim. I couldn't think what I was going to do. Andrew wants me to continue to live here with him as his wife and mother of Jason and Lorelai. He's insisting on calling me Kim even though I told him out straight that I'm Ruth but he doesn't want to see me as myself. He's even offered to pay me.'

280

'I wonder why that is?' Grace mused.

'I can't understand. I love the kids, don't get me wrong, they're great, but I'm not Kim and I can't play their mother or Andrew's wife either.'

'How were you able to walk away from your own situation for this length of time?' Grace asked.

'There's just my partner, we've no family.'

'Is he not anxious to have you back home?'

'Oh yes, and he is very angry now.'

'Do you have a job?'

'I work with my partner.'

'What business is he in?'

'Property.'

'Must be an amazing man if he agrees to let you play the role of another man's wife. Could be very tricky. Can you give me his name.'

'I'd rather not, he wouldn't want to be involved,' Ruth said, very nervous.

'Let me be straight. Does Andrew expect you to sleep with him?' Grace had to ask.

'He's only been home for three nights so I've found excuses, a headache, a touch of flu, I couldn't do that, not on Kim.'

'How does he react?'

'Angry.'

'I'll have to look into this.'

'But you said this was off the record.' Ruth's eyes were wide with fright.

'I won't involve you, don't worry, but I must find out what happened to Kim. Can you give me the address in London where she went?'

Ruth nodded, reached for her bag and pulled out the photocopy of the electricity bill.

'What was the date she left?'

She told her.

'Do you know the flight number, and the name of the hotel?'

She shook her head. 'All I know is that she took an early flight and left here about five in the morning.'

281

'That's enough,' Grace said, and stood up. 'Thanks for coming to meet me, Ruth, I appreciate it. When is Andrew due back?' she asked.

'Saturday.'

'Can you stay at the house until he comes back?'

'I hope so. But my partner is putting a lot of pressure on me, and if he finds out I talked to you he ...my life could be in ...' She stopped suddenly.

'Your life?'

Ruth's face paled.

Chapter Seventy-eight

John left the car parked some distance away from the house in Ranelagh where Grace McKenzie lived. He pushed up the hood of his black jacket, and hunched his shoulders. He drew near the house. She was home. The lights were on. The car in the driveway. There were low walls alongside a small gravelled area in the front and a wooden side door. It was only about five foot high and half hidden by a heavy growth of trees and shrubs. It could easily be scaled. He glanced around, the road was deserted. A strong wind blew and he was glad of that. He darted up the side of the house and hid among the bushes which twisted wildly and gave him enough cover to climb up over the gate and thump softly to the ground.

The area at the back was also gravelled, interspersed with flagstones and he took care where he put his feet as he crept around. A security light flashed on and illuminated the garden. He leaned back into the shadows feeling like an animal caught in the headlamps of a car and waited for something to happen. But he kept his nerve and didn't move. To his relief she didn't appear, and after a few minutes he relaxed. Standing there he mulled over possible ways to gain access to this house. If it was late at night the alarm would definitely be on and the whole neighbourhood alerted. Not that anyone took much notice of alarms but he had a dread of drawing attention to himself. He left the garden quickly the same way and returned to the car.

It was unusual for him to play the cat. Strange to pursue this woman. Watch her. And plan when he would make his move.

Chapter Seventy-nine

Grace had a meeting with the Super and received his agreement to contact the UK police and request that they check out whoever was living at the address Ruth had given her. Perhaps Andrew had properties in London and rented them out. Many Irish people had invested in England during the *Celtic Tiger* and she wouldn't have been surprised. But it seemed unlikely that Kim would be unaware of this.

And she was puzzled at Ruth's remark about her partner. It sounded as if he was a violent man, and would kill her if he found out she had talked with the Gardaí. What sort of person was he? Had he something to hide? If Ruth had given her his name then Grace could have checked up on him. Now she was worried about her safety.

The following morning Grace received a report from the UK. Andrew was apparently living with another woman in London. She was shocked. This information took her breath away. The audacity of the man. To live two lives in tandem and have each family ignorant of the other's existence. He had seemed to be the perfect husband. Well almost. Obviously stuff had been going on between Kim and himself in recent times. He was a bastard. Probably played around and then decided to settle with one of his women.

'I'm not surprised that Kim was suspicious, but what happened to her when she went over to the UK? Do you think she just went to the address on the electricity bill, knocked on the door and demanded to know what connection this Sara had with Andrew?'

Peter raised his eyebrows.

'I wonder did the woman Sara realise who she was and saw her as a threat?' Grace asked.

'Can we interview her, do you think?' Peter asked.

'According to the UK police this Sara knew nothing at all of a Kim Morris, and they didn't tell her that Andrew had another family here, although she is probably wondering now.'

'But Kim went to that house. That was her plan according to Ruth.'

'Difficult situation.'

'So Andrew's suggestion that Kim went off with another man seems improbable,' Peter looked down at his notes.

'I never believed that for a second. We'll bring Andrew in, see what he has to say,' Grace said. 'In the meantime, we'll check her movements. What flight she took. The hotel. Did she hire a car. Can you do that for me?'

'Yea, sure.'

The following day Grace went to Rathfarnham with Peter. He parked a little way up the road and she called to the house. She had talked to Ruth earlier, and found out that Andrew had already arrived home and was watching a football match. She asked Ruth to take the children out somewhere.

After they had left, Grace went to the house, and rang the bell. It took a few minutes, but eventually Andrew opened the door.

She smiled. Anxious to make this as pleasant as possible. 'How are you?'

'Fine, thanks,' he grinned. 'They're out. Gone for a walk. They left a few minutes ago for the park, you should catch them.'

'We can have a chat in the meantime,' she made a move to step inside.

'There's a match on, Man United,' he said. 'I'm watching it.'

'That will have to wait, I'm afraid.'

'What do you mean, Grace?' he stared at her.

'It's official, Andrew.' She pulled her ID from her pocket.

His face paled. He bit his lip, but let her in and walked into the lounge. 'What's this about?' he asked.

'Kim.'

'What do you mean?'

'That woman who has just taken the children for a walk is not your wife,' she said.

'That's ridiculous,' he burst out. 'Of course she is.'

'She's Kim's sister, Ruth.'

He stared at her.

'And she has told me that you know it.'

'Bitch,' he muttered.

'So you admit you're living with your wife's sister?'

He didn't reply. Turning away from her to stare out the window.

'I'll have to ask you to come down to the station with me.'

They held him in the interrogation room.

'Andrew, we have information that you have a second family in London. Tell us about that?'

He shook his head, and twisted his hands. He seemed very nervous.

His solicitor sat beside him.

'You have a partner and two children. Did Kim know about them?'

'No,' he muttered.

'Were you going to tell her?'

He shook his head.

'Did she go to London to see that woman Sara?'

He nodded.

'What happened when she went to that address in Staines?'

He covered his face with his hands, and burst into tears.

Grace glanced at Peter. They gave him a few minutes to control himself, and then began with the questioning again.

'Where did you meet Kim when she went to London?'

'At the house.'

'And Sara was there as well?'

'No, we were outside.'

'Did Sara know that Kim was there?'

'No.'

'Were you surprised to see her?'

He lowered his head again.

Each time they questioned him, he told them something else. A small part of what had transpired that night. How he had lost his temper. Their argument in the car. That she had threatened to tell Sara what was happening. And finally, how he had lost his head and strangled her. Slowly the bigger picture emerged. It was very difficult for Grace. Particularly when he described how he had disposed of her body. To hear this in his own words cut deep. The thought of him killing her dear friend was really too much and she gave up later that night and let Peter continue with another officer.

Before going home Grace called Ruth. Told her that Andrew was being kept in overnight for questioning.

'Do you think that he knows something about Kim?'

'I don't know yet, Ruth.' She couldn't have told her over the phone that Andrew was in the process of confessing to the murder of Kim. 'Are the children all right?'

'Yea, they're fine. What about Dolores and Noel? Should I phone them? Tell them what's happened?'

'I'll talk to them tomorrow. You're not expecting them this evening?'

'No, they usually call during the day.'

'How are you feeling?' Grace was very concerned about her.

'I'm up the walls, don't know what to think.'

'Phone me if you want to talk. Any time.'

Chapter Eighty

Ruth was stunned to hear they had held Andrew for interrogation. She sat in the kitchen staring into space, unable to get her mind around it. Did the Gardaí suspect that he had harmed Kim? Tears spilled down her cheeks. She hadn't been able to face it before, and vaguely thought that something may have happened to her sister, but all the time she had still hoped that Kim would come home.

A text came through.

Is he there? I'm outside.

I can't let you in. She texted back.

Ruth had begun to realise that perhaps she was better off without John. This man would never want to share a normal relationship with her. Always so sure that if they ever settled in one place she would be able to change him. She had been a fool. He only wanted to use her. To suit himself.

She stayed in the kitchen. Could hear him rapping on the glass, but was reluctant to stare him face to face, and ignored the noise. She was afraid, and wasn't going to give in. There was the safety of the children to consider. They were her responsibility now that Andrew had been taken into custody. She wondered how she would tell the children what had happened.

John continued knocking. The sound went through her head. She covered her ears, but it made little difference. The rhythm of his keys reverberated like a drum beat as he demanded entrance.

'What's that?' Jason appeared beside her.

'Just the wind, love.'

'It's loud,' he ran towards the sound.

'Jason?' she called. 'Come back here.'

He stood in the room staring at John through the patio door.

'It's the burglar,' he shouted.

She tried to take him out of the room, but he resisted her efforts. 'I'm going to shoot him,' he yelled.

'Let's go up to bed, pet.' She took his hand. In the last few days he had opened up a little more to her. Now he left his soft hand in hers, so trusting her heart missed a beat. This little boy. The little girl. It was only now she realized how much she would miss them. Ruth brought him back upstairs, feeling she should stay with him. It was difficult to keep him asleep these days.

'Why didn't you open up sooner, do you think I've nothing to do but hang around outside?' John shouted at her.

She didn't reply.

'Give me a drink.'

She poured a glass of whiskey and handed it to him.

He gulped it and wandered around the room. 'I've a job to do tonight and after that I'll be away. But when I return I want you back,' he muttered. 'This sister business is finished. Do you understand?'

'What job is that?' she asked. Suddenly curious. Normally she would never dare to ask him about work. 'Someone who has been on my back will finally be eliminated.' He swallowed the last of the whiskey, banged down the glass on the table and left without another word. Unexpectedly, Ruth remembered the evening when they had first met in the bar in Seville. She had fallen in love with him instantly. But it was only now she realised for certain that the man she knew then didn't exist any longer. As Ruth watched him disappear into the shadows, she had decided never to see him again. She waited for a while to make sure he wasn't coming back. And then picked up her phone. 'Grace?'

'Yes Ruth?'

'There's something I must tell you...'

'What is that, Ruth?'

'I'm not sure about this, but I think you could be in danger. Please take care.'

'What is it about?' Grace sounded puzzled.

'John was here.' Ruth had gone so far now, there was no going back.

'Who?'

'My partner.'

'And what has he to do with me?' Grace asked.

'He threatened to ...harm you.'

Chapter Eighty-one

Grace drove through the rain. A heavy downpour. Within a short time the streets sloshed with water. Parking the car in the driveway there was only one thing on her mind. The warning Ruth had given. Now she needed to be prepared. Without even picking up her briefcase or bag, immediately she ran for the doorway, opened it and stepped inside. The alarm access sound beeped and she punched in the code. As it ceased, she was aware of a shadow crossing behind her and swung in response to find that something hard had been pushed into her back. She knew instantly what it was. The thought of setting the alarm off again crossed her mind for a second but that was immediately dismissed, these crazies were unpredictable. And who would notice the alarm going off anyway?

Grace took a chance, pushed her body against him, glad when he lost his balance and stumbled. She ran up the stairs two at a time her fingers gripping the key to the landing door. She had to get to her own gun.

He was just seconds behind as the door opened and she flung herself along the landing and into the bedroom. But he caught up, wound his arm around her neck and forced her to a sudden halt. She managed to swing around and throw herself on him. Shouting. Fists swinging, automatically in *Karate* mode, and knocking his gun to the ground. But suddenly, he raised his arm and a shining blade snapped out of a black-gloved hand.

Grace froze. Her breath held. Knowing that it was insane to take another chance.

He held the knife close to her neck. The pressure of metal against her skin was cold. Her pulse raced. She dug fingernails into her palms to control any reaction which might startle him.

'The light,' he ordered, his voice rough, with a slight trace of an English accent.

Slowly she reached for the switch. The room was illuminated. Now it would be impossible to get the gun.

'Fuck ...' he muttered, his lips distorted through the black mask he wore.

He forced her backwards then. Hard. She lost her footing and fell on to the bed with him on top. The papers crinkled with the weight of their two bodies. So close she could smell him. A highly perfumed odour. She wanted to shout. To thump his face. To push her fingers into the dark glittering eyes. But forced herself to stay quiet, the knife still at her throat, knowing that this man wouldn't hesitate to cut her to pieces.

Terror swept through her. Flashes of another time. The beach in Tramore. The wind. The crashing waves. The struggle. Her screams for help. Just sixteen years old.

Through the opening in the balaclava his lips touched hers. She almost gagged. Suddenly an idea occurred. The wall of papers was close to her. The bundles tied with twine. The knife moved downwards and slashed through the fabric of her blouse. He leaned closer. His lips pressed on hers again, harder now, forcing her mouth open. She found it more and more difficult not to fight him. But her fingers slowly curled around the twine on the bundle of papers nearest to her, regretting the fact that she had tied it so tight.

The knife caught the centre of her black lace bra and it snapped. Grace was exposed to him. Her chest heaved as he pushed back the sides of the bra. His fingers traced the shape of her breasts. A shudder vibrated within her. The knife still hovered close to her skin and she was very aware of how lethal that shining blade was.

Grace tightened her grip around the twine, hoping that when she tugged it the tower above would be destabilised. One day while trying to push extra issues into the wall, something like that had happened and she had to lean against it to prevent the bundles from falling down on top of her. She murmured a prayer in her head. He slashed through the waistband of her skirt. She gasped as the blade cut her skin. It was painful.

'Fuck you,' she shouted, but paid the penalty as he brought the knife up to her forehead. Pressed the point into her skin. Blood dribbled down between her eyes.

'Bastard,' she dragged the bundle out with a jerk. There was an increasingly loud rumble and suddenly the papers collapsed down on top of them in a cloud of dust.

Grace was stunned. The weight of the man's body and the bundles of newspapers almost crushed her. It was difficult to breathe. He lay quite still and she struggled to get out from under him praying he was unconscious. She was weak and made little progress at first. But gradually managed to push her way out of the room through the piles of loosened papers.

She crawled along the landing. The key was still in the door. A huge relief when it clicked into position. That sound which told her he was held inside and couldn't get at her. She leaned against the door, aware that blood dribbled down her face. She tried to stop the bleeding with her hand. At the same time searching in her jacket pocket for her phone to call for help. It hit her then. She began to shake and burst into tears.

Grace had escaped today, but hadn't been so lucky all those years ago. Then a man had succeeded. Cut down her innocence with such brutality the horrific experience had overshadowed her life.

Peter arrived first. She sat at the bottom of the stairs smoking a cigarette, wrapped in a raincoat. Her face in her hands. He put his arm around her. 'What happened, Grace?'

'There's someone upstairs.'

He bent down to look closer at her. 'You've been hurt, you're bleeding. I'll call an ambulance.'

'No, I'm all right, I want you to go up, he's there,' she shuddered. 'But be careful, he has a knife and a gun. Here's the key.'

It was only when she saw the flashing blue lights outside that Grace began to feel safe. Other Gardai arrived after Peter, and they went upstairs, followed by the paramedics.

'Grace?' Mark appeared in the doorway. 'What happened, my love?'

'A man ...' It was difficult to explain exactly. Terrified to even think of it. She burst into tears again.

He put his arms around her. Pressed his handkerchief against the injury on her forehead. She smoked another cigarette and slowly managed to get control over herself.

Peter came downstairs.

'Has he come to?' she asked.

'No.'

'He's badly injured?'

He nodded. 'Yea.'

Her eyes widened in shock. 'He's dead?' she gasped.

'You were very lucky.'

She was stunned into silence.

'Crime scene guys are on their way, and we have to wait for the State Pathologist,' Peter said and hurried back upstairs.

'Grace, you'll have to go to the hospital,' Mark said.

She shook her head. 'No, they'll need me here, but ...will you stay with me?' Her eyes were large green pools filled with sorrow.

'You don't have to ask me that,' he said, and kissed her.

'Thank you ...I love you, Mark.'

Chapter Eighty-two

As the paramedics took care of Grace, Peter called Mark upstairs. 'I think you should have a look up here.'

Mark stared into the dark aperture. He was horrified. But not surprised.

'I can't let you in yet,' Peter explained. 'How she could have lived in such a place is beyond me. Downstairs is so different. This is the stuff of nightmares.'

'I had an idea there was something going on, but she wouldn't tell me. It's much worse than I had imagined,' Mark said.

'This is your field. You deal with it every day.'

'And it's surprisingly common.'

'Strange she didn't confide in you. You'd be the most obvious person.'

'It's difficult for someone to admit they have a problem. It means having to go back through their lives to try and pinpoint the origin. It can be very tough.'

'I saw a programme on television about hoarding. It was incredible.'

'There are many reasons why a person might begin to hoard. We all have an element of that in our personalities.'

'I know. My mother has an amazing amount of stuff collected at home,' Peter said.

'People hold on to things for sentimental reasons particularly. Then at a further stage they can't bear to see an empty space, it has to be filled with something,' Mark explained.

'It's sad, how will Grace ever deal with this?'

'I don't know.'

'We should insist she goes to hospital. Apart from the physical injuries there is an element of shock,' Peter said.

'It will be hard to persuade her, you know Grace.'

'Tell me.'

'It seems to have been a very personal attack, not a random burglary, would you agree?' Mark asked.

'Yes, and only for those papers she might be in a much worst state.'

'What do you mean?'

'It looks like the wall of newspapers over the bed collapsed. And he got the brunt of it. We'll find out from Grace exactly what happened later.'

'It must have been terrifying for her.'

The two men were silent for a moment. Then they came back downstairs.

Mark had been very worried about his relationship with Grace. He had been too blunt that last time. Although all he had wanted to do was help. Afterwards, he regretted his frankness, and knew he should have been more sensitive towards her. That row had been the worst yet. But now suddenly her words had given him hope. If she loved him as much as he loved her then surely nothing could stand in their way.

Chapter Eighty-three

It was only now that Grace understood why she had such a sense of sympathy with Elena, and all the other women who had been trafficked. When that man had attacked her, she knew only a primeval need to escape from him. Had felt his lips. His body. His hands. And was swept back into the past. To when someone else had forced himself on her. Aged just sixteen, she had been afraid to tell anyone, and held the horror deep within her heart.

He was her cousin. Someone she had known for years. She was a girl without any experience. Knowing nothing of sex. Messing around with boys consisted of kissing, and touching, terrified of going any further. One or two girls in the gang described how they had done *it*, but Grace hadn't met anyone who could have persuaded her.

But this boy had grabbed her and held her down in the sand dunes of Tramore beach. All those years ago she had to endure the rape. That ghastly loss of innocence. A savage act.

But tonight her own weakness had intervened and saved her life.

Mark took her home with him, and she lay in bed beside him but couldn't sleep. The images in her head a crazy mix of the beach in Tramore, and the man with the knife. Dark nightmares. Reluctant to smoke in Mark's bedroom, she had to get out of bed and go downstairs to have a cigarette more than once. Each time Mark followed her. Waited silently until she finished, put his arm around her, and brought her back upstairs again. They didn't talk. Grace couldn't have explained exactly how she felt. Although she was aware that all of this needed to be purged. She must move on, and leave the baggage in the past. And hope Mark would still be there for her in the future.

The following morning, as soon as Mark had left to go to work, Grace took a taxi to Dundrum Shopping Centre, and did some shopping for clothes. She didn't know when she would get back into the house and bought a few items to keep her going. The only visible injury was the cut on her forehead which was covered by a plaster and was just below the hair line. While bleeding profusely at first, it had only required a couple of stitches, and would heal naturally without scarring. She left her hair loose and it was almost completely hidden. The injury on her stomach was nothing more than a scratch. Then she went into work.

'What are you doing here?' Peter stared at her. 'You should be resting. You're not well enough to be at work.'

'I couldn't have stayed there thinking about it.'

'I suggested that Mark keep you at home and not let you near this place,' he said. 'And I was serious about that.'

'He thinks I'm there,' she managed a smile.

'Sit down.' He pulled out a chair.

'What is the situation with Andrew?' she asked.

'He is in court today. We have a full confession and he will be extradited to the UK when Warrants arrive.'

'What about the woman in England, the second family?'

'The UK police are handling that.'

'I wonder had she anything to do with Kim's murder?'

'Andrew said not.'

'Can we believe him, he's obviously a serial liar.' She bent her head. Tears suddenly brimmed. She covered her eyes with her hand.

Peter pushed a box of tissues across the desk.

'Has he given you more detail about what he did with …Kim?' she struggled for control.

'He said he'll take the UK police to the place, he can't explain exactly apparently.'

She pressed a tissue against her lips.

There was a silence between them. Peter busied himself.

'Where is the man?' she whispered.

'At the hospital. They've carried out a post mortem.'

'How did he die?'

'It was a freak accident. Whatever angle he was at, one of the newspaper bundles hit him and broke his neck.'

'Who is he?'

'No ID. But remember that guy you met at the club in Leeson Street on the prostitution case. You gave us a rough image. Well, the corpse looks a lot like him.'

'What?' She was taken aback. 'I can't believe I didn't recognize him.'

'How could you, he was wearing a mask.'

'Oh yea, he was.' She thought back. Tried to see similarities. Her memory of the night before was hazy. The order in which things happened very confused.

'He must have had it in for you.'

'Bastard,' she spat the word out.

The Super leaned back in his chair and looked at her. 'You don't look in great condition, how are you?'

'I'm all right,' she said, defensive.

'I want you to step back. Your life is in danger. The word may have already gone out, you don't know.'

'The job is dangerous,' she stated. 'Always was, always will be. And the only thing you say to me lately is to take time off.'

'So do what I say.'

'I enjoy the risks.'

'Grace, you're one of my best officers, I must protect you.'

She sighed.

'On the other matter, there will be an investigation into the way the man died at your house.'

'I've been thinking about that.'

'Is there any reason to suppose that you caused the collapse of the stacked newspapers?'

'Yes, I did,' she said.

'You were lucky that it was possible.'

'I pulled out one of the bundles. I was hoping the wall would fall before he managed to kill me.'

'So it was self-defence?'

She nodded.

The Super made a note on his pad.

'About the Andrew Morris case?' she asked.

'Now that he has confessed it should be all wrapped up without much trouble. You don't have to be part of this, you're too close.' His tone was brusque.

'There's just one thing I want to do,' she paused for a few seconds, hoping he would agree. 'And that is to tell Kim's sister that Andrew has confessed. Also I want to talk to the grandparents. And what about the children?'

'We'll send an officer around, with a counsellor.'

'No, let me,' she insisted. 'Please? And I'll take Mark. He knows them anyway so it might be easier.'

'All right, if you feel up to it,' he agreed. 'But keep a low profile. We don't know why this guy assaulted you, and if he's not working alone and is part of some criminal group then you're still in danger.'

'Who else knows about me?' Grace asked him.

He looked up sharply. 'What do you mean?' he asked.

'You know, the newspapers.'

'A few people,' he paused. 'I'm sorry, but under the circumstances it couldn't be helped. You should talk to Mark, he might be able to help.'

'I can handle it myself,' she said abruptly.

'How long have you been ...collecting?' the Super asked. It was a soft enquiry and held no accusation.

'I'm not sure, years.'

'Something like that builds up.'

'Have you known anyone else who ...?' she asked.

'Yes, a relative.'

She leaned forward across the desk. Suddenly anxious to find out what he knew. 'And did they manage to kick it?'

'With a lot of help,' he said.

Ruth opened the door, a look of dread on her face. Immediately Grace put her arms around her and hugged. 'I'm so sorry to tell you this, but ...' she murmured, finding it very difficult.

'She's dead, isn't she?' Ruth burst out.

Grace nodded, and held her close. It took a while before she stopped crying.

'I had hoped there was another explanation. I didn't care what that was. Even if she had set me up and run away ...but now, to know that she's dead is ...'

'Andrew confessed,' Grace said.

'It was him? How he could have done such a thing?'

'It's such a loss for you to lose your twin sister. You must have been so close.'

'We were at one time, but we hadn't met for many years, and that was all my fault,' Ruth said.

'I'm sure she was really happy when you made contact,' Grace said.

'It must have been hard when you realised that I wasn't Kim.'

'She was a wonderful person, and you are too,' Grace said.

Ruth shook her head. 'No I'm not, if you only knew.'

'I don't believe that.'

'There was something on the radio this morning about an inspector being assaulted. Was that you?'

'Your warning was too late, and thank you for calling me, it must have been difficult,' Grace said slowly. 'Can I ask you to tell me the name of your partner?'

'He's my ex-partner now, I've had it with him,' Ruth said, bitterness in her voice.

'We want to check him out, just in case he has any involvement. Although the man who assaulted me may not be your partner.'

'I'm so glad you're OK,' Ruth said.

'More or less,' Grace murmured. She didn't want to go through the experience of the night before, but knew she had to find out what Ruth knew. 'The man who attacked me is dead, we don't know who he is.' She took a deep breath. 'I wonder ...would you have a photo of your partner?'

Ruth went upstairs and after a moment reappeared and handed it to Grace.

She stared at it, and knew instantly that it was the man in the club.

'Could I ask you to identify the man who attacked me. You may know him,' Grace asked.

Ruth looked frightened.

'I'll be with you, and it won't take long. It's important,' Grace reassured.

Chapter Eighty-four

Ruth was nervous. While she had become very much afraid of John, she wouldn't have wished him dead. And had felt a terrible guilt that she had warned Grace against him. He hadn't been in touch since last night and she prayed that the person in the morgue wasn't him.

'Are you all right with this?' Grace asked before they went through the door. Mark and Peter had gone in ahead of them.

Ruth nodded, hating the atmosphere of the place. She had never been in a morgue before. Their footsteps were loud on the tiled floor as they walked down the long corridor. A man in a white coat appeared up ahead and ushered them into a room. She didn't want to look around, and kept her eyes downwards.

'Ruth?' Grace indicated a trolley up ahead. There was a body lying on it covered with a sheet.

She turned away, feeling sick.

'It won't take long, just a little further,' Mark murmured and took her arm.

The doctor lifted the top of the sheet. She stared, gave a little gasp and fainted.

Ruth came to almost immediately and stared up into Grace's concerned eyes.

Mark still had his arm around her, and now helped her walk out of the room and sit in the waiting room.

'Here, have some water.' Grace handed her a glass.

For Ruth, it had been horrific to see John lying there. His face white. Devoid of any expression. Skin like porcelain. And very obviously dead.

Chapter Eighty-five

It had been very difficult for Grace to go to the morgue, and although she had given her word to be with Ruth when she went to identify the man, she still struggled to deal with it herself. This was the man who had assaulted her. It was how she described the event. How her work colleagues described it. But she knew it was much more than that. For her. It was a defining moment. When she had been forced to stare into the eyes of the monster which had overshadowed her life since she was sixteen.

In those last moments at the morgue, Grace had hung back, reluctant to go any further, and left Ruth with Mark and Peter to make her final identification. But then suddenly she needed to see him. To satisfy herself that he was actually the man she had met at the club in Leeson Street. Tears moistened her eyes as she recognised him. Those smooth features now cold in death. Suddenly she could see the face of her cousin superimposed. The images merged. She turned away. Sickened. Her attention taken by Ruth who had fainted.

Grace stayed in the house at Rathfarnham with Ruth that night. She couldn't have left her alone, but it made the loss of Kim all the more painful.

In the morning, Ruth took the children to school and when she returned they sat opposite each other at the kitchen table. At first there wasn't much conversation. A relaxed silence between them. Outside the large patio window the trees twisted this way and that in the wind. Leaves scattered on the patio, and Grace remembered a day in the summer when they had been invited here for a barbeque with Kim and Andrew's friends and family. It was an exceptionally warm day and people sat around in the sunshine enjoying a glass of wine. The kids screamed with excitement, and Grace remembered how Mark and herself had played a game of football with them, run ragged by the end of it. Tears moistened her eyes.

'I suppose we'd better get started,' Grace smiled, reached into her bag and put a tape recorder on the table.

Ruth stared at it, a look of fear on her face.

'I'm sorry but I have to keep a note of everything you say.'

She nodded.

It took a while but with some gentle encouragement from Grace, she began to explain how she had lived with John.

'He forced you to get involved?' Grace asked.

'I didn't want to at first, but I love him ...loved him then. I worked on the computer mostly. And then collected and delivered money. It didn't seem real. I might have been playing a game.'

'Can you tell us the names of the other people involved?' she asked.

'I only knew the first names of a couple of guys, but didn't know the people I met when doing collections. Although I remember some of the places I called to.'

'We'll have you look at some mug shots. You might recognise one or two of them.'

Ruth glanced at her watch. 'I'll have to pick up Lorelai from school but I'm worried, how will I tell the children about their Dad?'

'I don't know, it's a very difficult one. We won't do anything just yet, I'll talk to Dolores and Noel. It's going to be very hard for them.'

Ruth nodded.

'There is something else and I hope it won't upset you too much,' Grace said, 'I wonder would it be all right if we checked out your home.'

'The place in Dalkey?' she asked.

'If you don't mind.'

'We've only been there a few weeks, I don't really consider it home.'

'Then you won't mind so much?'

She shook her head. 'I'll give you the key.' She opened her bag and searched for it. 'There's a security code …'

'I'll make a copy and get it back to you,' Grace promised.

Chapter Eighty-six

Victor met Dave at the usual place. He ordered two pints. They drank slowly for a time. Talked about the soccer match which had been played the night before. And argued whether or not a penalty should have been allowed.

'John's dead. And the woman is talking to the *Branch*,' Victor said in a low voice.

'I heard.' Dave gulped his beer.

'Do you think she'll give them everything?'

'Incriminate herself then.'

'Hardly likely to do that. It would be crazy.'

'If they manage to break into the computers then we're finished. What do we do?'

'John was going to re-locate. Switzerland. Wind up the operation.' Victor stared across the pub.

'We'll have to do the same, get out while we can,' Dave grunted. 'I've been in Spain for the last couple of weeks, suppose I could stay on and continue the business from there.'

'Not if that bitch opens her mouth.'

'Should we eliminate her?' Dave asked.

'Yes.' Victor's voice was cold and full of purpose.

'She's been staying somewhere else lately, John wasn't too pleased about that.'

'Been looking after someone's kids. He asked me to keep an eye on her. She has a regular routine. School runs. Shopping. Swimming. The park. She's there most nights.' Victor took a notebook from his back pocket.

'We'd have to make it fast, will I do it?'

'No, I will.'

Chapter Eighty-seven

Grace and Mark stood outside the front door of the home of Andrew's parents, Dolores and Noel. He rang the bell. Grace was nervous. Hating the thought of this.

The door opened. Noel stared at them. A look of fear on his face. He didn't say anything.

Dolores appeared behind him. 'Is there something wrong, Grace?' she asked immediately.

'We have something to tell you,' Grace said.

'What ...?' Both spoke at the same time.

Grace felt panic inside her. 'Maybe we should talk in the house?'

They moved down the hall and into the living room.

'Please sit down,' Grace said.

There was an air of questioning between the couple.

'This is going to be difficult for you but ...' Grace went on to tell them what had happened.

Dolores burst into tears.

'For a minute I thought you were going to tell us there had been a plane crash,' Noel burst out.

'He couldn't possibly murder Kim, it must have been someone else or maybe an accident. I don't believe it. Not Andrew. There's no way ...not my baby.' Dolores sobbed.

'He's our son, he loved Kim, they were so happy together,' Noel wiped his eyes, he was as distraught as Dolores. 'And we only saw her yesterday or the day before. How is all this possible,' he demanded.

'That wasn't Kim. It was her sister Ruth,' Mark said.

Noel put his arm around Dolores. She collapsed into him.

'We're so sorry to give you such terrible news,' Grace said, gentle.

'Where is Andrew now?' Noel asked.

'He's in custody, and will be sent to England for trial. He confessed,' Mark explained.

'Why is he going to England?' Dolores raised her head.

'Kim had gone over to see Andrew and it happened there.'

Grace left it at that. She didn't go into the detail of why Kim was in the UK. She felt it would be too much for the couple to take on that as well as the fact that their son was going to be tried for his wife's murder. They would find out in time. She tried to comfort them.

'Where is Andrew now?' Noel asked.

'Mountjoy.'

'And Jason and Lorelai?' Dolores asked.

'They're at home.'

'We'll go over to see them, the poor things.'

'They don't know anything yet, it's going to be a very difficult situation for them.'

Ruth invited them in. The children were excited to see their grandparents. Dolores and Noel hugged and kissed. But they didn't take much notice of Ruth. It was painfully obvious they were suspicious of her now.

'Do you want to come over to stay with us?' Dolores asked.

'Yes, yes,' the children screamed.

'I'll get their clothes,' Ruth said and went upstairs.

Grace followed her. She wondered whether the kids should go with the grandparents, but thought it probably was for the best. 'I'm sorry about this, Ruth, but we might need to talk further with you so they'll be looked after, and won't realise there's anything going on.'

'But will I see them again?'

'Yes, of course you will,' Grace reassured. 'You are their aunt.'

'I don't think I could bear it if I didn't.' Ruth pressed a tissue to her eyes. 'I love them.'

309

'I know you do.' Grace held her close. 'I have no children myself, but I can imagine how it is for you. Even though you were only looking after them for a short time you must be very attached.'

'I always hoped to have a baby, but John didn't want that.' She took a deep breath. 'And Jason and Lorelai were like my own children, my very own.'

'I understand,' Grace said softly.

'I must see the children again. I must.' Ruth clenched her hands together and cried, tears drifting down her cheeks.

Peter brought Grace up to date. 'The information held on those computers at the house in Dalkey is a potential gold mine, Grace,' he said. 'It was some job to get into the basement of that house. We had to break in by sea through the boathouse. There were offices. Banks of computers. An armoury. Incredible stuff. The lads have already deciphered some of the codes, and if they continue then we'll get to the basis of that sex trade operation. And it's international. We're on to Interpol. And we've found passports for women from all over Europe.'

Grace was so taken aback she couldn't speak. So glad that some of those girls would be saved from a life of hell. They deserved justice.

Chapter Eighty-eight

Ruth hated the silence. It was eerie without the children. She could hear their voices raised in laughter or argument behind the door of the playroom, or television room, or from the garden. But they were never where she expected.

It hurt. No-one waited for her to make breakfast. Or help them bathe. Dress. Put on shoes. There was no reason to bake a pie, or juice up fruit. No piles of clothes to be washed or ironed. The realisation that she would never see Kim again suddenly hit her. To have found and lost her sister in such a short time was heart-breaking. Ruth went around the house and touched some of her things. Buried her face in those clothes belonging to Kim which she hadn't worn, and breathed deeply. It was a final farewell.

Ruth watched from the windows aware that the men she had named wouldn't hesitate to kill her, and even John had been capable of such an act. She rushed upstairs, and retrieved her small haversack. Kim had hidden it at the bottom of the wardrobe in the spare room. Moving so often, there were some basic items she always took with her. And now she checked the bag for her passport and a photo of her parents.

Although she knew that the Gardaí would probably have given her protection, she didn't want that. Caught up in this thing, she had revealed everything she knew about John and his associates, and that meant they would always be on her heels. Her life threatened.

That evening, she sat on a bus which travelled north out of Dublin and continued on to Belfast. The first lonely step on her journey. Her time here was spent.

Chapter Eighty-nine

Grace opened the front door of her home and stepped into the hall. She had received permission from the Super to return. But was extremely nervous as she switched on the light and entered the code for the alarm. All the time looking over her shoulder in case some intruder had followed her inside. Once it was disarmed, she looked upstairs. Newspapers protruded from the door at the top and cascaded down on the stairs, interspersed by *crime scene tape*.

Suddenly the urge to go up there swept through her. That hadn't changed at least. As ever, she longed to breathe in the aroma of newsprint. Touch it. Kiss it. And was now drawn up the stairs, stepping through the drifting papers which whispered to her like fallen leaves. She reached the landing. Pushed through the unlocked door and walked into the darkness. Her hands slid along the velvet walls until she came to her bedroom. She reached to switch on the light. The room was illuminated. Filled with the bundles of newspapers which had collapsed down in an enormous heap.

Once again, the blade of the knife hovered in front of her. The masked face grew closer. She could feel the weight of him on top of her. So heavy it was difficult to breathe. She turned, ran to the top of the stairs, and looked back with a sense of horror. It was as if she had allowed her cousin to take over her life all those years ago and force her to live it the way he wanted. Until now another man had attempted to end it.

Downstairs, Grace lit a cigarette with shaking hands and took a deep pull. Then quickly she packed a bag. She stood at the front door and looked back. Realising she couldn't continue to live here any longer, and would have to force herself to stay away from whatever was upstairs and which had turned her life into a hideous caricature.

Grace stood outside Mark's house. She rang the bell. After a moment he opened the door. He smiled, stepped down and pulled her close. Pressed his lips on hers. Tender. Intimate. He cupped her face in his hands and looked into her eyes. Then he gently kissed her forehead, drew her inside and closed the door.

TO MAKE A DONATION TO
LAURALYNN HOUSE

**Children's Sunshine Home/LauraLynn Account
AIB Bank, Sandyford Business Centre,
Foxrock, Dublin 18.**

**Account No. 32130009
Sort Code: 93-35-70**

www.lauralynnhospice.com

Acknowledgements

As always, our very special thanks to Jane and Brendan, knowing you both has changed our lives.

Many thanks to both my family and Arthur's family, our friends and clients, who continue to support our efforts to raise funds for LauraLynn House. And all those generous people who help in various ways but are too numerous to mention. You know who you are and that we appreciate everything you do.

Grateful thanks to all my friends in The Wednesday Group, who give me such valuable critique. Many thanks especially to Muriel Bolger who edited the book on this occasion also, and special thanks to Vivien Hughes who proofed the manuscript. You all know how much we appreciate your generosity.

Special thanks to Martone Design & Print – Yvonne, Martin, Dave. Couldn't do it without you.

Thanks to CPI, Cox & Wyman.

Thanks to all at LauraLynn House.

Thanks to Kevin Dempsey Distributors Ltd., and Power Home Products Ltd., for their generosity in supplying product for LauraLynn House.

Special thanks to Nisheeth, of Rasam Indian Restaurant, Glasthule.

Thanks also to Irish Distillers Pernod Ricard. Superquinn. Tesco.

And in Nenagh, our grateful thanks to Walsh Packaging, Nenagh Chamber of Commerce, McLoughlin's Hardware, Cinnamon Alley Restaurant, Jessicas, Irish Computers, Abbey Court Hotel, and Caseys in Toomevara.

Many many thanks to all at Cyclone Couriers – especially Mags – who continue to support us by storing and delivering the books free of charge.

And much love to my darling husband, Arthur, without whose love and support this wouldn't be possible.

CYCLONE COURIERS

Cyclone Couriers – who proudly support LauraLynn House – are the leading supplier of local, national and international courier services in Dublin. Cyclone also supply confidential mobile on-site document shredding and recycling services and secure document storage & records management services through their Cyclone Shredding and Cyclone Archive Division.

Cyclone Couriers – The fleet of pushbikes, motorbikes, and vans, can cater for all your urgent local and national courier requirements.

Cyclone International – Overnight, next day, timed and weekend door-to-door deliveries to destinations within the thirty-two counties of Ireland.

Delivery options to the UK, mainland Europe, USA, and the rest of the world.

A variety of services to all destinations across the globe.

Cyclone Shredding – On-site confidential document and product shredding & recycling service. Destruction and recycling of computers, hard drives, monitors and office electronic equipment.

Cyclone Archive – Secure document and data storage and records management. Hard copy document storage and tracking – data storage – fireproof media safe – document scanning and upload of document images.

Cyclone Couriers operate from 8, Upper Stephen Street, Dublin 8.

Cyclone Archive, International and Shredding, operate from
19-20 North Park, Finglas, Dublin 11.

www.cyclone.ie email: sales@cyclone.ie Tel: 01-475 7246

THE MARRIED WOMAN

Fran O'Brien

Marriage is for ever ...

In their busy lives, Kate and Dermot rush along on parallel lines,
seldom coming together to exchange a word or a kiss.
To rekindle the love they once knew, Kate struggles to lose
weight, has a make-over, buys new clothes, and arranges a
romantic trip to Spain with Dermot.

For the third time he cancels and she goes alone.

In Andalucia she meets the artist Jack Linley. He takes her with
him into a new world of emotion and for the first time in years she
feels like a desirable beautiful woman.

Will life ever be the same again?

Available now online
McGuinness Books
www.franobrien.net

THE LIBERATED WOMAN

Fran O'Brien

At last, Kate has made it!

She has ditched her obnoxious husband Dermot and is
reunited with her lover, Jack.

Her interior design business goes international and TV
appearances bring instant success.

But Dermot hasn't gone away and his problems encroach.

Her brother Pat and family come home from Boston
and move in on a supposedly temporary basis.

Her manipulative stepmother Irene is getting married
again and Kate is dragged into the extravaganza.

When a secret from the past is revealed Kate has
to review her choices ...

ODDS ON LOVE

Fran O'Brien

Bel and Tom seem to be the perfect couple with successful careers, a beautiful home and all the trappings. But underneath the facade cracks appear and damage the basis of their marriage and the deep love they have shared since that first night they met.

Her longing to have a baby creates problems for Tom, who can't deal with the possibility that her failure to conceive may be his fault. His masculinity is questioned and in attempting to deal with his insecurities he is swept up into something far more insidious and dangerous than he could ever have imagined.

Then against all the odds, Bel is thrilled to find out she is pregnant. But she is unable to tell Tom the wonderful news as he doesn't come home that night and disappears mysteriously out of her life leaving her to deal with the fall out.

Available now online
McGuinness Books
www.franobrien.net

WHO IS FAYE?

Fran O'Brien

Can the past ever be buried?

Jenny should be fulfilled. She has a successful career,
and shares a comfortable life with her husband, Michael,
at Ballymoragh Stud.

But increasingly unwelcome memories surface and
keep her awake at night.

Is it too late to go back to the source of those fears
and confront them?

THE RED CARPET

Fran O'Brien

Lights, Camera, Action.

Amy is raised in the glitzy facade that is Hollywood.
Her mother, Maxine, is an Oscar winning actress, and
her father, John, a famous film producer. When
Amy is eight years old, Maxine is tragically killed.

A grown woman, Amy becomes the focus of John's
obsession for her to star in his movies and be as
successful as her mother. But Amy's insistence
on following her heart, and moving permanently to
Ireland, causes a rift between them.

As her daughter, Emma, approaches her eighth
birthday, Amy is haunted by the nightmare of
what happened on her own eighth birthday.

She determines to find answers to her questions.

Available now online
McGuinness Books
www.franobrien.net

FAIRFIELDS

1907   QUEENSTOWN   CORK

Set against the backdrop of a family feud and prejudice
Anna and Royal Naval Officer, Mike, fall in love.
They meet secretly at an old cottage
on the shores of the lake at Fairfields.

During that spring and summer their feelings for each
other deepen. Blissfully happy, Anna accepts Mike's
proposal of marriage, unaware that her family have a
different future arranged for her.

**Is their love strong enough to withstand
the turmoil that lies ahead?**

**Available now online
McGuinness Books
www.franobrien.net**